THE REBELS

THE REBELS

SÁNDOR MÁRAI

*Translated from the Hungarian
by George Szirtes*

ALFRED A. KNOPF

New York

2007

THIS IS A BORZOI BOOK
PUBLISHED BY ALFRED A. KNOPF

Translation copyright © 2007 by Alfred A. Knopf,
a division of Random House, Inc.

All rights reserved. Published in the United States by Alfred A.
Knopf, a division of Random House, Inc., New York, and in
Canada by Random House of Canada Limited, Toronto.
www.aaknopf.com

Originally published in Hungary as *A Zendülők*
by Pantheon-Kiodás, Budapest, in 1930.

Copyright © Heirs of Sándor Márai. Vorosvary-Weller
Publishing, Toronto.

Knopf, Borzoi Books, and the colophon are registered
trademarks of Random House, Inc.

Library of Congress Cataloging-in-Publication Data
Márai, Sándor, 1900–1989
[Zendülők. English]
The rebels / by Sándor Márai ; translated from the
Hungarian by George Szirtes.—1st American ed.
p. cm.
ISBN-13: 978-0-375-40757-4
I. Szirtes, George, 1948–   .   II. Title.
PH3281.M35Z4213 2007
894'.511334—dc22   2006025572

Manufactured in the United States of America

First American Edition

THE REBELS

I

THE DOCTOR'S SON LAY ON THE BED, STIFF with cramp. His whole body was covered in sweat, and he felt feverish. He stared at the expanse of window in which the angles of the street, the single tree, a roof, and three further windows were slowly fading. A vertical line of smoke rose from the chimney opposite. By now it was darker in the low-arched room than it was outside. Through the window pressed the stifling early summer heat and in the steamy twilight the gas lamps outside glowed faintly green. Sometimes on spring evenings an invisible fog descends that lends a touch of green to the streetlights. The servant was singing and ironing in the kitchen. In the pane of the partly open window sputtered a ring of sparks from the iron: it was like the striking of a match in the darkness. The girl in the hallway was swinging the fiery metal box above her head.

He lay in a cramp, stared straight ahead, lost in thought. The gang had gone by three o'clock. Without transition it seemed to him that he had woken from some terrible nightmare and that everything would be all right now, he just had to be fully awake, step back into life, and, exercising his best charm and desire to please, make something of it. He gave a painful grin. Slowly he struggled upright, becoming conscious of his limbs, dangling his feet, gazing dreamily at the world around him. His movements were leaden as he raised himself from the bed, made his way to the basin, felt around in the darkness for the jug of water, lowered his head to the tray, and splashed the warm standing water over his damp hair and brow. Dripping with water, practically blind, he found the door and tapped around for the light switch. He sat down at the table and distractedly began to dry his hair with a thick towel.

The alarm clock was ticking on the bedside table. Seven o'clock; he was expected. He had been lying there for four hours, cramped, unmoving. He turned his head like a man with a tight collar, inserting his finger trying to adjust it for comfort. He found it hard to swallow. He went to the basin, washed his hands, rinsed his mouth, swilled the mouthwash round, gargled. Having stopped singing, the girl in the kitchen doorway noticed the light in the student's room. The boy buttoned his collar and took a few steps round the room. His aunt would not be back before eight.

A long time ago, in his childhood, his aunt had told him that she would leave her treasure to him. That "treasure," according to her, was stashed away in a secret place where no "agents and brokers" could get at it. Auntie hated the stock market, though she never really explained her loathing. In the child's imagination the stock exchange remained a dark cave at whose mouth Ali Baba and the forty thieves were grappling with a few powerful, armed men determined to guard their treasure. The bad luck associated with Fridays also played a part in the aunt's account whenever she spoke of treasure. She spoke of treasure often, with a significant emphasis, telling him that she had checked its secret location that day and that it was all right. Ábel should not worry about the future because the treasure would be his and their lives were almost certain to be free of further trouble. The boy once sought out the secret place, a tin box in the drawer of his aunt's washstand, where he found some old, no longer valid Lombard Street bills, a few banknotes of the Kossuth era, and some worthless lottery tickets. Auntie's treasure could no longer help him. He stood at the mirror staring at his creased face, then sat back down at the table. It was a moot point whether money was of any use now, he thought. Perhaps there were matters where money, and all that money could buy—time, travel, distance, health— was of no help at all. He sat before the desk. He pulled open the drawer where notebooks and sheets scribbled over with writing lay in a heap, picked up a poem, and read it. Forgetting all else he read it in an undertone, craning over it. The poem was about a dog lying in the sun. When had he written it? He couldn't remember.

The girl appeared, stopped in the doorway, and asked whether he would be staying home for supper. She posed there lazily, leaning against the doorpost, one hand on her hip, with a teasing smile on her face. The student ran his eyes over her and shrugged. She had brought the sharp, piquant tang of the kitchen with her, a damp smell hidden in the folds of her skirt that made him wrinkle his nose. He asked whether his aunt had returned yet. No, she wouldn't be home before eight, she replied.

Nowadays it seemed to him that there were moments when his whole life flashed past him. It was as if the change he had lived through had trapped everything he had experienced on the surface of his memory, so he could see his childhood, his father, and hear the lost voice of his mother, experience it all in individual movements of Aunt Etelka as she bowed before him. He looked around him amazed. The girl followed his eye movements, uncertain what to do.

The room was in a sorry state. The gang had wreaked havoc in it: torn books and magazines lay under the bed, one volume, *Fidibus,* was soaking in a pool of liqueur from an upturned bottle that gave out a hideous sweet-sickly stench. A muddy footprint was smeared across the plush cover of one of the chairs. Cushions were strewn about the floor. He had finished his exams at eleven in the morning and had waited in the schoolyard for the three members of the gang who had followed shortly after him in alphabetical order, and they had come directly back here to his place, taking no detours. Béla, the grocer's son, only called his father once they had arrived, telling him that he had passed and that they should not expect him home for dinner. Tibor did not contact his family, keeping from them the news that despite his patently strenuous efforts he had failed; his critically ill mother could wait to find that out in the evening, or the next day come to that. This was such an insignificant matter for the time being, it counted for so little, they didn't even mention it. In six weeks' time they would be in uniform and, with one great effort, even if the training dragged on, they'd be out at the front by the end of August.

He sat down on the bed. He looked at the girl. If I were not so timid, not so lacking in courage, thought the student, I'd pull her to me and lay my head on her breast. A decent sleep is the cure for everything. Pity she smells of the kitchen, as I can't stand kitchen smells, but that's because I've had an upper-middle-class upbringing: my grandfather was a landowner and my father is a practicing doctor. There's a reason for everything. It may not reflect well on me but sometimes a smell is more powerful than reason. It might be that she cannot stand my smell either, the way the Chinese find the smell of white men disgusting. There are certain barriers between people. The girl had been working there a year and the thought of her full body sometimes haunted his dreams and worked on his fantasy, and often, at moments of adolescent boyish regression, he imagined her as a model. She had a nice face, pale and soft, a blond pigtail amusingly perched on the crown of her head.

The girl started putting the room in order, and in an unintentionally quiet voice he asked her for a glass of milk. He took tiny sips of it, the bland standby drink of childhood, because for days on end they had been drinking wine and spirits, sweet sticky liquor that he quaffed with a stoical obligatory manliness though he didn't like the taste of it, nor could his stomach digest it. Milk felt good, the drink of that other, lost world. He went to the wardrobe, took out a clean collar, and brushed his coat down while the girl tidied and made the bed. She was sweeping the remnant of a pack of cards from under the table: he suddenly remembered he had no money. Searching his various pockets he found just three crowns, and couldn't understand it at first for his aunt had handed him twenty crowns in the morning before he set off for his exams. Under normal circumstances this would have constituted a healthy sum and he had to stop for a moment and recall what he had spent it on. After his aunt's celebratory dinner they had started a game of Ramsli with the German "William Tell" pack and he had lost. His memory of it was somewhat blurry, but he seemed to recall he did not want to play but someone—was it Tibor? was it Ernő?—made him. He stuffed the remaining money into his pocket and told the girl not to expect him for supper because he might be home late. He stopped in the doorway. One of the pack, an ace of hearts, lay on the threshold so he absentmindedly picked up the greasy and none too clean card, the rest of the pack being strewn on the table where the maid had deposited them. The top card there was another ace of hearts. He reached for it carefully with two fingers and examined it, turned it this way and that way, comparing it with the one he had found on the threshold. In the packs supplied by Piatnik there was usually only one ace of hearts. The two aces looked equally greasy, spotty, and well-used, inviting confidence, both with similar blue backs. He sat down at the table and sorted the pack into its four suits. He discovered two acorn aces as well, and two tens, one of leaves and one of bells. The four cards represented four winners at *vingt-et-un*. After Ramsli they would often go on to play *vingt-et-un*. The doubled cards were exactly like all the others in the pack. The cheat had been careful: they might have been using the pack for months by now. In any case the cards were foolproof. He himself had fished out the pack from a drawer in his father's writing desk. It was a very old, much-used pack.

He pocketed the cards. He went over to his father's room. People know the precise moment when they leave a place forever, a room, for example, where they have spent a long time. There was no thought in his head but he stood on the threshold and looked back. His mother had had this room at one time. Three generations of his family had occupied the house and this room had always been the women and children's room. It might have been because of these bright feminine furnishings: the light-colored cherrywood furniture, the low arches under which there swam the constant odors of childhood illnesses, of chamomile tea, violet-root, almond-flavored milk, and baby food. His mother had spent a very short time, perhaps only some three years, in the house, but all those highly potent oriental scents, so powerful that it was enough to leave one bottle unstoppered for a day for the room to be saturated with them for years, like the memory of her own presence, completely filling the house. Certain objects continued living their taboo lives: his mother's glass, her sewing table, her pincushion survived as if in a bell jar, separated out, though this was something they never spoke about. He couldn't think of his mother as anything but a very frail, much younger elder sister, and he knew that this early-departed woman lived in his father's memory the same way. He looked back at the room where he had spent his childhood, where he had been born, where his mother had died. He switched off the light.

In the low light of the streetlamp his father's current room felt like someone had been buried there, quite recently, someone whose memory the survivors did not dare disturb. There was something trancelike about the condition of the objects, the way the belongings of the dead remain frozen, rather as in a museum. True, his father was still alive, and was at this very moment standing at the operating table of a field hospital, sawing off a leg. Or maybe he was smoking a cigarette in his room, tugging at his beard with one hand, taking off his glasses. For the sake of piety and tidiness Etelka had covered the operating table in the room with a crocheted cloth, and the old surgical chair had taken on the appearance of an unfashionable rocking chair. He didn't light the lamp. He stood in the doorway, his hands deep in his pockets, his perspiring fingers toying with the cards. A great tide of heat rolled through him. The card parties had started at Christmas when the gang first broke out in a fever of ungovernable anxiety that had dominated their lives ever since. It was possible that someone had cheated in that first moment: he himself had certainly been losing constantly since then.

His tutorial fees, the aunt's little contributions, the sums his father occasionally sent, everything. Was it the winning individual who was the cheat? Perhaps it was precisely the opposite, the loser who had started cheating, now, near the end? He saw their three faces before him and closed his eyes.

In recent days he had been keenly aware of the figure of his father. His father had come to his bedside in dreams and leaned over him with his sad, solemn eyes. Naturally, everyone had a father. Everyone was born somewhere. How much is it possible to know of such things? Perhaps, once all this was over, if he was still alive, when he had developed a portly belly and grown a mustache, he would be walking down a foreign street and would suddenly have to stop because there was his father coming towards him with a face that was swelling to monstrous size as faces in the cinema tended to do, taking on superhuman proportions, and then, coming even closer, his father would part those giant lips of his and say something, pronouncing the single word that explained his whole life. That's what would happen: he would turn up sometime in a town in the dark that was glimmering ever so slightly, then growing ever brighter, so you could see every leaf on every tree, and the gates to the various houses would open, people step out into the street and start talking. Finally one mouth would bend over another mouth and the eyes close, then faint away.

The room was chilly. The surgical instruments sparkled in the glazed cupboard. In one of those drawers Father kept his slides, sections of diseased brain tissue he had once written a book about and published at his own expense. Several hundred copies of the work lay untouched in the library. In the days just before the war started his father was no longer seeing patients, only the three regulars he had somehow managed to keep on from the old practice: the magistrate, the old woman with the constantly shaking head, and the paranoid Gypsy band-leader who would turn up in the middle of a meal and play the violin for them while they were eating. Father treated these three like members of the family. His invalids respected him. Usually they sat in this very room after supper as if they were part of the family circle gathered to pay each other unctuous compliments. The lady with the shaking head sat with Etelka as they both plied their cro-chet, the magistrate sat solemnly, ceremoniously, vaguely expectant, under the great chandelier, holding the boy on his knees, and the Gypsy bandleader stood by the piano, leaning a little to one side, his bow in his hand, his violin under his arm, in the careless pose adopted by many famous concert artistes. They could stay like that, silent for hours, as if waiting for something to happen, not say-ing a word while Father took no notice of them and exam-ined the slides at the desk. At eleven o'clock he would raise his hand to signal that they could go. They would bow deeply and take their leave. It was rare for his father to say anything at these gatherings, and the three invalids' expressions would be full of respect and an almost ago-nized seriousness as they turned towards him to acknowl-edge a chance remark like "It's been a cold day," then, having bent their heads, they would withdraw once more into a world of profound meditation. The woman with the shaking head would indicate her agreement by rapidly batting her eyelids, the magistrate and bandleader would frown and concentrate on the deeper implications of the observation. His childhood was full of such incidents.

He recalled two specific occasions in the room. One of them underlay every memory involving his father. He would have been four or five years old, sitting on the floor of this room, playing. His father steps in, sits down beside him on the floor, and without further ado begins to sing:

> . . . *Au clair de la Lune*
> *Mon ami Pierrot . . .*

He knows the song. Etelka has taught it to him. His father's mouth opens and closes, the face is curiously twisted as it laughs, the song emerges from between those enormous teeth with a kind of whimsical childish lisp. He immediately understands that his father wants to put everything right, all that had passed between them from the moment of his birth, the silence, the isolation, the distance, the magic spell under which they had hitherto lived together; this single gesture is to release them from it, that's what this sitting beside him and singing in such whimsical manner is about. Has he gone mad? he wonders. His father's voice is losing confidence. He is still singing:

> . . . *Non, je ne prête pas ma plume*
> *À un vieux savetier . . .*

but then he stops and they are left staring into each other's eyes. There is a statue in the main square, an enormous bronze soldier, pointing his rifle at the tyrant's chest: it's as if the soldier had leapt off its plinth, fully armed and uniformed, and was running along on all fours. *Vieux savetier . . . ,* he repeats, his lips trembling, to console his father for whom he now feels a terrible pity. He starts crying. His father slowly gets to his feet, goes to the table, rummages among his books as if searching for something, notices that the child is watching him even through his tears, shrugs his shoulders, and hurries out of the room. For a long time after this they are like two people joined by a lie that degrades them both: their eyes do not meet.

Much later, some ten years later. Father is sitting at his table examining a slide under the table lamp when the boy enters. It's an early afternoon in winter. The boy stops in the half-light but the father extends his hands towards him and invites him to come closer. There is some dry blue matter between the two sheets of glass, something with blotches and lines on it, like the map of the country he sees in his geography book. The father's bony finger is following the lines of this peculiar map, moving along its branches, its curves, carefully tracing every kink of one particularly sinuous line, and where the line, somewhere near the edge of the slide, breaks, he taps at the glass.

It is my most beautiful slide, says his father.

The boy knows that his father's finger is moving over a section of a brain. The image is full of variety, of dangerous, restless twists and turns. "What a map!" he thinks. His father bends close to the sheet of glass, the light intensely illuminating his face whose expression is of agonized, helpless curiosity, transforming his normally self-disciplined gaze into a mask that is almost grotesque. Involuntarily, he too leans closer. His father's finger is delicately, circuitously following some point in the image where the crooked line gathers into a knot, then moves off in several directions. Like a cartographer who cannot quite orientate himself on a strange map, like a doctor feeling round a body to discover the secret of a diseased organ, he is helpless and impatient.

This was a Ruthenian peasant, his father explains, preoccupied. One day he slaughtered his entire family. His parents, his wife, and his two children. It is my most beautiful slide.

He bends over the dried-up blue substance. His father's face clears: it is no longer full of painful tense curiosity, it empties, loses expression, the bony hand pushes away the slide and two pairs of eyes look blankly in front of them.

In the evening his father played the violin. He played the violin every night and no one was allowed into the room while he was playing. After supper he would retreat into his room and spend an hour wrestling with the obstinate, rebellious instrument, conjuring a set of tortured sounds from it. His father had never been taught the violin and some kind of shyness and embarrassment prevented him from taking lessons now. His playing was riddled with errors, and entailed, or so the boy felt, a kind of bad faith. He himself knew his efforts were a hopeless, obstinate experiment, and he couldn't bear it if anyone made a pointed remark about it in his presence. Nevertheless the tortured sounds of his violin filled the house. The awareness of his father's increasing embitterment as night after night, alone in his room, he struggled with the instrument, made him feel as if his father were engaged in some ugly, shameful habit in the solitude of his room while being overheard by the other gleefully malevolent dwellers in the house. At such times he too would lock himself in his room, sitting in the dark, his hands over his ears, biting his lips, staring and waiting. It was as if his father were doing something low and treacherous. Now the violin lay on top of the cupboard.

When he imagined his father's death it was like an avalanche. Nothing unusual had happened to him so far, except for the fact that he was more silent than usual when he came back on leave.

Automatically bowing in the direction of the writing desk, he clapped his hat on his head and left the room.

HE MET HIS AUNT IN THE STAIRWELL. SHE WAS dressed in her Sunday best, and groaned as she stopped. They kissed each other. She encouraged him to put a coat on and not be back too late. For a second he entertained the possibility of sinking to his knees and telling her everything.

The stairwell curved in a half circle with wide steps, and with its engravings of the town's old public buildings gave an impression of grandeur. The stair carpet was of a multicolored folk design. The verandah had once served as his father's waiting room and was soaked through with the smell of other people, the sickening, pungent iodine-and-ether smell of his father's medicine cupboard only faintly detectable through it. Ernő's father smelled of flour paste and raw leather. Béla's walked around in a haze of eastern spices, herring, and leftover fresh fruit. Tibor's house was discreetly scented with lavender, the smell of genteel poverty and sickness, combined with the rather more combative smell of cured leather. Smells characteristic of their fathers' occupations filled their homes. Ábel always thought of his own house in terms of the sobering light trance of ether, a mixture of acid and narcotic.

And so each nook and cranny of the house lived on in him, sorted according to smell, and providing he followed the magnetic needle of scent he could imagine each room with its own life. His aunt kept her arcanum of a hundred domestic substances—turpentine, benzine, chlorine, petroleum, a large quantity of each since they were rare items in the shops—in the dark corridor between kitchen and dining room. She was just returning from one of her secretive household expeditions. She was carrying her booty of two kilos of starch, rice, and freshly roasted coffee in her crocheted shopping bag. Her black hat, with its short veil in permanent mourning for some unknown deceased acquaintance, was perched on the topknot of her hair. Her sharp yellow nose felt cold against the boy's face. Etelka entered the house like a guest or a distant relative who was only making a brief visit—and, after his mother's death, had somehow remained there like a servant, a mother substitute, unpaid, always steadfast and ready to leave at the drop of a hat. Ábel loved her. She was "the other world" as he called her, and he loved her because she spoke softly and attached herself to them, to both of them, to father and son, with all the inexhaustible and ruthless love of the barren and constructed her life around them. She was the sort of old maid who kept people instead of dogs and cats for pets. Ábel knew that Etelka would happily give her life for him. It was a long time since they had been able to bring themselves to talk to each other. With each day that passed that low, oppressive, one-story dwelling was becoming ever more like a hothouse. There was something steamed up, close, and damp about it. Its yellow walls sank under the weight of its double roof. Red guttering framed the yellow façade and the gate, from both sides of which hung cast-iron lamps, lacquered green. Even the garden, that tiny old urban patch of grass, with its minimal cramped proportions, felt like a terrarium. Tall fire walls surrounded it on three sides. In the summer it was densely overgrown with lush weeds. The three of them, Etelka, Father, and Ábel, had lived there, in that house and in that garden, in utter seclusion since the death of his mother, with an occasional, rare change of servants. Later Ábel wondered if Etelka nursed some feelings for his father, if there had been a time when there was more than she let on in her heightened devotion to him. But no one ever spoke of that. He too only recalled it the way one remembers something that has failed to happen, like some mood before a potential shower in childhood, when the room darkens for a moment but no downpour follows the vexed dark that is immediately dispelled by the sun. Only the sensation of waiting remains embedded in the nerves.

You slept for a long time, his aunt was telling him. I wanted to wait until you woke up. I noticed you had been drinking spirits, sweetheart. Beware of hard drink, it can be harmful at your age. I'm just an old woman, Ábel, and can only beg you to look after yourself. You are launched on life now, my child. Do be careful what you do at night. Boys are so impulsive at this age. When is the party to be? It doesn't matter how late you come home: look in on me. The cost of starch is up again. Eggs too. Should your father come home he should bring some provisions with him. We'll write him a letter tomorrow and tell him you have passed your exams. Give me a kiss.

She tipped her head towards the boy's face and squeezed it. They remained like that a moment. People live together but there are long periods when they know nothing of each other's lives. Then one has the sensation that the other has vanished off the map. This was one corner of the world: his aunt's furniture inherited from his mother, the garden, his father, the fiddle playing, Jules Verne, and the walk in the cemetery with his aunt on All Souls' Day. This world had such power that nothing external could destroy it, not even the war. Just once each year some unforeseen thing broke through a chink in it, another world. Everything changed. That which had hitherto been sweet was now bitter, that which had been sour was now like gall. The hothouse became a primeval forest. And his aunt like a corpse, or less than that.

He slammed the glazed door, the bell swung and rang,

the sound swam through the air and penetrated the silent house. He looked back from the gate: his aunt stood at the glazed door, her hands linked, and stared at him.

THE WINDOWS OF THE THEATER WERE LIT. A CAR was waiting by the side door that led to the upstairs boxes. He cut across the high street and decided to call on Ernő's father.

The cobbler had returned home some eighteen months ago with a serious wound in his lungs and had been spitting blood ever since. He lived in a high apartment block down a narrow alleyway among fishmongers, in a cellar that was five shallow steps down from the street and served as both his workplace and his accommodation. The entrance was surrounded by painted signs that he himself had made, signs involving mysterious pictures studded with captions in a hodgepodge of biblical language, exhorting any passerby to live modestly and to come to Christ. "Young man, hold high your Shield of Faith," proclaimed one sign. "God takes no pleasure in your great knowledge, your rank, your strength, or your declarations of religion, but if you give your heart to Jesus He will put a veil between you and your past and prepare you for the glory of the Lord," said another. "Raise our hearts, almighty Savior, like the serpent of brass, so that those who are disappointed in life might be cured by embracing You," said a third. And one in particularly large letters declared: "Neither will death always begin with dying. There are many among us living yet coffined. Dedicate yourself to death; lay your life in the hands of Jesus and you will no longer fear death."

People stopped, read the texts, shook their heads, and walked on in astonishment.

The workshop was densely shrouded in the half-light and a simmering bowl full of paste filled the room with its ripe, sour, acid smell. The cobbler was sitting hunched by an oxyacetylene lamp next to a low table, like a huge shaggy insect hypnotized by the circle of light. Once he noticed the boy he carefully arranged everything he had been working with on the table, including the large uncured leather sole that had been lying on his lap, the shoe knife, the thread, and a scrawny yellow half shoe, and only then stood up and bowed deeply.

"Blessed be the name of the Lord. He who confirms us in our faith and leads us to victory over our foes."

What Ábel liked about him was that he issued his grandly ceremonial greetings in such an indifferent, commonplace manner he might have simply been mouthing "your servant." The cobbler was a short, shriveled man entirely consumed by his disease. The weight of his leather apron seemed to drag him down. One leg was shorter than another, a condition he contracted before the bullet found his lung. A long mustache dripped from his wasted, bony face, adhering to his tousled beard and uncut hair that would not lie flat, but covered his skull like a wire wig, a shrub full of thistles. His great black eyes shone and turned with a confused light deep beneath his brow, the whites as large as a Negro's.

"The young gentleman is looking for my son, Ernő,"

said the cobbler, his peculiarly small white sickly hand gesturing him to take a seat. There was considerable natural grace in his movements. He himself did not sit down, but leaned on a short crooked stick to address his guest. "My son Ernő is not at home. We must be reasonable about such things. We cannot ask him to spend all his time with his parents. The young gentlemen have taken their exams today and have therefore moved up a step in the eyes of God and man."

He spoke in a flat voice, with as little emotion or expression as ever, as if he were praying or reciting the liturgy.

"My unworthy son, Ernő, has today been allotted his place among the gentlemen sons of gentlemen fathers," he continued. "Judging by the available evidence it seems it was not the Lord's will that my son Ernő should be a prop to his parents in their old age. He wants my son to live among gentlemen, and to become my enemy. It would be foolish and absurd of me to rail against God's will. Today my son has entered the superior rank of gentlefolk, and he must needs be the enemy of his lowly parents, his relations, and everyone who knew him."

He made a gesture in the air with his hand as if bestowing a blessing. "He who recognizes the hand of God in mortal affairs rejoices in sickness, misfortune, and enmity between his kinfolk. My son Ernő is a quiet boy who rejects the forthrightness the great source of Light has bestowed on me, his father, so that I may fulfill my obligations. The way has opened unto him: mountains have collapsed. It is utterly certain that the hour has come when the ruling social order must demand bloody sacrifices. Millions are lying dead in the ditches of the world and, insignificant as I am, I have been allowed to survive while the ruling classes offer involuntary sacrifices unto the earth and its waters."

Yes, Mr. Zakarka, said Ábel. May I speak to Ernő?

"Indeed," he continued undisturbed. "Be so gracious as to consider the scale of the matter. We have been used to seeing how the ruling class, with its remarkable refinement, its extraordinary achievements in each and every field, remained immune to all natural disasters such as earthquakes, flood, fire, and war, providing God's finger had not picked them out specifically. We have been used to there being two classes in the world, one living in close proximity to the other, but having less to do with it than do locusts with bears. Please be so gracious as to remember that the last days are here. The sons of the ruling class are lying in the same lime pits as the sons of the low. The prophets have risen and their words are becoming audible; the Lord has marked even my humble words out for hearing and for following."

The cobbler threw a long shadow in the hissing light of the oxyacetylene lamp. He gave an occasional cough adding "Beg your pardon" each time as he trundled off into a corner of the workshop where he spent some time hawking and spitting.

Ábel sat there, leaning forward. He knew he had to wait until the cobbler had had his say. The Bible lay on a shelf on the wall among a few old mugs and pots, with a child-sized meter-high crucifix on the wall beside it. The cobbler swayed as he walked, very much dependent on his stick. After he had finished coughing he continued in a cracked voice.

"As concerns my son, Ernő," he began, tucking his hands under his leather apron, "the young gentlemen were kind enough to accept him into their company, for which he will owe them an eternal debt of gratitude, a debt that will linger long after the young gentlemen have gone. By any human estimation my son Ernő, with his stunted body and inherited diseases, is likely to outlive the young gentlemen who treated him with such kindness, and who have proved more amenable than my unfortunate son to following the examples of their heroic gentlemen fathers. It goes to show that there's a point even to illness and deformation. The young gentlemen are going where all are equal in the eyes of death, but Ernő is staying here. He will become a gentleman since the hour of trial will pass from the face of the earth, and those who remain will be the recipients of God's special favor. It is my intention to remain alive long enough to see that hour."

Having announced this he gave an easy courteous bow, an almost apologetic bow as if there was nothing he could do about any of this. Ábel looked at the crucifix. The cobbler followed his gaze with a stern expression.

"The young gentlemen were kind to my son. Especially the son of the much respected Mr. Prockauer. I must not forget this. Young Master Prockauer, though not personally respectable, enjoys such an elevated position in the world owing to the very high respect in which his honorable father is held, that his friendship is an honor of which my son will be forever sensible. Ernō is aware how much he owes to the gentleman. It may be because of his natural taciturnity that he has not spoken of his gratefulness to me, though, naturally, my poor understanding cannot gauge the deeper meaning of what gentlemen say. But what the waking will not say, the sleeping will occasionally utter. My son has often addressed young Master Prockauer by his first name when asleep."

"Tibor?" asked Ábel. His throat was dry.

The cobbler stepped into a chamber of the cellar that was hidden by a curtain. "I slept here at his feet," he said and waved in the direction of a box bed with drawers under it. "I took to the floor, which is harder, and gave up the bed to my son so he should get used to the gentlemen's style of doing things. That's where I heard, more than once, my son shout out the first name of young Master Prockauer. A person only calls to someone else in his sleep when he is suffering. I have no way of telling what caused my son to suffer in his sleep so that he should cry out the young gentleman's name."

He allowed the curtain to fall as if covering up some shameful sight. So this is where Ernō lives, thought Ábel. He had never dared imagine where Ernō slept, what he ate, or what they talked about at home. He had visited the workshop often enough recently, but always when Ernō was away, and the cobbler had never shown him the room where he and his son lived. But this was where Ernō slept with his father. His mother probably had her own bed in the place.

"Perhaps it was out of gratefulness that my son shouted

out Master Prockauer's first name," said the cobbler. "The young gentleman had long honored my son with his company. Even in the lower years at school he allowed my son to take home books belonging to his father, the colonel. And later, when the young gentleman was, with perfectly excusable carelessness, neglecting his studies, the colonel's boy bestowed on my son the distinction of allowing him to be of help to him. The good graces of gentlemen are indeed inscrutable. It was thanks to the offices of the good colonel that I was permitted to take part in that great cleansing at the front."

"In what?" Ábel leaned forward. The cobbler straightened. "The cleansing. It is not the proper time to speak of everything just yet. The only man capable of being cleansed is he who has undergone humiliations. The good colonel, whose son showered such favors on my son, made it possible for me to be cleansed, when he chose me in the absence of his official aide. I had three opportunities to be cleansed."

He extended his hands before him.

"For one who gives life, all methods are equally suitable when employing an aide for the taking of life. Be so kind as to consider all we have to thank the noble gentlemen of the Prockauer family for. My son not only had the privilege of educating a high-ranking officer's son, and, in due course, to appear in the company of gentlemen of which he would become one even while wearing his cast-offs, but I, his father, am in the colonel's debt for having been allowed to participate in the great cleansing appointed by the Lord, in a triple cleansing. With these two hands. Is the young gentleman unaware of this?"

"You, Mr. Zakarka?" asked Ábel and stood up. He wasn't shocked but he was filled with wonder.

"I had three opportunities. Didn't my son Ernő mention these to the young gentlemen? Perhaps he didn't want to brag about his father's cleansing, and if so, he did right, because it is proper that the lowly should retain his modesty, even when, out of their goodness, gentlemen permit him to join them. I had three opportunities of being cleansed. Be so gracious as to be informed that the war which the Lord in his goodness allowed to happen so that we might see our sins, offers us mortals few opportunities for cleansing. Aiming a gun and, at a certain distance, bringing down a man is not the same as snuffing out a life with our bare hands, and I do mean precisely that. It is different closing one's hands about a person's neck and breaking his vertebra, different from, say, using a sharp implement and wounding a fellow human being, and different again from bombarding someone at a distance with the assistance of certain explosive materials. Cleansing can only occur when a man is directly in touch with death. And, what was more, all three were gentlemen."

"Who were they?" the boy asked.

They were standing eye to eye. The cobbler leaned closer.

"Czech officers. Traitors from the motherland's point of view. It was a peculiar act of grace on the colonel's part, an act for which I will remain eternally grateful to him that he entrusted me with officers, not common people. As I have said, my family stands in especial debt to the Prockauers. I hear the condition of the noble lady has deteriorated."

"When did you hear?" asked Ábel overeagerly.

He immediately regretted asking the question. The cobbler's eyes roved round the room then suddenly found and buried themselves in his own, the feeling hot and sharp. It was like looking into dazzling light. He closed his eyes. The condition of Tibor's mother had been giving cause for concern for several days. It was a strange feeling, this anxiety. They didn't talk about it. The colonel's wife had been bed-bound for three years: her condition changed but she didn't rise from her bed. Her elder son, who had returned a few months previously as an ensign, having lost an arm at the front, stubbornly kept repeating that she was perfectly capable of getting up and simply didn't want to. He told people that once the boys were in bed at night she would rise from her sickbed and walk about in the apartment. If there was indeed a change in the condition of Tibor's mother then something had to be done quickly for the colonel might appear any day. He didn't dare look at the cobbler who stood directly in front of him and who seemed to have grown somewhat in the twilight. Ábel knew he was the same height as the cobbler but felt as though he were being forced to look up at him. The light in the cobbler's eyes slowly went out. They both looked down.

"It's nothing to do with me," said the cobbler. "I humbly beseech the young gentleman not to mention the matter in front of Master Tibor. The elder son of Colonel Prockauer was here earlier, also seeking my son Ernő. He mentioned it in passing."

"What?"

The oxyacetylene lamp flared up. The cobbler limped over to the lamp and carefully turned the flame down.

"As people do in conversations. Young Master Lajos, if I may so refer to him, being a fellow soldier on the front and a comrade in arms, has made a significant sacrifice for the homeland. Soldiers who have served at the front look each other up when opportunity affords. We talk of a good many things at such times. Young Master Lajos also made mention of the fact that young Master Tibor was worried. I must not neglect to mention that apart from losing an arm in that great bloodbath, young Master Lajos made a spiritual sacrifice too. He doesn't remember very much of what he has said. And when he says something, pretty soon after he doesn't want to know anything about it. In the course of conversation he mentioned that it was not absolutely impossible that there had been some deterioration in the noble lady's condition. We must prepare ourselves, he said. That's how I know."

Ábel knew nothing of this for certain. It could be that the one-armed invalid had imagined it all. The elder of the Prockauer boys was given to strange behavior at times. Once he had avoided and laughed at his younger brother's circle of friends and their amusements: now he was forever seeking them out. Little by little they included him in everything. He was the first to make the acquaintance of the actor. Ábel thought about it: they had known the actor by sight for a long time, but the one-armed Lajos was the first to introduce himself and get him to meet the others. No doubt he had been his loquacious self.

He talked with the cobbler about Tibor's anxieties, anxieties that resulted in him betraying their common secret. It would be good to know how far Lajos had taken the cobbler into his confidence. The cobbler was inclined to talk, admittedly in his own peculiar way, though much depended on whom he was addressing. Ernő told them his father was not a frequenter of bars and that he kept his set speeches about the new order between rich and poor, and on the collapse and rebuilding of the world, for a selected audience.

He had never doubted that the cobbler was not quite right in the head, but the manner in which he performed his speeches was so calm and disciplined that, eye to eye, he did not feel he was talking to a madman any more than when listening to certain views of adults generally. In its proper context, in its own way, everything he said was sober and to the point. When he thought about it he couldn't quite free himself of the uncomfortable feeling that there was something attractive in the cobbler's obsession, something he couldn't just skip over, get on with his life, and ignore. The cobbler fascinated him, but not like Ernő did, or like Tibor, not even like the actor—nothing like them, quite the contrary in fact, but that contrary was irresistible to him. From time to time he felt obliged to seek the cobbler out.

The cobbler was Ernő's father, and Ernő was one of the

gang. Indeed, Ernő was one of the pillars of the gang. Each time they launched out on something afterwards it seemed to him that the silent and secretive Ernő had somehow initiated it. He hadn't known, of course, that the cobbler had actually hanged men at the front. Ábel was taken aback but felt no horror. He looked at the cobbler, at those hands that had furthered the process of "cleansing," and neither hated nor shrank from them. It was beyond his comprehension: his mind could not grasp it. The whole thing had happened too quickly: childhood, the hothouse, Father's sessions with the violin, then that something else that other people called the war, but which changed nothing in his life, and suddenly there he was, standing among adults, burdened with guilt and lies, hatching life or death schemes with the gang whose members a year, a day, or one hour earlier were as much children as he had been, living in a different, gentler, tamer world, knowing nothing of danger. They didn't have time to bother with what the adults were doing. Their fathers went away, their elder brothers were called up, but these obscure and, as far as they were concerned, far from terrible but boring and everyday occurrences, indeed anything anyone did in those faraway places, were of no interest to them. He couldn't begin to cope with excess knowledge, such as the knowledge that Ernő's father had hanged people. That was something to do with fathers and elder brothers. One heard of other things like that. The world he had known had smashed and he felt he was walking on its shards. It might be that in a few weeks or a few months he too would have to hang people. If Mr. Zakarka regarded this as a form of cleansing, that was his business. People cleanse themselves as best they can.

The cobbler often employed the term "cleansing." Ábel found it attractive but couldn't understand what exactly he meant by it. The cobbler quoted the Bible. Ábel liked his turn of phrase. His manner of speech affected him like a kind of seductive singing, a singing that was off-key and full of missed notes, yet the voice was alive and full. It had something of the wayside preacher in it. At one point he had referred to himself as "a minor prophet" and lowered his eyes.

Sometimes he had the feeling that the cobbler knew everything about them. He knew some surprising things about the town. He rarely left his miserable room, yet it was as though he had invisible emissaries: with a word here and a word there he let slip that he knew what was going on and kept his eyes on everything. He hardly ever spoke when his son was present. When Ernő entered their poor quarters the cobbler would give a deep bow and fall silent. He would speak respectfully of his son even in his presence but he would never address him directly. Ábel watched him with amazement. Each time he came he had to restrain himself from pouring his heart out to him. Sometimes, just now in fact, as he was walking down the street, he felt an irresistible temptation to call on the cobbler and tell him everything. Perhaps I should ask him to turn the light off, he thought. It would be easier in the dark. It was only a few months since he had made the acquaintance of Ernő's father, up till then he had known nothing of him. Thinking it over, he didn't think he was mad. The cobbler seemed to be of no particular age. He felt closer to him than he did any ordinary adult. It was as if the cobbler, like the gang, was living in that transitional state between childhood and adulthood. The cobbler was neither adult nor child. Like them he seemed to hover in a world between good and evil. He felt the weight of this knowledge as intensely as he would the burden of a terrible secret. He was frightened of the cobbler, though sometimes it felt as though he were the only man who could help him. He was like an adult to look at, but Ábel's sense of him was of someone in disguise, a child wearing a false beard.

He could never decide whether the cobbler was friend or foe. He employed broad terms: The gentry, he said. The poor. Only sinners may be cleansed. At such times his voice rang like a true preacher's. His frail, flat tones filled the narrow room.

"As I said," he ended without any change of pace, "my son Ernő is in the coffeehouse with the young gentlemen. Custom now openly permits him to frequent places reserved for adult gentlemen."

He bowed and sat back down on his chair and picked up his work as though there was no one else present. Ábel stood beside him and watched him as he leaned, bent-backed, over the sole and pricked a series of tiny holes at the perimeter of the leather strip with his auger. Ábel had come to tell him everything, to talk about Tibor and the actor, to ask him for help in the face of the danger that was threatening them all. Now that he was staring at the cobbler's wire-wig hair his nerve failed him again. Whatever is said out loud has life. He quietly and timidly took his leave, though the cobbler was no longer paying attention to him. When he reached the steps the cobbler spoke. Astonished, Ábel turned round and saw the cobbler was laughing.

"We will all be cleansed," said the cobbler and raised his leather-knife. His face was radiant.

IT WAS INDEED POSSIBLE THAT THEY WOULD ALL be cleansed. He walked slowly beside the wall, aimlessly, as if he had no particular place to go. The gang would surely be waiting for him by now. The pack of cards was weighing down his pocket. It was a warm evening, uneasily warm. Some time that afternoon there must have been rain that covered the street with a thin, soft sheen of light, but as evening approached a wind got up in the hills and within a few minutes had dried the surfaces. A balmy haze of warmth drifted through the air conveyed to town by freshly swollen fields when the mist of the spring evening rises and dew begins to settle in the pores of the skin.

He had turned eighteen in April but looked younger than that. Down the school corridors, just before you reached the conference rooms, there was a group of old class photographs on display. He had often studied them, surprised at how different he and his generation looked from those who had graduated ten or twenty years ago. They were enormous mature men, almost without exception. Though most of their faces looked young, there were those among them who seemed fully adult. There were one or two with fine curling mustaches. Next to them Ábel's friends looked like children in short pants. It was as if with every year that passed the generations had grown softer and more childish. He found the picture of his father's graduation year. There was Kikinday the judge, Kronauer the colonel in the medical corps, and there was his father too: all proper adults. Kronauer had a sharp mustache, checkered trousers, and a coat after the French fashion. He held a tall hat in his hands. His father was manly, broad-shouldered. He was practically all man, differing from the figure Ábel knew only in that he lacked the latter's addition of a beard. But you could imagine him bearded even then, twenty-four years ago. He wondered how he himself would look if he grew a beard or a mustache. Thinking that, he gave a bitter grin. It was unlikely he would get that far because his face was still completely smooth and white, lacking any sign of whiskers, lacking even the ghost of a mustache. His hands were small too, like a child's. Perhaps humanity degenerated year by year. But it was also possible that they were evolving. The Japanese were small too, refined, and yet looked older.

He had begun to read two years ago. He read unsystematically, whatever came to hand. One day he wrote something. He was fifteen. When he saw the piece of paper with his writing on it he got a fright and hid it in his drawer. The next day he took it out and read it. It wasn't poetry but it didn't seem to be quite prose either. It scared him so he tore it up. His fear persisted for days. At that time he was still inhabiting "this" side of life. There was no one he dared talk to. What was this? Why did he write it down? What does it mean when a man picks up a pen and writes something? When something simply comes to him and it appears there, complete, in his writing? Why should he have done that? Is this what writers do? He had come across a book once that someone had brought home from the front. It was a Russian book, full of Russian script. A novel. The author was anonymous. He could not help but feel shaken when he thought of it. Somewhere in Russia there lived this anonymous figure conjuring characters, events, and entire tragedies out of nothing, committing them to paper, a spirit floating over an immense distance, and here he was holding it in his hands.

He stopped in front of the bookshop window and ran a melancholy eye over the books. Books hid some secret, not precisely in what they said, but in the reason for them being written at all. There wasn't anybody he could discuss this with. He did try occasionally with Ernő, but Ernő always seemed to be speaking of something else and they failed to communicate with each other. Ernő talked about the books' "contents." He knew that was of secondary importance. What he wanted to know was why the books existed. Do they bring joy to those who write them? He felt they must cause more pain than pleasure. And if you write something down, is it then lost, does it have nothing to do with you any more, is there only a memory, an ache, left behind, as if you had been found guilty of something, something for which, sooner or later, you would have to answer?

He wrote a few poems. He described somebody's

appearance or a conversation he had overheard in the street. No one knew he had done this, not the gang and certainly not his aunt. Tibor was only interested in sports, the theater, and girls. For Béla it was fashion and girls. The one-armed one was utterly fixated on girls. It was difficult to know what interested Ernő. He was a passionate chess player. An excellent mathematician. But the mystery of why someone sat down each night to commit whatever he had seen or heard to paper was of absolutely no interest to him.

He sat alone in his room at night, a sheet of paper before him, but it was his father's secret sessions with the violin that came to mind, which made him blush, so he quickly rose from the table, lay down, and immediately turned off the light. He knew what he was doing was not the real thing. It was no more than what his father was doing when he played the violin. And it wasn't simply a matter of someone writing down what he had seen and heard during the day. There was always something beyond such events, some secret, some meaning, some connection between them that he should discover, seize on, and artic-ulate. One day he found a copy of *War and Peace*. When he got as far as the scene where the prince returns from the battlefield and sees his dead wife whose expression seems to be asking "What have you done to me?" he shuddered. He felt someone had expressed a thought that could prob-ably not be articulated in words. It was something that affected the whole realm of human experience. "What have you done to me?"

He reached the high street. The city shimmered with

weak light like an invalid's bedroom. Couples were still strolling in crowds down the avenue: in the theater the performance had just begun. Some officers were standing around in front of Béla's father's delicatessen, chatting with the hunchbacked chemist who had an intimate knowledge of the town and its affairs. They were sizing up the girls and the chemist was helping them by revealing their interesting little secrets. Now and then they burst out in a storm of laughter. They were on leave, wounded, each one wearing one of the uniforms of the front. The chemist covered his mouth with his hand.

Opposite the theater, in front of the café, stood the actor leaning on an advertising pillar. The one-armed one was with him, loudly explaining something. When Ábel reached them the actor greeted him with a profound bow.

"We were waiting for you, my angel," he said.

THE ACTOR HAD ARRIVED IN TOWN WITH THE company in the early autumn, saying he had had a contract in the capital first, but the theater had closed. He was forty-five years old but claimed to be thirty-five. Not even the gang believed this though they eagerly swallowed everything else he told them. He tended to play comic, dancing roles but referred to himself as a ballet instructor. The contract laid down that the company was obliged to supply divas and leading men each season for a few highlights from popular operettas. It was the comedian-dancer's task to teach them the appropriate elements of ballet.

He had put on weight, developing a proper paunch and jowls, a rare thing in the world of comedians and dancers. The audience liked him because he included a lot of current gossip in his act. He wore a wig of light chestnut color. His head was large and equine. His jaw was thrust forward and he was so near-sighted that he couldn't see the prompter's box, but he refused to wear glasses out of vanity, not even in real life, as he put it.

His stage name was Amadé: Amadé Volpay was how they billed him. He spoke with his mouth full as if chewing on a dumpling. He wore generously fitting, light suits that skillfully disguised his fatness as did his corset that was laced so tightly when he was on stage that his face was practically red, so that he didn't look half as fat as he did in life. It was as if his girth were no more than some kind of misapprehension that existed between him and the world at large, and he never ceased talking about it. He spoke eloquently and at length to both intimates and strangers in the effort to persuade them that he was not fat. He produced precise measurements and medical tables showing average proportions to prove he was as slender as a flamingo and that his figure was in all respects the manly ideal, his belly swelling as he did so because, in his passion, he forgot to hold it in.

Bearing this in mind he would walk down the street like a ballet dancer, practically mincing. He propelled his substantial body along on points, with delicate, genuinely airy steps, as if it weighed nothing, as if he feared being blown away by the next gust of wind. He always shaved his jowls to the same dazzling pale blue sheen. He would then apply powders and creams to them, and arrange them carefully in the space allowed by his folded-over collar as if they were a discrete and separate part of his body. Occasionally he would touch them tenderly with his short, pudgy, remarkably pale fingers to check that nothing was awry, that everything was where it ought to be.

The actor spent all day on the street, on the most frequented stretch of the high street, between the church and the café, from which he could keep an eye on the side entrance to the theater. You could see him there at all hours, patrolling up and down, usually holding forth and surrounded by a gaggle of people. It was only after supper that he retreated to the middle picture window of the café where anyone passing was obliged to acknowledge his presence and from which position he, in his turn, could keep track of everyone. He didn't play cards. He didn't drink. He appeared to avoid his fellow actors. His clothes carried the sweet but choking smell of cinnamon. It was this smell that emanated from him to the outside so that anyone passing him would know that Amadé Volpay was around.

He wore two rings on his fleshy fingers, one signet ring with a red stone and a wedding ring. He never denied that he was Jewish and unmarried. The rings were only for show.

THE GANG HAD ALREADY FORMED BY THE TIME the actor first appeared in town. There is in the development of every human association a period of jelling, a process of crystallization of whose laws we remain ignorant. They had in fact been in the same class since fourth grade. Ernő was the only one who had spent eight full years at the institute. Béla, the grocer's son, had shuttled between three schools before arriving there; he was a whole year at a school in the capital. He had been educated at boarding establishments, in places where there were thirty boys to a dormitory. Even in childhood he had worn a sword with his house uniform, a ceremonial smallsword to be precise. Tibor arrived in the fourth grade when the colonel was posted to the town. Ábel entered the school in the third grade having been taught at home before that.

There had been fifty of them in the fourth grade. Only seventeen remained to graduate. The war, of which they never spoke, silently took its toll of their numbers, secretly, half-unnoticed, as it tends to do in such remote nooks of life, even in a grade at the middle school of a provincial town. When war broke out they were entering fifth grade and there were still fifty of them. Now, four years later, only seventeen remained to graduate. Many of them simply failed to reappear. The peasant boys went home to take their fathers' places. Many couldn't afford the school fees. Many more just failed to attend without telling anyone why. Perhaps they were sick. Perhaps they had died. Many did indeed die, and their bodies were borne out with flags of mourning and wailing choirs. About a million had died on the front in those years, it was said. Or was it two million? There were even some who claimed three million. But they lived their obscure and remote lives behind the lines, among the mountains, the town wrapped in silence as in cotton wool. The war filtered through to them down channels no wider than a hair's breadth. These hairbreadths sucked the life from the town as if driven by an invisible vast pump that replaced it with the stench of war, a peculiar, pestilent gas that arrived directly from the front, diluted a little, thinned out, but percolated through with enough strength to stiffen limbs, to fry lungs, and to destroy the weak. You couldn't positively say this or that student was a victim of the war. But when the war broke out there were fifty of them and by the time they posed for the class photograph there were seventeen.

For two years, until seventh grade, the members of the gang took no notice of each other. They lived separate lives in close proximity to each other. Tibor gave himself over to his passion for sport. Ábel devoted himself to literature. Ernő was wholly absorbed by his studies. It is very hard to say what brought them together, especially at this rather early age when there are no mutual concerns that help to develop friendship. You couldn't say that the members of the gang ever liked each other. Not even that they felt any common sympathy. Béla sat at the back of the class and was, for some years, one of the low achievers, and had hardly exchanged a word with Ábel or with Tibor. Ábel did occasionally spend time with Ernő but was always dismissed on a minor trifle, some hardly registered, unspoken rebuff that for a long time separated him from the cobbler's boy. Generally it is not mutual feeling that unites people. On the contrary, people usually find the process of being thrown together painful and embarrassing. It is not a particularly amusing experience for two people to find themselves in company.

For three years Ábel sat in the middle of the third row from the door. Ernő was stationed behind him, Tibor to his right in the front row. That's how they spent three years. One day at the beginning of the fourth year Ábel was staring blankly ahead, bored with physics, slowly surveying the rows of other desks when his gaze settled on Tibor who had his head in his hands oblivious to everything, absorbed, reading a book under the table. It wasn't that Ábel was particularly taken by the sight, nor was he the subject of some miraculous instantaneous illumination. Indeed, his first response was indifference and he decided to shift his attention elsewhere. But what he found, astonishingly, was that he couldn't look away for long. His eyes wandered over the room, aware of the sleepy hum of fat autumnal bluebottles trailing their gross little bodies over the window. He couldn't look away. Once he had convinced himself that it was Tibor's head that was demanding his attention, he turned round to regard him with renewed interest. Was there something about Tibor he had failed to notice before? Maybe he had combed his hair a little differently today or was wearing a strange new tie. Ábel examined him carefully. He couldn't see anything particularly different. Tibor's hair was cropped short in military fashion. He was wearing a khaki-colored outfit and a green bow-tie. His fingers were automatically soothing his brow. He kept reading. At one point he put a finger to his nose, picked something, and rubbed it between his fingers absently while turning the pages with his other hand under the desk. For all Ábel could see he was fully absorbed in his book. He was probably reading the sports annual. Something about horses or football. Ábel watched him, trying to understand what it was that was so fascinating about him. He considered Tibor's ears. They were small and pointed, close to his head. The fingers with which he was stroking his brow were bent like hooks yet the hand itself was soft and round. Ábel looked at his nose, Tibor's face in quarter profile. The face had clear angular lines. He was the softer mirror image of Colonel Prockauer, only some thirty years younger and a touch freckled. Ábel gazed at him thoughtfully, and frowned. Later it would seem as if everything he had previously known about Tibor was brought into focus in these few seconds. For instance he knew that he had freckles on his neck as well as his face: they were there where his blond hair made a narrow arch above the topmost vertebra. The marks looked as if flies had dirtied that very pale skin of his.

Now Tibor moved, pushed the book under the desk, and looked around inquiringly, returning to the world. For a moment Ábel could see those fleshy, sulky lips head-on. They indicated a state of bored annoyance. He felt shaken for a second. Out of the blue, without even thinking about it, the words *How beautiful he is!* came to him. These four words decided the matter. Then Tibor bent down again and Ábel could only see the crown of his head, the boy between them hiding him from view. This caused him such pain it was as if someone had forcefully robbed him of a unique, once-in-a-lifetime experience. It was a bodily pain occasioning a terrible sense of loss, the kind a dog feels when you snatch his half-eaten dish from him, or what anyone might feel when a breathtaking landscape is suddenly obscured by a tunnel. He felt such pain and fury it made him want to groan out loud. There were practically tears in his eyes as he shifted slightly to one side and rose a little from his seat in order to see Tibor, now, immediately, now while the beauty lasted, for one second too late and it would be gone. And it was true: for when they met at break and he could look calmly, with even a certain curiosity, into Tibor's eyes, he was disappointed to discover that he felt nothing at all.

But when he was alone in his room that afternoon, while he was drawing something, just as he had pushed away the drawing board and was starting to fiddle with the brush, somewhere between the two movements the feeling returned, much more powerful now than it had been in the morning. It was so strong that his whole body ached as he shifted: it reared up at him as he bent over the desk. He is beautiful, he cried out, half audibly. It was a wholly intangible feeling. It was a kind of happiness he had never even dreamt of. There was a sweetness to it, a taste that brought tears to his eyes. It made him shake. He is beautiful: Tibor is beautiful, he repeated with bloodless lips, feeling a touch chilly. His hand was cold too, bloodless and trembling. He stood up and ran about the room a little, avoiding the furniture. There were tears in his eyes: he felt dizzy and would have liked to hold on to something. A desire for oblivion flooded through him. This was the ultimate thing, this beauty. There was nothing else. The world could offer no more. The tame world he had so far inhabited was split wide open, its contents ran out: he stood naked and shivering.

A week later the gang was formed. It takes hardly a moment to form a crystal from the appropriate miscellaneous elements: you cannot know what process preceded the formation, just as we cannot know what drives certain people together, people who hitherto knew nothing of each other, but who immediately form a solid body under conditions that create more anxiety than guilt ever does: so it is with parents and children, so with lovers, and so with murderers. They launched forth from the four corners of that room, each greedy for the others, as if they had been waiting years for precisely this, as if they had a thousand things to communicate and share. Within a week the four of them were as one though they had hardly said a word to each other before. Béla, on whom they had slightly looked down, was practically breathless in the effort to join them before it was too late. Once all four were together in a nook of the corridor they looked into each other's eyes and started to speak. Ernő took off his pince-nez and they suddenly fell silent. Tibor stood in the center. He started to say something but the words stuck in his mouth. The other three were looking at him. They waited, silent a while, then all four slowly shuffled back to their places.

THEY WERE STANDING BY THE REVOLVING DOORS of the café. The actor took his hand for a second. The

46

Roman emperors had been absolute rulers. There was something of Nero in Amadé. Nero himself had been an actor. Fine. In any case you are the first adult whom I can address familiarly as *tu,* with whom I am on *tutoyer* terms, as an adult with adults. He says he has visited Barcelona. He might be lying. One should check up and make sure. Father is sitting down to supper. He might have amputated four legs by now, legs as substantial as this actor's. Here's Lajos. He has half an arm missing. Amadé is wearing a pale brown necktie today: this is the fourth necktie he has been seen wearing. Here comes Mr. Kikinday whom someone seems to have sentenced to death. His necktie is dark blue with white spots. Yellow silk with green stripes. White silk with big blue spots. Etelka has a blouse that is white silk with big blue spots. She no longer wears it: it is a year since she last had it on. Amadé always has that cinnamon smell. We were playing in the garden with the janitor's daughter, then we went to the shed and played a game in which I punished her so she had to lie down and I pulled up her skirt and beat her bare bottom till it was red. Then Etelka turned up, saw us, and gave us a beating. I was four. The girl three. Etelka was forty. Once she left the door open to the cupboard full of underwear and I pulled out a shred of cloth and played with it, tying it round my head the way the maid does her headscarf. Etelka grew quite red when she saw me, snatched the cloth from me, and smacked my hand. Today I know the thing I was playing with was her brassiere, that the piece of cloth she dashed off with was a brassiere fresh from the laundry. I was four. How do I know now that the shred of cloth was my aunt's brassiere? No one told me. And what was there so outrageous about the fact that my aunt had breasts that required support? How warm that hand is. His hand is so soft that my index finger sinks into the pad of flesh in his palm. Amadé's wig is nicely fixed. When I found my aunt's hair in the cupboard behind the books I thought I had finally unmasked her. My aunt had no wig but she did wear hairpieces. I discovered two fat shiny pigtails. I might tell Tibor that later in the evening. Or perhaps Amadé. Maybe neither, but just Ernō. If I told Amadé he would answer with some nonsense rhyme like "Round pig, little pig, open mouth, and jig-jig-jig!" And he'd open his mouth and stick his fleshy tongue out between his thick lips as he always does. He's laughing now and I can see his gold teeth. The actor released his hand. They went in through the revolving doors.

THE REVOLVING DOORS MOVED ROUND WITH them and they entered the café. It was the sort of hour at which cafés in provincial towns are empty but for the usual roster of dubious characters. The only signs of life were in the separate card rooms. In one room sat two lawyers, the editor of a local paper, and a very short man with hair carefully parted in the middle, his outfit selected with painstaking refinement. Opposite the door sat Havas. He was holding cards in his hand, his bald head glistening with drops of perspiration. Now and then he dipped his hand into his pocket and wiped his brow with a red handkerchief. The man who used to run the mill, now the owner of the town pawnbroker's shop, declared, *Three-card run, two aces, game,* as they passed him. The actor and Ábel stopped to greet them. Havas made as if to rise from his chair but never moved: the vast body remained glued to his seat. He congratulated them. Your friends are already here. He seemed absent-minded, radiant with a kind of happiness that quickly drew him back to his cards. He declared himself in for the next round. The air in the card room was sour, worse than in the main part of the café. This might have been because the card players, having played for several hours, had grown careless of social niceties, or because it was difficult to air those little booths and the players were perspiring rather heavily. They threw their cigar butts on the floor. One or two of them spat on the remains and the dying stubs filled the lower regions of the café with acrid smoke. The gang sat in a little booth as they used to do when the café was still strictly out of bounds to them. The actor immediately sat himself at the head of the table. Ábel took his place by Ernő.

Someone has cheated, he announced calmly.

He took out the cards and spread them out on the table. He had never felt so calm before.

I don't want to take ages over this, he said, and noted with astonishment his own perfectly level voice.—I had no idea what I was going to do about it on my way here, what I was going to do or say, or if indeed I was going to say anything at all. But there we are: now I have said it. I don't know if he has been cheating for long or whether this was the first time. He brought two aces with him, one heart and one acorn, and two tens, a leaf and a bell. While we were weighing things up he dropped a ten instead of an ace, or picked up three cards including a ten and didn't ask for more, but secretly added an ace. Have a look at the cards: their backs resemble those of the ones we are using. It is impossible to tell the difference between our cards and the cheat's.

Ernō raised his head to take a deep breath, removed his pince-nez, and frowned furiously. Béla pressed the monocle he was wearing in public for the first time into his pale, puffy, acne-covered face. Tibor opened his mouth a little way and ground his teeth.

Let's just go back to my place right now, said Béla. Right now. Go through my drawers, my cupboards, my books, try every pocket of all my suits, and why not cut the linings open while you're at it? Do it all. Search the entire apartment. If you want to frisk my person you can do that immediately, right here.

You're an idiot, said Tibor. Sit down.

Tibor's face was not so red now. In fact he looked extremely pale. Under his blond hair his brow looked as white as a lime-washed wall. His lips were trembling.

He's right, you're an idiot, Ábel continued.—It's not about frisking you. Not you, not me, not Ernō, not Tibor. None of us is to be frisked. *Lajos was only messing about.* Look, here's the proof. Two aces, two tens. Someone brought cards with him, either in his pocket or up his sleeve. One of us must therefore be cheating.

Keep your voice down, said the one-armed man.

They drew closer together.—What's terrible about

this, he continued in a low voice, is that we will never know who it was. Understand? Never. We could search everyone individually but we are, each of us, equally innocent and equally under suspicion. It's not a matter of money. In any case, who came out as winners this afternoon?

They counted back. Béla and Ernő seemed to have won roughly an equal number of times, Béla playing a high-risk game, Ernő more cautiously. Ábel and Tibor both lost.

The loser might just as likely have cheated, said Ábel. Perhaps he cheated because he was losing. Everyone is equally under suspicion. You can treat me as a suspect too if you want. It is true that I was the one who discovered the cheating but it might be that I get a kick out of flirting with danger. I might have cheated then made a deliberate point of launching the accusation and taking pleasure in seeing all of you torturing yourselves. That's why I say we would be idiots to frisk each other. We are all equally under suspicion.

Everyone is suspect, the one-armed one declared happily, grinning.

They weren't listening to him. Ábel looked up with a pained expression on his face.

But maybe I wasn't the cheat, he said slowly and speculatively. The strange thing is that we could imagine any one of us cheating so the cap fits all. It seems everyone that may be suspected might be guilty.

That's an exaggeration, said the one-armed one.

The actor ordered ham with pickled cucumber, a soft-boiled egg, and tea with lemon. They didn't look at each other. The actor hadn't yet said anything; instead he thoughtfully adjusted his wig, and apart from a little chomping, began to eat in the most delicate and refined manner. He held the dessert spoon lightly with two fingers, cracked the shell of the egg with a demure, slightly amused tap, used the ends of two fingers to break off a pinch of bread and dip it into the yolk, cut the fatty edge off the ham with infinite care, and conducted a tricky surgical operation to excavate a sliver of muscle from it. He raised the knife with one hand like a conductor with his baton.

"That's an exaggeration," he pronounced with a mild but firm voice that brooked no contradiction.—"Lajos is right again! Have you noticed how Lajos has always been right recently? You exaggerate, my friend"—he turned forty-five degrees to address Ábel.—"We are all aware of your tender, sensitive soul."

He stuffed a slice of ham into his mouth.

"Don't take this amiss, but only very young people can say that kind of thing. My general experience of the world, or so I have observed on my travels, is that people get over everything. That is providing they survive of course."

He bent over the egg and sniffed it.

"You are of a philosophical bent, that is all. Naturally, it is an unpleasant episode. We have every reason to believe what our friend Ábel says. One of you has cheated. It's not such a bad thing."

He clicked his tongue.

"What does it mean? Perhaps it wasn't the money that

he cheated for. People never know what they are going to do next. It's a puzzle, a real puzzle. He came prepared of course, for he brought the cards. Maybe he just flirted with the thought. Life is just a big game, my friends."

He touched the cards carelessly, put down his knife and fork, and leaned back. He looked around him in a dreamy fashion, surprised by the rapt attention he noted on their faces. He had got used to the fact that people never took serious note of what he said, that they heard him with mocking or indifferent expressions. In this company each word of his hit home. He gave a smirk of satisfaction.

"I am not thinking of the unmasking of our friend, Ábel," he said with a dismissive gesture. "What are cards? What is money? It's something else I have in mind. When through my friend Lajos's kind attentions, I was invited to join your circle ... my young friends, my very young friends ... the first question I asked myself, having acknowledged the charming impression you immediately made on me, was what holds them together? Because something does hold you together. I have considerable experience in gauging human relationships. I said to myself: something joins them together but they do not speak of it. Yet each of them thinks about it. And one of them is cheating."

He ate with great gusto. The ham slice became a ham sliver, the egg a hollow shell. Everything he picked up, even the salt cellar, seemed to be on familiar terms with him.

He spoke quietly, ceremoniously, with feeling. He even

closed his eyes for a moment as if communing with himself. Havas's voice could be heard from the next cubicle, and the slapping down of cards. A woman was moving through the café with a bucket and mop in her hand. The waiter sat by the billiard tables in the half-light, like a monk by the window of his cell at twilight. Lajos ran his eyes around the company with lively, friendly interest.

"It is probably unimportant that the person in question has now extended his cheating activities to a card game," the actor continued. "He is your Judas, and we don't really know him. He is someone I dare not even begin to suspect since the four of you are equally dear to me, and yet he must have been cheating you for a long time, cheating in his every word, his every look. The only reason he cheated at cards was because he wanted to round off his triumph in that way. He wanted to experience the full physical delight of having cheated you.

"There's a nice expression: *to sweep something under the carpet.* It is an excellent expression. Don't rack your brains, my friends. We are together. It's been a wonderful day. You are no longer responsible to your masters. I thought we could celebrate the event tonight."

The actor continued his meal with patent satisfaction. Here's to a good time tonight, he said, his mouth full.

A calendar hung in the enclosure. Ábel stared at the date: May seventeenth.

We'll have a nice little haroosh, said the actor and chomped a little more.

Ábel slowly gathered up the cards one by one. Technical terms of the game. *Bank, clear-out, castle, take one, flush, no flush.* Ernő never offered up a flush. The cards clicked in Havas's hands. Who is Havas? The proprietor of the town pawnbroker's shop. Why has he been dreaming about him for weeks on end now? He dreams that Havas enters the room, wipes his walrus mustache with the back of his hand, and unbuttons his collar in leisurely fashion. He is laughing so hard his eyes are quite lost in the folds of fat. His breath is like the stink of a kitchen: it smells of lard and dishwater. Tibor's mouth assumes that defiant suffering look.

He has put the cards in his pocket.

They watched each other carefully, bent over the table again, made eye contact with one brief last look, and immediately shifted their gaze. The waiter stood up and went to the door, turning on the lamps as he went. Guests were arriving. Two officers, then the town clerk. The Gypsies shuffled in.

HAVAS STOPPED AT THE DOOR OF THE CUBICLE. Cigar ash was clinging to his crumpled and swollen waistcoat. He took the cigar holder from his mouth.

Greetings, Amadé, he puffed, out of breath.

Greetings, Emil.

They turned to him.

"Your servant, gentlemen," said Havas. "My compliments."

"Soon be time for the May picnic," said the one-armed one.

They had discussed the May picnic in the afternoon. It

had been the one-armed one's idea, and was generally welcomed. They liked the thought of it and talked about the recent mild weather. They were bound to agree if the one-armed man thought of it. They would hold the picnic in the grounds of The Peculiar on top of the hill. They had already sent a messenger to inform the innkeeper. They had reasons for choosing The Peculiar. The one-armed one had had a very productive afternoon in town. Everything was ready. He had ordered lanterns, had spoken with the teaching staff and got most of the alumni to agree. The Peculiar was already green and leafy. They could always go inside if they needed to at night. Cost of ticket, five crowns. Those paying no school fees half price. Dear Guests Are Cordially Invited. Havas sat down with them. He made sucking noises with his cigar holder. He said a May picnic was a jolly good idea. The weather was good, quite summery. He himself had never liked outdoor parties. One sits down at night on damp grass, one's rear chills down, it leads to looseness of the bowels. Havas would have preferred the party to be in the Petőfi café.

"I went to nothing better than an ordinary state school," he said with satisfaction, "but I have no hesitation in commending the Petőfi. It's not much to look at. It's a single-story building with a not particularly attractive entrance. But inside, gentlemen, a man can feel at home. The proprietor spent four years in jail for pimping. That was in peacetime. So he made mistakes. So what? It's like being at home. I have even danced on the billiards table there. Should anyone wish to dance on the billiards table I propose the Petőfi café. A bottle of *reservé* costs eight crowns."

He gazed sleepily in front of him. The actor finished eating.

"No news from your dear father?" the pawnbroker asked Tibor.

His voice was deferential and respectful. Amadé stared at his plate. Ábel raised his head and sneaked a look at Tibor. The one-armed one looked bored. Tibor moved. He made as if to leap to his feet.

No news, he said.

"A hero," Havas declared. "The colonel is a hero. The hero of Valjevo."

He drew his chair closer to the table.

"Now here's a remarkable thing, gentlemen, for young Lajos is a hero too. The hero of Isonzo. And now young Master Tibor too will have the opportunity of showing what he can do. A heroic family."

"That's enough, you old fool," said Ernő.

The pawnbroker gave a forced laugh. They breathed a little more easily. Ernő was the only one who dared talk to the pawnbroker like this. The pawnbroker was a friend of Amadé. When people met the pawnbroker they tended to avert their eyes.

The pawnbroker was professional and polite in his official capacity. *The article please. Write it down, miss: a lady's gold pocket watch, 80 grams, estimated value 120, deposit 100, less handling and interest 4.60, there we are 95.40. Next please.* He did not look up. He didn't even look

57

up when Tibor brought him the silver. The well-known Prockauer silverware, complete with monogram. Aristocratic Prockauer. The actor had talked with him that morning. They were taking his mother into the hospital for two days, for tests. That was six months ago already: *October 13, 1917. Date elapsed: April 13, 1918. Write it down, miss. One set of silverware for 24, 22 kilograms, with monogram. Estimated value 800. Deposit 600.* He didn't look up: his nimble fingers pushed the money under the glass screen.

"I, for example, would never eat only cold ham for supper," said Havas. "It's not the food, I believe. My friend Amadé claims it's the diet. But please, what use is a diet to me? I lose not an ounce of weight, I get a headache, and it's such agony I want to curse all day. A body needs decent sustenance I say. And a spot of exercise. Love has a slimming effect too. Love, gentlemen, take it from one who knows. But how is one to find a little love nowadays? It's scarce. A man has to rely on himself."

"Fat pig," said Ernő and turned away from him.

They laughed awkwardly. So did the actor. The actor was showing his false white teeth as though Ernő had said something remarkably witty. They cackled as though compelled to do so. Ábel blushed. There was something painful yet welcome about the way Ernő had addressed Havas. Havas weighed close to two hundred and ninety pounds. Ernő knew that unless a miracle occurred everything depended on him: they were all dependent on Havas being in a good mood. Tibor's mother hadn't yet noticed the silverware was missing. But the colonel might arrive home any day on leave or wounded and he might decide to inspect it. It did not bear thinking about what would happen if the silverware was not in its usual place. The colonel had once knocked the driver of a dray cold with his bare fist. It wasn't just Lajos and Tibor's fate at stake: it was all their fates. If the silverware was lost, if Havas didn't want to hang on to it until they found some money, it was possible the colonel wouldn't stop short of setting the lawyers on them. Their affairs would not bear close examination. It was a private matter. All that had happened in the last six months was their business and no one else's. If only Havas would grant them a few weeks' grace. Just until they had finished their training. True, the matter of the silverware would have to be faced even so. The colonel might follow them to the front and threaten them with a sound whipping even in the heat of battle. There was no limit to the power of fathers.

Ernő spoke to Havas as though it were degrading to address remarks to him. The pawnbroker put up with it. Ernő had some hold on the pawnbroker, though no one knew what that hold was. Maybe he knew something about him, was aware of a piece of dirty business, had information about his usury. Ernő would turn away whenever the pawnbroker approached them. He pulled a painful face, as if the disgusting sight were enough to make him spit. The pawnbroker pretended not to notice Ernő, nor to hear his insults. He hastened to agree with anything he said. He kept smiling. The hairs of his mustache bristled as he smiled. Tibor said Havas was frightened of Ernő.

The actor looked as if he were daydreaming and occasionally glanced away.

"It is all settled," he told Tibor. "Havas is a friend and he knows you to be gentlemen. There is nothing in the conditions that obliges him . . . He won't demand anything."

Havas did not demand anything. The money, like all money in the last few months, drained invisibly away: they were having to save Béla with it. Amadé was embarrassed, since he too was in receipt of some. He kept quiet for now. He smiled. He could smile so stiffly while looking straight ahead that one would think he had a glass eye. His bluish jowls sat stolidly in the vent of his collar. His brow practically shone. It was like precious china. He smiled, a toothpick dangling from his lips, and looked fixedly into the distance with his glass eyes. The pawnbroker fitted a new cigar into the holder. They stared at each other, smiling icily. The actor gave an almost imperceptible shrug. They both smiled.

"Master Ernő is right," said the pawnbroker. "I am a fat pig. I have got used to it. What can I do about it? So I'm fat. Should I torture myself with the thought? I am the kind of fat man who is fat because he eats a lot. Amadé is the kind of fat man who eats practically nothing and yet is still fat. I'd die if I couldn't eat properly. A fine, solid piece of roast pork, in a nice crispy roasted skin, accompanied by potatoes boiled with onions and some pickled gherkins: it's a pleasure biting at the crisp skin. That's the stuff for me. And *lángos* with cabbage. This is my fate in life. You should try to see me as the helpless creature of fate."

Everyone looked at him and Ábel noted the pained courteous smile on Tibor's face. It was this smile that he particularly liked about him. There was something distracted and troubled about it, a kind of noblesse oblige. Tibor was trying to smile indulgently at Havas's corpulence. Béla was giving him a fish-eyed look as if he had never seen him before. Ernő was screwing up his nose.

"Yes, just imagine it . . . ," he said with a shudder of disgust.

"You should see me undressed," Havas continued, calm and solemn. He drew loudly on his cigar holder. He nodded. "Yes, terrible. And I should also confess that I wear a girdle. Not a full girdle, just a thing that goes round my stomach. When I take it off my belly simply drops."

He surveyed the assembled company. The actor gave a croak.

"Are you staying with us, Emil?"

The pawnbroker rose slowly to his feet. He put on his hat so it was tipped back over his head. His brow was glistening with sweat.

"Thank you for the kind invitation," he said quietly. "I will not remain with the gentlemen tonight."

Tibor made a sudden movement.

"I would like to speak to you tomorrow, Mr. Havas."

The pawnbroker's eyes disappeared under his swollen lids.

"At your service, Mr. Prockauer."

"Not at your shop."

"Just as you please," said Havas. "Two o'clock at my apartment then. At your service." He looked around. "Perhaps Master Ábel would like to come too," he added.

Ábel blushed. Tibor turned away. "Yes, I'll come too," said Ábel quickly.

The pawnbroker nodded as if he thought this the most natural thing. He did not shake hands with anyone. Once he had gone Tibor sat back down and rubbed his eyes.

"And now we shall have the most splendid party," said the actor.

2

THE TOWN DOZES AMONG MOUNTAINS, PRE-
served in cotton wool, its three towers pointing
indifferently at the sky. There is electricity and running
water in its houses. A train in the station is blowing its
whistle. Three mountain peaks surround the town: inside
the rock, some copper and a little magnesite. A river
rushes through, a brisk mountain stream, the air above it
sharp and hard and delivered into the heart of town while,
in the opposite direction, the dense forest swarms up the
mountainside. The middle peak retains its cap of snow for
a considerable time: the locals are proud of the alpine
backdrop it so picturesquely provides. A narrow-gauge
train carries passengers from the railway station to the
main square. The houses too are narrow and long, tending
to shoulder up against each other because the town was
once a fort and people have lived here for generations. The
seminary is yellow: mornings and evenings you can see the
monks in their brown robes, their rope cords, and sandals
carrying their rosaries as they make their way to church for

their devotions. The bishop's palace has a wide wrought-iron balcony, its spikes complete with baroque ornamentation, the flag-holder above them. The bishop walks out with his secretary every afternoon at three, the secretary's hard hat glimmering with silk and a tassel dangling behind from the hat's rim. The bishop makes a point of grandly greeting everyone who greets him. He rises early because he is an old man who sleeps badly; by dawn he is standing at his high desk forming tiny pearl-like letters. Others are measuring out wine in the cellars of the town hall, the wine stone cold. The vaults of the cellars are made of heavy slate: a century ago it was Poles who were drinking the wine here, the smoky marks of their torches still visible on the walls. Damp keg smells, the delicate, dense smell of alcohol and stearin candles. A bread ticket. Closing time. An endless sequence of barely noticed trains passes through town. One rumbles past now: it measures at least two or three hundred meters but the platform guard doesn't even look up and the trains roll on carrying holidaymakers and the wounded, for here is the resort and here is the station. Some open the doors of their cars for an hour or so and the smell of carbolic and iodine oozes out to an enormous silence. The smell wafts downtown but is particularly acrid near the station. Big buckets of lime wait on the platform, for it sometimes happens that certain passengers have to be carried from the train and need to be sprinkled with it. But this is the fourth year of hostilities and the town has gotten used to it, especially those people whose job it is to sprinkle lime. They are very quiet now. There are no longer attendants in snow-white garments with red crosses on their armbands waiting at the resort station: the lady volunteers of the town are gone along with their shining uniforms that looked as crisp as those worn by wax nurse dolls displayed in the pharmaceutical department of the big store, to be replaced by, at most, two sanitary workers whose uniforms do not shine and are not crisp, and who grunt *hey-upp* when called upon to act as stretcher bearers. The war is a long way from here. There is only a kind of ash or soot, the kind that is carried from a distant fire and falls some distance from its source. The war will never reach as far as this. There were only telegrams at the beginning, and then the trains that passed through town. An elementary school had to be turned into a hospital as did half the monastery. A number of people were awarded distinctions for their services to the nation. The stationer's window still displays the maps of Russia and France, but the nimble, plumpish old proprietor no longer nips out each morning to pin tiny flags on them to mark the victories of the Central Powers with his own fair hands; in fact he tends not to put pins anywhere and has lost a little weight for no one pays attention to the maps now. The town has become accustomed to the war. No one talks about it, rushes out for special editions of the local paper, or bothers to pick up the national press at the station. The town has become accustomed to the war in the way one can get used to old age, the thought of death, to anything at all. The roads are a little neglected, a lot of people go about in mourning dress, some familiar faces have disappeared, but you can't deny that a few sprigs of well-being are blossoming in the ruins. The war is a distant hourglass, sand mixed with human remains, but this morning you could see the treasurer in his gray morning suit and yellow elastic-sided boots in the public gardens, girls who were children only four years ago but are now slender young ladies strolling down the promenade, girls to whom men turn their minds despite the war. It is a small, clean, and colorful town, a toy town in its gift box. There is a lot of litter everywhere now, houses are not repaired, old notices in groceries inform the public that salted fish are expected, but that's about all. Red, blue, and yellow advertisements on street columns. And, here too, those who are doing well can find opportunities for helping themselves. Every afternoon the town clerk may be seen ambling through Szent János Square with his vizsla hound, heading for the embankment to play fetch. The movie house is pretty popular and the theater is almost always full when they perform operetta. Amadé Volpay is the comic. One day Ábel will be sitting in a big city and will pronounce the words "world war," but recall only Tibor and Amadé, and a certain anxiety and curiosity. One's hometown is not merely the church tower or a square with a fountain though, it is flourishing trade and industry, it is the doorway where some thought first crossed your mind, a bench on which you used to sit pondering something incomprehensible, a moment in the shower where you seemed dizzily to remember fragments of an earlier existence, a neatly polished pebble found in an old drawer that you can no longer think why you stored there, the scripture master's hat, brown with an unbecoming patch, the cold sweat before a history lesson, strange games whose rules no one understood and you were too embarrassed to explain, a lie the consequences of which gave you nightmares for the rest of your life, an object in someone's hand, a voice you hear at night through an open window and cannot forget, the way a room is lit, two tassels under a pair of curtains. War is not precisely what we tend to think about it. Ábel will not be telling tales about it to his grandchildren as they sit on his knee, because in him too the war awakens memories of fear and anxiety, but the fear is in respect of Tibor and the anxiety is focused on Amadé. The population numbers sixty thousand. There are tennis courts. The town happens to be asleep right now, the mayor has problems with his heart and lies spread-eagled in his bed, his dentures in the glass of water beside him; in musty rooms omnipotent fathers sleep in nightshirts beside their wives. In the woods above town animals are waking. The actor is saying: Sad to say, you don't know real vodka. The real pure stuff turns everything you see a blue color.

THEY BEGAN STEALING AT THE BEGINNING OF November.

There was a short period, a few weeks in the gang's existence, when they could amuse themselves perfectly well without money. They would meet at Ábel's or Tibor's place. Sometimes they could spend the whole night at Ábel's, if they kept their heads down until his aunt had dozed off. At that early stage they didn't need to pay for entertainment. Cash only became an issue afterwards once their experiments and exploits developed more complex requirements. Béla was the first to commit a theft.

It was he who had sought explanations and raised objections, who labored to excuse himself. No one had prevailed on him to steal but once he started making excuses, they spontaneously shouted, indeed howled him down. Béla had stolen thirty crowns from his father's cash-box in order to buy a pair of brown, handmade, double-soled shoes he had coveted in the display of a recently opened shoe shop. He bought the shoes, brought them over to Tibor's, tried them on, and walked about in the room for half an hour. He didn't dare go out into the street wearing them because he was terrified at the thought of meeting his father who would notice the shoes on his feet and might get to asking where they were from.

The way things worked at his father's big grocery store allowed Béla, once most of the assistants had been drafted and schoolkids had to be engaged to take their place, to remove money inconspicuously from the box, small sums at first, then ever larger ones. Some afternoons, when his father took a nap Béla would slip unnoticed through the gloom of the shop into the glass booth where his father kept cash in the drawer of his desk. The daily intake was substantial enough to allow his theft of ten or twenty crowns to go unremarked.

Béla worked fast. He bought himself a miscellaneous set of clothes. He was rather fastidious. One relative, the district magistrate, had hanged himself from the window catch in the third year of the war because he feared his wife and children would starve to death. His father-in-law's shop cellars might be stacked with millstone-shaped Swiss cheeses, herring, wheat, potatoes, rice, and sardines but they failed to reassure him and the thought of starving gripped his family's imagination. Whether at home, at table, or in the shop, Béla, who was able to take his pick of such delicacies even at times of strictest rationing, found little satisfaction in his father's rich Canaan store. He spent the stolen money in other grocers' shops, surreptitiously purchasing Baltic herring, Turkish delight, sardines, and anchovies in oil at inflated prices, all goods the traders had bought from his own father.

Béla was as terrified of his father as simple people are of natural disasters. The mere mention of his name left him pale and trembling. In the gang's imagination Colonel Prockauer was one of the Fates of Ancient Greece, the Fates who could strike out of the blue and wreak universal carnage, leaving behind a flat plain and the smoke of ruins. Béla's father was not, like him, an act of fate but part of their common, wholly undramatic lot, an ordinary accident. His bony hand would come into contact with his son's face and administer light but very powerful blows with a cold methodical regularity, the kind delivered by people with heart problems, anxious—for the family's sake—not to get themselves overexcited. Once he threw a knife at an apprentice boy, a great big blade he used to cut cheese with, that lay on the counter covered in cheese parings.

For a long time it was only Béla who stole. They even took care to ensure that it should be Béla alone who spent the stolen money. He had to consume the food he had bought with it in front of the others without any assistance from the gang. Ernő sat opposite the thief, his penetrating gaze fixed on him, checking that he ate it all up, his cheeks crammed, his eyes bulging.

He hid the items of clothing he had bought at Tibor's apartment. He bought other things too: a double-barreled shotgun, a powerful magnifying glass, an enormous papier-mâché globe, a pair of leather leggings with fine straps, a Browning revolver. It was when he bought the bicycle he never dared to ride because he didn't know how to and because some acquaintance might see him and tell his father that the moment of decision about the hiding place arrived. The purchases were multiplying. Tibor, who was afraid that his father would suddenly turn up, no longer felt up to acting as Béla's unclaimed luggage office. They had to get rid of the things somehow.

They began by ordering Béla about. Béla grimaced and obeyed. Within two days he was told to buy an entire fireworks display that would be thrown into the river the next evening. Ernő was the fount of their best ideas, for example the one where Béla had to steal sixty crowns and send a bouquet of flowers to the prior at the monastery. According to the messenger, the reverend father received the gift with considerable astonishment. He blushed in embarrassment, made a clumsy bow, and stood there with the flowers in his hand, covered in confusion.

They did more than play cards at Ábel's place. They told tales of passion, lying their heads off. The stories had to begin with the words: "This afternoon I was passing the theater when I met a sailor, the captain of a ship." The town lay thousands of miles from any sea. They had to inquire of the sea captain how he came to be in town and what he was doing here. The extraordinary story that developed out of the meeting with the captain had to be built up, detail by detail, out of facts that could be checked or were thought to be at least credible, complete with witnesses who actually lived in town a few streets away and could testify to the truth of the narrator's account. The core of the story was pure fantasy but the details had to be simple and clear.

They went around as a foursome. They took up the sidewalk and, at all hours of the day, would be found padding down the narrower streets like a wary military detachment, wholly preoccupied. Ernő and Ábel took care that their exploits should be interesting and should remain within the bounds of the feasible. They fastidiously rejected certain ideas the group threw up as a whole. After a few weeks Béla too learned the ropes. Tibor, with his refined instincts, had no problems adapting to group existence. If the games and exploits they undertook had any rules, they remained unacknowledged, the only criterion being that they should have no practical use. Ernő described their activities as self-justifying. Béla stole and bought useless things with the stolen money, clothes he would never wear and items of technical apparatus whose application was beyond his understanding.

They even came up with the idea of having some kind of gang uniform made, something they could wear at home, but they rejected it. Another time they enthusiastically agreed that they should find a tailor out of town and order garments they could never wear because they were too big, or because the trousers or the jacket were hilariously tight, all to be made from the most expensive material that could be found.

One day Ernő brought them the address of such a tailor.

Each of them looked him up individually. Tibor ordered a tailcoat made of white sail canvas with yellow silk lining. Ernő chose an enormous checkered suit that would have accommodated several of him, the trouser legs being attached at the ankle by means of elastic bands. Ábel ordered a cutaway coat that reached down to his heels. The one-armed one chose a suit that had no sleeves at all, the jacket smoothly stitched at the shoulders, tight and armless.

Béla decided on a simple riding costume, a scarlet hunting coat, long black trousers. He also procured spurs and a top hat. They spent hours at the tailor anxiously getting themselves measured up, measuring the tails of Ábel's heel-length jacket to check that it should not be, even a centimeter or two, longer than it needed to be. The tailor thought they were preparing for a carnival.

He delivered the various articles of clothing in one single lot. The day they first tried them on was March 3, 1918, the day of the Brest-Litovsk Treaty.

THE NICE THING ABOUT FRIENDSHIP IS THAT IT is unselfish. From time to time they took an inventory of their possessions and divided them up among themselves.

Béla offered the double-barreled shotgun and a pair of spurs to Ernő with a cordial smile. By way of return Ernő presented him with three raw leather soles from his father's shop along with a little china Virgin and Child.

Once the habit of exchanging gifts was established it was impossible for the others to refuse. Ábel started by stealing books from home: the second volume of *Sons of a Stony-Hearted Man* and *The Lives of the Saints*. The books were dutifully acknowledged. When Tibor stole the colonel's horn-handled knife, Ábel, in a rush of enthusiasm, offered his aunt's fortune to the gang. They discussed the offer with a certain reluctance. The word "fortune" awed them: for them it suggested wads of paper money, books full of savings, and any number of precious stones. Eventually they agreed that Ábel should bring them the fortune one afternoon. They put on their specially made costumes for the occasion, and carefully went through the tin box Ábel had delivered precisely on time, rendering an account of all the out-of-date lottery tickets, pawnbrokers' bills, and worthless old banknotes in a pocket book, before Ábel surreptitiously returned the box to its usual place.

Everyone contributed to the common store according to his talent. The guiding principle was that the worth of any contribution depended on the peril involved in the object's removal rather than on its fiscal value. It was reckoned a piece of derring-do to extract an officially stamped book from the school library and to sell the volume to that exploiter of poor students, the secondhand book dealer. This was in fact an exploit full of danger because the punishment for taking a valuable institutional book was expulsion, possibly followed by legal proceedings. Ernő took responsibility for the mission and carried it out with remarkable success. Allegedly he hypnotized the second-hand-book seller into accepting the sale. The money made from such an exchange had to be "used for the good." As to what that good was, each had his own opinion: with the money they had put together they bought a little gold chain from the local jeweler but, having bargained long and hard with him, left it on the shelf and never returned for it.

The gang made a decision that the various teachers they had tormented over the years, according to the usual unspoken compact whereby staff and students torment each other mercilessly, were off-limits: staff should now be treated with due care and consideration. They sat in class quietly, folding their arms in rapt attention. Béla would rush from the back of the room to the front in order to assist the staff member with impeccable courtesy. Occasionally they combined to astound one or another teacher with their exhaustive knowledge of the set topic and to encourage order and respect among their fellow students. The class regarded all this with suspicion but that didn't bother them. They were aware that they were partaking of far higher amusements than these other blockheads who hadn't got beyond age-old idiotic pranks and the crude taunting of teachers: they could be polite, appear to be infinitely conscientious, and could lull and eventually disarm their suspicious, tortured superiors. This was far more amusing than crude, disruptive jokes. Not long before

Christmas the form master felt obliged to deliver a short speech to the class presenting Béla and Tibor as exemplars, greeting them like reformed black sheep.

Béla couldn't control himself. He bought skeleton keys and rubber gloves he had absolutely no use for, for no better reason than that he had unobstructed access to the ready cashbox in his father's desk. He no longer knew what to do with the money. The gang stuck stubbornly to its "for its own sake" principles, and the ten or twenty crowns they daily procured were spent on equally useless items. Béla developed a double passion for cosmetics and fashionable clothes. After his fervent pleas they allowed him to order two elegant up-to-the-minute suits, along with a silk shirt, a high-quality necktie, fine deerskin gloves, and lacquered shoes with antelope inlay. He also purchased a soft, pale-colored rabbit-fur hat and a light bamboo cane. Once a week he was permitted to dress up in these at Tibor's apartment, while the gang passed the items to him, the one-armed one being tireless in his efforts to beautify him. Once Béla stood there, fully dressed at the mirror with the hat on his head, the gloves on his hands, and the cane at his side, they made him walk up and down the room like a mannequin at a salon, while they passed critical comments on his outfit. Once this was over he sat in a chair opposite the mirror, grinding his teeth, gazing and gazing at his reflection. Then he slowly undressed. Tibor took the clothes and carefully locked them away in his wardrobe while Béla donned his inelegant school clothes again, the trousers of which were made from an old pair of his father's.

As far as the cosmetics were concerned, his addiction had to remain a secret from the rest of the gang. His obsession with such items as pomades, scents, face creams, combs, and fine soap did not meet with their approval. He was not allowed to use the expensive lotion he had bought to treat his spots: the gang seized it, made him strip, and spread the cream that, supposedly, could make all spots and warts disappear in a matter of days, over his buttocks.

Their rebellion regarding the function and use of various objects and matters extended to include some peculiar sacrifices. For example it was regarded as correct and admirable to spend days fretting in the attempt to learn some ten lines of text from a Swedish book, a language no one in the region could speak. Ábel won considerable prestige by parroting such phrases. At the same time it was considered a mortal sin to cram for the next day's Latin or history class. They did not reject intellectual effort in itself but prized it only when it yielded no practical result. There were equally stringent rules regarding sins of the flesh. Tibor was an outstanding athlete, passionate about the long and high jump, so found it hard to resist leaping over a fallen chair or some other obstacle. They let him indulge the joy of leaping, but only when attempting to leap a distance or height that was clearly beyond his capacities and there remained a good chance that he would bruise himself in the process.

The hoard grew and grew. Everything was shoved into Tibor's room for the time being. It was only the arrival of the bicycle that rendered the space too narrow. The Prockauers lived in a single-story building, and one could only get into the boy's room by passing through the room where his sick mother lay. The situation was rendered slightly less problematic by the fact that the windows in his room opened onto the yard, so the heavier and more awkward articles could be passed through the window. The window was also useful as a means of entrance and departure though someone usually had to be posted to engage the mother's attention. The person most frequently entrusted with that task was Ernō, who would sit with hands clasped by the woman's bedside, his hat on his knees, his eyes fixed on the ground, while the traffic continued in and out of Tibor's window.

It was hardly possible to move now in either Tibor's or Lajos's room. The purloined objects covered the table, the top of the cupboard, and the beds. The gang had started competing with one another. Ábel had brought his father's pliers and pincers, an old camera, and parts of his aunt's girlhood trousseau whose lilac ribbons and yellowed papyrus colors spoke eloquently of the expectations of an unrequired maidenhead. Out of sheer good manners Tibor attempted to match Ábel's offering with a complete set of his father's riding gear. Useful household items began migrating from one home to another, swapping places. This was all just a game for now, a test of skill and courage. Tibor would wake some nights with sweat pouring off him to gaze astounded at the crowded room: he dreamt his father had arrived home unexpectedly and ordered him to account for the bicycle, the canvas tailcoat, the medical pliers and pincers. It was Béla alone who, having stolen money, faced a more pressing danger. It wouldn't have counted for much that he never spent it.

They decided to seek a proper repository for their loot. Ábel's aunt, for all her credulity and infinite patience, did nevertheless notice the saddle and full set of equine apparatus in his room. The colonel's wife started feeling better that fall and talked of rising from her bed. There was no immediate danger since at the beginning of every season Mrs. Prockauer tended to forewarn the world of her imminent emergence, predicting that she would soon be up and walking, but nothing had come of it in all these years. One fall afternoon they hired a cab and drove out to The Peculiar. They dined at the inn. The one-armed one set off to explore the house with the result that he discovered some rooms-to-let in the mezzanine.

The Peculiar was built on a gentle slope, a half hour's coach ride from town, in the middle of a partially cleared forest. Behind it loomed a dense bristling wall of pines, with the bare crags of the mountain rising to a peak above it, a peak whose glittering cap of snow might make anyone think they were in the Alps. The place had once been a spa, and a few empty neglected buildings, which used to be popular with the local bourgeoisie in the summer at the end of the last century, were ranged round the inn. Ábel had a faint memory of how, a very long time ago, in the early years of his childhood when his mother was still alive, they had vacationed here in August. A bitter, sulfurous water still bubbled from the spring. The long tobacco-smelling dining room of the inn with its pendulous oil-burning chandeliers, the ceiling decorated with old boughs, reminded him of the so-called Anna Balls, named after the ball first given in his daughter's honor by one János Szentgyörgyi Horváth back in 1825. Along the floor, where it met the walls, dry rot fungus grew in luxuriant forms. When the weather was very hot some summers, groups of picnickers might find their way here. The inn itself was still approached through a mass of tipped-up tables on white gravel in a garden with a few straggling trees, surrounded by rotten stakes that served to support empty tin lantern casings. Glass domes prevented wind blowing the candles out on the tables. The place was sticky with damp and neglect, a neglect that seemed to symbolize the human condition at large.

"No," said the man, "no one comes here in the fall."

He was elderly, with a Slavonic accent, and had been struggling to maintain the property that he had acquired decades ago at an auction and was now stuck with. He told them that a few years ago, in peacetime, which they wouldn't be able to remember, couples from town used to make excursions here. The happy memory of once playing mild Cupid to a generation of genteel lovers flickered across his tired, careworn face. That was when he had fitted out the three guest rooms upstairs. This gay, salacious period came to an end with the outbreak of war. Nowadays, it seemed, couples no longer thought it necessary to avoid the public gaze. The rooms had stood empty for years. There was nothing to stop them installing a couple of iron stoves there. He and his wife spent the whole winter here.

The gang hemmed and hawed. Should they or shouldn't they, they wondered as they chewed their tasteless salami and Liptauer, sipped at their beers, and silently pondered the idea. The one-armed one stuttered and offered arguments but they ignored him. Ábel was lightly aware of his heart beating. Without having exchanged a word on the subject they felt they had come to a turning point. Taken aback by the idea, Béla spoke with his mouth full, "Well, well, friend . . ." They were all preoccupied by the thought of a hiding place, regretting they hadn't discovered one before. Had they done so earlier, having one would have prevented them sneaking about and relieved them of the constant sense of shame. They proceeded silently up the rotting wooden stairs, in single file. Years of unattended rubbish and gloom had gathered in the room. The windows opened onto the pine forest. The beds lay bare, without sheet or blanket, as if glued to the walls that were themselves hung with cobwebs. Mice had clearly been busy at their work of destruction. The tabletop was covered in mouse droppings.

"Wonderful!" cried the one-armed one. "No one could possibly live here now!"

Using his thumb and forefinger he carefully lifted a woman's comb from the dust on one of the bedside tables. The filthy object suggested something lascivious, the lost illusions of a long-forgotten affair. They examined it, bright-eyed. The notion that no one could live here now allowed them to consider the room as their own.

It was Béla who struck the deal for two rooms. The following week they made the most thoroughgoing preparations for the move. The proprietor thought the young gentlemen were after a location for various discreet rendezvous. By the end of the first week he had to admit he was disappointed in that hope. There were daily deliveries, the arrival of the bicycle signaling the end of all the comings and goings. Every day it was a different young man with a knapsack full of peculiar hard-to-explain items. Had he not known that he was dealing with students he might have felt rather uneasy. But seeing it was the son of Colonel Prockauer and his school friends what was there to worry about? Each arrival vanished into one of the rooms, locked the door, and spent a long time in there fiddling with things. After they had gone the proprietor would carefully creep in and take a look, but a few strange items of dress, the great globe, and those harmless books suggested no cause for alarm.

The gang relaxed its ideals regarding uselessness. The knowledge that they had their own, and to a large degree independent, hiding place, a space they could do what they liked with, a room they could safely lock, slowly intoxicated even the most sober of them. They spent entire afternoons in their foul-smelling lair by the sweating iron stove, swimming in demonic cigarette smoke, arguing, making up pointless games, and refining their rules. This was the time of proper games. It was a second childhood, guiltier than the first but less restrained, more exciting, more sweet.

They would arrive as soon as they could in the winter afternoon, immediately after lunch. The bicycle was used by whoever turn it was to arrive first and light the stove.

By this time they had supplies of tea, rum, brandy, and tobacco. The smell of rum saturated the walls of the airless room, and according to Ábel anyone who came in would think he was in a ship's cabin. All cabins smelled of rum, Ábel insisted. The saddle lay on the bed, with the hunting rifle next to it, and a visitor was more likely to think that he had entered the lair of a criminal on the run, and that the fugitive occupant was resting his exhausted limbs somewhere while his hard-driven horse was ambling about in the snow. The hideaway served all their purposes. It offered a shelter unknown to fathers, teachers, and the powers-that-be. It was somewhere real life could finally begin. That life resembled nothing they had hitherto known. It wasn't like their fathers' lives, lives that did not appeal to them in the least. Here they could discuss whatever remained unfinished or unexplored. Here the discipline that governed every aspect of their childhood lives could no longer threaten or haunt them.

They had long ago stopped being children, but here, in this room, they discovered that they dared to do what would have shamed them in town, even in front of each other, that, somewhat shyly, they could continue playing at childhood, indulging a part of themselves that could never properly be developed in childhood, a part they still retained. It was only from this vantage point that they could clearly see the adult world as it was and discuss their experiences of it. The one-armed one entered this game with real passion. His nervous stuttering laughter grew more relaxed here. This bolt-hole in The Peculiar was the only place where, occasionally, even Ernō could be seen laughing.

THIS WAS WHERE THEY GOT TO KNOW EACH other. The secret and secure comradeship that had separated them from the rest of town gave them an opportunity to explore each other's characters in ways they hadn't tried before. Everyone had to tell "everything that had happened." It was self-evidently the case that this "everything that had happened" referred only to the time they had spent under the watchful eyes of their parents. It slowly became clear to them that it was no coincidence that had brought them together like this.

They arranged "afternoons of fear." Everyone had to reveal what it was they had been most afraid of "in the early days." In this way they discovered that each of them had something they had not hitherto shared. These "fears" were located in the misty past, at some uncertain distance in time. One such afternoon when it had grown dark and they were squatting in a circle round the dying stove, the one-armed one said the time when he was most afraid was not in the flickering light of the field hospital, on the operating table, but when, at the age of seven, through the glass door of the verandah, he saw his father looming over his mother, the pair of them wrestling, until his mother used both her hands to push his face away and ran off into her room. He had felt so scared at that moment he thought he was going to die. As soon as he had said this he started stuttering again and had a spell of nervous hiccups. In the meantime Béla, who was sitting in the window watching the light reflected off the snow, tried to collect his own feelings.

"Being afraid is good," he said.

It was a painful process trying to explain what he understood by the "pleasure" of fear. Tentatively, over several weeks, he had tried to analyze the roots of his own fear while the others were looking for ways to communicate with each other. Once he discovered that he could not get beyond a certain embarrassing point in his life, he stopped in shock and fell silent. Ábel and Ernő subjected him to a strict cross-examination.

"I am ashamed of it," he confessed in pain.

He was given two days to collect himself. It was strange that he who had been so excitably lewd and foul-mouthed so far had now to defend his peculiar modesty. The gang was all the more surprised by this sudden shyness regarding his memory, especially since, as it turned out after extended interrogation, there was nothing salacious in it. It was more comical than anything but it was only after a prolonged period of agonizing that he could bring himself to tell them.

We were living on the ground floor then, he started, perspiring and red in the face. Turn your faces away!

It was as if that had been the most trying part of the narrative, for now he spoke in a fever, rapidly, telling them how the end of the ground-floor passage opened onto the neighbor's garden. Béla had been a timid child with a strict upbringing who even at the age of six would be so alarmed by harsh words that he wet his pants. Whenever this happened he would dry his trousers but would bundle up his underwear and throw the incriminating evidence into the neighbor's garden. He had disposed of eight pairs of underpants that way. The expectation that his deeds would be discovered and that he would be humiliated and punished brought him to such a pitch of anxiety that he would suffer even more such childhood accidents. And once he actually was discovered and his father had given him a sound thrashing, he felt such a wave of relief flooding through him, such a sense of happiness and well-being, as he had never felt before.

Please understand, he croaked out as quickly as he could, that being afraid was a pleasure. I had calculated what my punishment would be and anticipated it. I learned to calculate it over a period. I knew what it was that would get me a box on the ear, what resulted in a beating, what in being made to go hungry: all that was calculable. It was dreadful living in anticipation of what was to come, but once it came it felt good.

ERNŐ SPOKE UP EVENTUALLY.

You know my father, he said. It took him a long time to become the buffoon he is now. He even learned to read late, only once he had grown up. He read just two books, the Bible and a cheap old eighteenth-century reference work, *The Little Threefold Mirror,* that everyone knew. I'm not ashamed of him, but then you know nothing about our relationship. He's right when he talks about the division of wealth. Wealth does not consist of having money. It's something quite different. I shall never possess it, while you—every one of you—has had it from the moment you were born.

My first real knowledge of fear was when one day my father stood in front of the mirror. I can have been hardly more than a toddler. I was sitting in a corner of the workshop on a low stool. We had a lame crow that my father had brought home. We had its wings clipped and it lived with us. I was sitting on the stool, playing with the crow. My father was working away in the room. At that time he had no beard, nor did he hobble. Suddenly he stopped, stood up, and as if I were not there at all went over to the chest of drawers, lifted the mirror off the wall, brought it over to the table, and looked at himself. I stared at him, speechless, nursing the crow in my lap. My father grasped his nose between finger and thumb and pulled it upwards. Then he bared his teeth. He began to swivel his eyes and twist his mouth and pull faces the like of which I had never seen. He carried on doing this for a long time, completely absorbed in it. My mouth gaped wide open as I stared. At first I felt like laughing, but I quickly realized it was nothing to laugh about. My father's expressions when he swiveled his eyes and twisted his lips were so strange that I began to be afraid. He took a step backward as if preparing to burst into laughter and opened his mouth monstrously wide. He knotted his eyebrows and snarled furiously. Then he began to weep. Suddenly he leapt towards me as if only just noticing my presence. I screamed out, in fear that he wanted to kill me. He leaned over me, his face deformed in a way I had never seen a face before, nor since for that matter. With one hand he grabbed the crow, squeezed the creature's neck, then threw it in front of me on the floor. Having done so he rushed out.

The crow lay before me lifeless. I had been playing with it for about a year. I picked it up and, since its body was still warm, began to rock and nurse it. That is how I was discovered by my mother, though I never told her what had happened. I think I must have felt that it was not to do with her. My father didn't come home that night. When he returned the next morning he brought a box into which he placed the crow, took my hand as if nothing had happened, and led me out into the yard.

Here we buried the crow. My father lavished such care on digging the grave and talked to me so cheerfully as he did so that I couldn't understand what he had been so furious about the day before and why he had to strangle the crow. But ever since then, when I'm left alone in a room with a mirror, I feel afraid in case I too should stand in front of it and start pulling faces.

THE WHITE TAILCOAT FITTED TIBOR SO SNUGLY he looked quite a man of the world. They did dress up sometimes. Béla sprawled in a chair wearing his red tailcoat, a top hat on his head, his gloves in his hand. The pettiest things made adequate toys for them in this mood. They could amuse themselves with an idea suggested by an object or the whim of a moment as long and as intensely as a child can play with a simple bell. Now each of them discovered an aptitude for acting.

The one-armed one became a passionate producer. He gave them their tasks in a few words and immediately set up the scene. They played out scenes in court, in close family circles, in recruitment offices, at teachers' conferences, on the bridges of sinking ships. Every child is a gifted actor. They clung to this forgotten talent, their one recompense for the world they were losing. This world glowed faintly behind the familiar world. Ábel believed that he could recall some episodes and sentences from it.

When they stood facing each other like this in the room, in costume, far from town, with the key turned behind them, in the acrid smoke of stove and tobacco, by the light of two flickering candles, among their stash of stolen things, joined like this in a compact whose rationale they never fully understood, only felt instinctively, there were times, between two sentences of some game, when they fell silent and stared at each other for a while as if there ought to be some explanation for their being together, for the game, for their lives. After one of these shocks to the system that was inevitably succeeded by an interval of wry, ironic dawdling, Ábel suggested that they should play a game of Raid. Ernő and the one-armed one left the room and the three remaining put on their fancy clothes and adopted poses of leisurely relaxation such as might be assumed by anyone in a secure hiding place. Ernő gave the door a loud knock. Their task was to explain, employing whatever outlandish vocabulary was available to them, why they were together like this and what they were doing here. Ernő and the one-armed one represented the forces of the outside world. They had no particular office. They could have been teachers, detectives, a military police patrol, or simply fathers who had sought out their "underlings"—that was the expression Ábel insisted on using—to get them to account for themselves.

Ernő asked the questions. The one-armed one stood at attention behind him like a member of the domestic staff behind the headmaster, a common foot soldier behind a general, or like a less powerful adult—a nasty uncle, say—behind a father. Ernő wore a hat and Béla swung his bamboo cane and held his deerskin gloves in his hand as they both walked up and down the room. Every so often he removed his pince-nez and held it before him between finger and thumb to clean it. He had come to a conclusion, he announced, and having discovered them in flagrante, established that they, the pupils, had for some time now been breaking the rules and had without permission of their parents, teachers, their betters, and of civil and military authorities generally, consciously decamped from town so that they might lock themselves away in one room of an inn set in a far from reputable bathing place, where they indulged in smoking and drinking alcoholic drinks and remained there for hours at a time. The sight that greeted the entering authorities was certainly strange.

"Prockauer, stand up. Putting aside the question of your progress, which is regrettably slow, I must admit your recent behavior in school has given no particular cause for complaint. I am sorry to note however that the evidence I see around me constitutes a breach of the rules. What is this? Rum. And that? Grape cider. This box? Rollmop herrings! And what do I see here, Ruzsák? Stand up. Would I be mistaken in assuming that those coffee beans have been purloined from your father's grocery?"

Béla stood up, fiddling absentmindedly with his gloves.

"Wrong. I only stole money from the shop. I bought the coffee elsewhere with the stolen money."

So they went on from item to item. Ernő's interrogation was thorough and formally impeccable. No one denied anything. They were all prepared to admit the provenance of every object. Lajos exchanged indignant looks with Ernő. Ernő's cross-questioning proceeded slowly, with the sharpest questions addressed primarily to Ábel and Béla.

"Not a word, Prockauer. I shall have particular things to say to you. What is the meaning of this clown costume? Is this how you prepare for exams? How you prepare for life while your fathers are fighting at the front?"

"Excuse me!" Ábel exclaimed. "We are not preparing for life."

Ernő placed two candlesticks on the table and politely invited the one-armed one to take a seat.

"What is this nonsense?" he asked. "What else can you be preparing for if not for life?"

"We are not preparing at all, headmaster sir," Ábel replied calmly. "That is precisely the point. We have taken particular care not to prepare. Life can prepare for whatever it likes. What we are concerned with is something quite different."

"Utterly different," Béla nodded.

"Hold your tongue, Ruzsák. You bought coffee beans with stolen money, and therefore have nothing to say. What are you boys up to?"

"What we are trying to do," answered Ábel in his best school voice, "is to nurture comradeship. We are a gang, if you please. We have nothing to do with what other people get up to. We are not responsible for them."

"There's something in that," agreed the one-armed one.

"But you yourself are responsible," Ábel retorted. "You agreed to serve and have your arm cut off. People have died on your account. People have died because of Ernő's father too. In my humble opinion anyone who takes part in this is responsible for what happens."

"You lot will shortly be called up," said Ernő coldly. "Do you think you will be talking like this then?"

"Naturally not. We won't be talking then, we will all be responsible, but until then I feel no obligation to acknowledge the rules of their world. Nor those of the music lessons I am currently missing because of a faked parental note, nor those that say it is forbidden to urinate against the walls of the theater in public. Nor those of the world war. That is why we are here."

"I understand," said Ernő. "And what are you doing here?"

They kept silent. Béla examined his nails. Tibor rolled a cigarette.

"Here we are none of their business," said Ábel. "Don't you understand yet? I hate what they teach us. I don't believe what they believe. I don't respect what they respect. I was always alone with my aunt. I don't know what will happen now. But I don't want to live with them, I don't even want to eat their food. That's why I'm here. Because here I can thumb my nose at their rules."

"They? Who are they?" asked Ernő.

They all began to shout at once.

"The locksmiths for a start!"

"The lawyers!"

"Teacher, baker, what's the difference?"

"All of them! All of them!"

They kept shouting whatever came into their heads. Béla was bellowing fit to burst. Ábel stood on the bed.

"I tell you we have to escape," he cried. "On bicycle, on horseback. Now! Through the woods!"

"You can't cycle through woods," Tibor remarked like a true sportsman.

They felt they were making progress. Now perhaps they were getting to the heart of the secret. Ábel was shouting himself hoarse.

"Your father is a great idiot!" he bellowed and pointed accusingly at Ernő. "What have I done? Nothing. My aunt kept sending me into the garden to play because the apartment was damp. So I played there. Your father goes on about the rich. That's not it: there's another enemy far more dangerous. It doesn't matter whether one is rich or poor."

He made a funnel with his hands and whispered through it. "It's all of them," he said, his face pale.

"We will become adults too," said Ernő solemnly.

"Maybe. But until then I shall defend myself. That's all."

Eventually they collapsed on the bed. Ábel's face was burning. Tibor sat down beside him.

"Do you really think it's possible to defend ourselves against them?" asked Tibor in a low voice, his eyes wide.

It was spring and visitors had started calling at The Peculiar. The gang became more circumspect in their gatherings. Once or twice a week they managed to get away there in the afternoon but only on Sunday for a whole day. Occasionally they discovered people picnicking in the garden.

So far everything that had happened was entirely between themselves and they felt no guilt about it. They had nothing to do with the mechanisms, rules, and policing of that other world. The "other world"'s significance lay as much in not being allowed to smoke in the street as in the world war. The insults the world showered on them roused them to a similar degree of fury: it was the same whether it was being unable to get bread without ration tickets, the unfair marks awarded by the Latin teacher, someone in the family being killed in action, or being prevented from frequenting the theater without express school permission. They felt that the system that worked against them and dragged them back acted as perniciously in insignificant matters as in great affairs of state. It was hard to say what hurt most: having to offer obsequious greetings to adults they met on the street or the thought of having, in all probability, to salute some sergeant major a few months later.

It was this spring that they lost all sense of proportion. It was not exactly that their games had turned more solemn. Lajos would go off by himself on long walks while they kept a wary eye on him. In certain respects they regarded Lajos as an adult. He was free to do what he wanted and, just as he excused himself from adult ranks as and when he chose, so he might, at any moment, choose to rejoin the enemy. He started wearing his army uniform again and spent the day hanging around with the actor. It seemed he had grown bored of meetings at The Peculiar. He was back in the café. The gang even discussed barring him but then the one-armed one turned up and just at the beginning of the season introduced the gang to the actor.

The introductions took place in Tibor's room. The actor immediately won their confidence when, out of sheer good manners, he climbed in through the window.

Tibor was the center of the group. Everything revolved around him: they had come together to please him. It was to him they brought their sacrifices and offerings. When the gang abandoned the "for its own sake" principle, there slowly developed a kind of material competition for Tibor's favors. Ábel wrote poems addressed to him. Béla would bring him presents. Ernő carried his books, polished his shoes, and undertook all kinds of servant-

and-porter tasks for him. Tibor, who had always been courteous, remained remarkably generous and courteous as the object of all this warmth and furious competition.

The younger son of Colonel Prockauer, apart from a passing phase of acne, was, for the gang, that mysterious being, the epitome of all physical perfection. The reputation of Prockauer Junior was much the same in town: so beautiful, so charming. Despite the various boyish accomplishments of running, swimming, riding, leaping, and excelling at tennis Tibor presented a somewhat soft, almost effeminate appearance. His very pale skin and the curiously wavy blond hair that kept falling over his brow covering his blue-gray eyes confirmed the impression. He had inherited his father's raw fleshy lips as well as the strong oval hands with their short fingers. But the lines of his nose and brow were delicate and mild and the fascinating discrepancy between the upper and lower regions of his face made for a certain uneasiness. His face lacked the normal adolescent's state of grotesque half-preparedness. It was as if the development of what was boyish in him had been suspended at a particularly fortunate moment in childhood, as if the sculptor had got so far, taken his hand away, and declared with satisfaction: let it remain as it is. Even at thirty Tibor would still look like a boy.

In every movement, in each appearance, whenever he laughed or spoke to somebody, whenever he thanked another with a smile, a characteristic rhythm or pace made itself felt, a light and almost shy courtesy. Unlike Béla and Ernõ, or his contemporaries generally, he seemed to utter foul language with a kind of reluctance, as if he had first to overcome some better part of himself. His profanities appeared to be a form of good manners, an aspect of his courtesy to the others whom he did not wish to shame by remaining silent while they swore.

He did not say much. Something about his being, the way he looked, suggested astonishment. Whenever Ábel or Ernő were speaking he had the knack of moving in close and with wide-open eyes paying them the utmost attention, then asking the simplest and most admiring of questions, always acknowledging the answer with a graceful smile. It was hard to tell whether the consideration that he radiated had been intensely cultivated or was the result of an entirely unselfconscious curiosity. Books frightened him whenever Ábel wanted to share his own enthusiasm for what he happened to be reading, and it was always with the utmost nervousness that he took a book in his hands, as if it were a highly complex, slightly mysterious object not altogether pleasant to the touch and he would only touch it in order to please his friend.

He lived with them, among them, and took no sides. He exhibited the patience of a good-hearted, high-born gentleman of leisure moving among impatient but decent courtiers, with the foggy sense that his place in relation to theirs was permanently fixed by his birth and destiny. He had a vague feeling that the gang was some inevitable part of that destiny, and as with all matters of fate the fact seemed to him both painful and ridiculous. These boys, from whom he was separated for only a few hours at a time when they were sleeping, to whom he felt bound by a power whose meaning and purpose lay beyond him, that was stronger than any other human bond, were not even particularly sympathetic to him. He wasn't really attracted to their form of rebellion: they seemed to have chosen it by some act of incomprehensible, intangible aggression. The environment in which they lived, the disorderly order, the unknown, unbearable, disintegrating world outside had also brought him close to a state of internal rebellion, but it was a simpler, more tangible, more violent form of revolution that appealed to him. He felt fully part of everything they did: he couldn't resist the tantalizing spell it cast with its peculiar means of protest and negation and the way it permeated all their games, a spell whose power emanated from Ábel or possibly Ernő. His tastes though ran to less complex forms of resistance. For instance, Tibor would never have argued against a scheme whereby they set up a machine gun in front of the church and fought a battle of self-defense, and if one of them were to suggest that they should set fire to the town one windy night it would only have been the practical details that gave him food for thought.

The boys—this gang—in whose midst he suddenly happened to find himself, who seemed to have material-ized around him, were not entirely what he would have chosen. He never dared confess this to anyone. He was ready to sacrifice his life to the gang because the gang would have sacrificed theirs for him. The military ethos of his father had somehow percolated through to him and exerted a certain influence. All for one and one for all. That "one" was Tibor.

He observed other groups, other gangs, with a kind of

embarrassed longing, admiring the pranks of his school-mates who, despite the yoke the world imposed on them, seemed to bear their lot lightly with wild practical jokes, fiercely competitive sports, and, above all, by giving themselves to the cult of the body. Tibor admired nothing so much as physical courage. The gang, however, violently rejected such acts of physical bravado along with all other forms of bravado that had any practical application as an entirely alien mode of being.

He couldn't understand why he was with them. He couldn't—he didn't wish to—dissociate himself from them but he continued to feel that he was a guest in whose honor they had gathered together. Everything they did filled him with a sour and vengeful delight. What is to become of all this, he thought and curled his lip. But he was incapable of disengagement. He sensed that there was a latent meaning in their games, that behind the games there glimmered a world he too remembered, a fresh, just, inexpressibly exciting world out of whose splinters the gang wanted to construct something, a small bell jar under a vast sky, within which they might hide themselves and stare at the world outside through the glass, their faces bitterly contorted.

He was the only one among them who didn't care whether the jar cracked or not, whether he would be drafted. Fear of the war? Could it be worse than the funk before exams, the humiliating concealments, the servile subterranean life they were condemned to live as things stood? War, in all likelihood, was just another form of servitude and humiliation invented by adults to torture one another and people weaker than themselves.

But he remained part of the gang because he felt that association with it protected him from the one overriding yet incomprehensible power, that of adults. Nor had he ever tested the strength of the ties that bound him to the others. They, who acted under no orders and lived in a constant state of rebellion against all sources of power, came to him gently and trusted their fates to him. Perhaps it was pity that he felt as he moved among them, pity and a touch of forgiveness and goodwill. They asked little of him—a smile, a minimal gesture of the hand, or simply his presence among them—and they would have suffered keenly if he refused them.

AND IT WAS ONLY IN THIS ROOM AT THE PECU-liar, solely in these past few months, that he showed an occasional, faint partiality for Ábel. They were bound, barely discernibly bound, by particular hatreds they had in common, more closely bound than the other half of the gang by class, by a vague similarity between the shapes their memories assumed, their upbringing and way of life. There was something they shared that was peculiar only to them, maybe no more than that they had both been beaten as children for matters such as not holding a knife and fork in the proper manner, or for not greeting somebody prop-erly, or for not responding properly to someone else's greeting. Ábel was skinny, freckled, and pale ginger—there was something about his physical being, particularly about his hands, that engendered in Tibor a certain sympathy he did not feel for the others. Maybe it came down to what Ernő had said, that wealth was not a matter of money but something else.

The sense of guilt shared by the two of them that—unlike the other two who were perhaps closer to the realities of life—they had something private going on, an advantage of a rather worthless sort but one that could not be made up, not in this life at least, by the others, established a bond between the two within the terms of the bond between the gang as a whole.

The itinerant career of Colonel Prockauer had seen him stationed in various melancholy towns, and somewhere in the recesses of his mind Tibor carried childhood memories of a range of barracks and garrisons. Lajos, the one-armed one, was rather like his father in many respects: pleasure-seeking, greedy, and violent. Tibor was sometimes astonished to note that the one-armed one, whose own childhood, like his, was restricted and spent in barrack squares, under the terrifying rule of his father, was just as drawn to the gang as he was, drawn by a longing for that irreplaceable lost "other world." Tibor was astonished that Lajos, who had returned from the adult world with partial paralysis and with only one arm, having only a few months before set out from their shared room and a school bench, should have voluntarily re-entered their company, as one among other suffering victims wearing the ball and chain of fate. There was a nervous humility about Lajos's manner when in the gang's company, a humility sometimes broken by an ungovernable rush of fury.

He wanted to share in their anxieties and sometimes he too smoked in secret. He was happy to walk down narrow side streets at night in their company and, heart racing, would steal into desolate bars at the edge of town with them. He, to whom everything that one's parents had forbidden was allowed, who was free of that complex hierarchy of superiors in which parents' friends played as threatening a role as did teachers or military patrols, now humbly volunteered once more to share with them a fate that no longer bound him.

Some sense of incompleteness emanated from the one-armed one ever since he had returned from the front. He never talked about the front in detail or directly. Ernő told the gang that the one-armed one was paying frequent visits to the cobbler. They would apparently talk in low voices for hours at a time. When confronted with this Lajos stuttered and tried to avoid answering by going off somewhere. The gang kept a dubious eye on these examples of backsliding whereby Lajos kept seeking out the company of adults. Lajos oscillated anxiously between the world of the gang and that of the adults. It was as if he were seeking something, an answer, some missing item he had utterly lost track of.

Béla suggested he was looking for his other arm. They waved away this ridiculous idea so Béla felt ashamed and fell silent. Surely he can't be looking for his missing arm because he knows where that is: first it was stored in a bucket, then thrown into the lime pit. People don't search so feverishly for trifles, Ernő declared in a superior manner. Ábel proposed that Lajos was looking for his place in society. He couldn't bring himself to believe that the things he so much desired—freedom and the rights and privileges of being an adult—were worth less than the gang's form of comradeship. He was seeking something he might have missed before, something adults could not give back to him.

They spoke of adults in general rather than in particular. The word "they" was self-explanatory: it was obvious who "they" signified. They spied on them, described each other's experiences of them, discussed possible developments. When Mr. Zádor, the bishop's secretary, who never went anywhere without his top hat, tripped and fell into a puddle in the street it was as much a victory for them as when Judge Kikinday had a toothache and couldn't sleep for nights on end. They made no distinctions and forgave nothing. They agreed on the principle that in a state of war any means might be employed to destroy the enemy. They never doubted, not for an instant, that the war they were fighting was quite distinct from the ones in which the adults were engaged.

Lajos was their spy. He could work behind enemy lines and render a reliable account. There were very few opportunities for a more effective assault: the enemy was armed, suspicious, and ruthless. His enormous claws were already extended towards them and would pretty soon drag them away.

. . .

THE ACTOR WAS FROM THE ENEMY CAMP BUT HE did enter theirs through the window. He was an adult: he had a belly, his shaven face had a bluish tinge, he wore a watch on a chain, strange clothes, and a wig. Lajos brought him along after long negotiations and they received him in the same suspicious manner as they would an enemy.

Immediately, within the first hour, he suggested they employ the familiar *tutoyer* mode of address. This put them on their guard. The actor sat, walked, chattered, and held forth. He seemed to have a vast amount to say. He smoked their cigarettes, talked of other towns, and told smutty jokes. He discoursed on the life of the theater, and on the doings of the female members of the company, supplying names and specific details. One had to take proper note of these details as they offered insights into what the enemy might have up its sleeve.

The actor was an object of suspicion in every respect. He used terms like sea, Barcelona, steerage, Berlin, underground train, three hundred francs. The actor would say, "Then the captain came down and the blacks all leapt overboard." All this was highly suspect. He sounded just like the sea captain they knew whom they tended to meet most afternoons in front of the theater. The actor said, "By that time I hadn't slept for three nights and my baggage had been left in Jeumont so I was overcome by drowsiness. Suddenly the train stops, I look up, and it says, Cologne! Well, I think, Cologne. We shall have to think of something really clever now." You could listen to stuff like this for hours. But all the time the suspicion grew that reality lay elsewhere, that this was merely the actor's reality. It ran counter to their practice to place their pooled trust in anyone. They had learned to sense it in their pulses: when others attempted to communicate with them it was either to punish or to plead, but whatever the case it was always with an ulterior motive. It was also difficult to believe that the actor, who could after all have been sitting in the window of the coffeehouse or strolling up and down the high street with his top hat and long-stemmed pipe, possibly enjoying the attentions of chorus girls and divas, should have chosen to spend time with them arguing for hours on end without some particular aim in view.

They never mentioned The Peculiar in front of the actor. He had had to climb through the window as they could not have met openly in public. They couldn't stroll down the street with him in public either. To have been seen walking with the actor would immediately have brought the wrath of teachers and relatives down on them. The actor was aware of this and sensitively adapted himself to the demands of the situation, lurking with them in a befitting manner.

He was equally nice to them all. He delivered his humorous anecdotes with a serious expression and furrowed brows. Listening to the actor you could come away with the impression that life consisted of a series of extraordinary events that began tragically but inevitably ended up as comedy. "The little blackies," the actor would say. Once he talked of how "the little tower thingamabob at Pisa" didn't in fact lean as much as people said it did. Everything was addressed in baby talk: in his mouth, which was forever chewing on a dumpling, the mighty universe itself became "our little cosmikins." You just had to get used to it.

As you also had to get used to the idea that he wanted to spend his time chatting to them in the first place when it was impossible to work out his game or to discover what made him tick. He'd sit on a chair in the center of the room in his checkered suit, his chin shaved to a brilliant high gloss, his wig stuck to his scalp as though fixed there by resin, his lilac handkerchief billowing from his cigar pocket, his legs crossed with lacquered shoes glimmering on his feet and his bright, slightly myopic eyes running all over them like some tiny insect while he discoursed on the affairs of the world in a thin frail voice. Clearly, it was only distant affairs that interested him.

One day Ábel said: "Watch him. Whenever he says something particularly good he stares straight ahead with a sad look on his face."

At such times every feature of the pale-blue shaven face relaxed and drooped; his nose seemed to lengthen in melancholy fashion, his thick fleshy lips pouted, and his eyes disappeared under half-closed lids. His nimble, plump white fingers flopped exhausted into his lap. He'd sit there, alone, always precisely at the center of the room. If there happened to be a table there he pushed it aside, drew up a chair, and settled on it, deliberately, exactly in the middle.

You also had to get used to his various fragrances. You had to get used to his constantly chewing licorice. Sometimes, on particularly melancholy days, his scent was quite nauseating. Normally he used a cinnamon essence, but when he felt very low he would splash the stuff on wildly, mixing musk, lilac, chypre, and rosewater, and walk round as if in a trance with clouds of perfume billowing about him, every so often raising his specially perfumed necktie to his nose to take a deep sniff.

There was a curious inner suppleness about his large, ponderous, and melancholy body. When he stood up he would give a little spin as though performing a pirouette. When he gave a bow he stood on tiptoe, one hand to his lips, his arm carving a wide arc before being allowed grandly to drop. As soon as he'd done so he would add: "This is how the strolling players would do it." And his eyes would be sad as if this were a fact that simply could not be helped.

He explained each and every movement he made. He could talk for hours about why he did this or that or what he did not like. "I loathe it," he'd shudder. And "I adore it!" He was not much given to the middle way. But when he found himself making too frequent use of the two expressions, he would hesitate and exclaim: "How crude this all is! Quite hysterical, don't you think? I loathe! I adore! Only women and comedy actors talk like this."

He had a particularly low opinion of women and comedy actors. He would employ the same disparaging collective tone for them both. Every time he mentioned his fellow professionals his face twisted with fury and pain. He would weep and complain when talking about the rehearsals that took up his mornings. But in the midst of his griping, suddenly it was as if he had given himself a slap: he'd stand up, shrug, and declare: "So what? When it comes down to it I am just a strolling player."

But his manner suggested that it was only when it came down to it really, in the very last analysis, that he was a mere strolling player.

A couple of weeks after he had made their acquaintance he invited them to his apartment.

The actor lived in a sublet, on the second floor of a tenement block in a wide side street, his windows opening onto a big, dirty courtyard. All the furniture in his room was pressed up against the wall thereby increasing the illusion of spaciousness. A broad carpet covered the floor in the middle and the entrance hall between the two windows offered the visitor his own reflection in a tall standing mirror.

A widow rented the room out, a young military widow who was struggling to bring up her child in the demanding conditions of the time. When the mother went out the actor would give her little rickets-stricken girl ballet lessons, teaching her the elements.

"There are people," he said, "who look to buy freak children, children whose bodies, like those of animals, are partly covered in fur. Children with two heads. I knew someone like that. He had heard of a little girl who was half covered in fur whose mother was unwilling to sell her, and of a boy with three hands. He kept a record of them. Occasionally he would get on a train and visit them, observe their development, and correspond with the parents. Then he'd sell them on to a freak show. He made a fortune."

The gang felt an undeniable excitement when they called to see him. They wouldn't have been surprised to find a colony of seals ranged round his bed when they entered. He received them in a black suit with a flower in his buttonhole. He greeted them with the utmost courtesy and showed them to their seats with a worldly grandeur, offering one the bed, one the chair by the basin, one the windowsill. He was an aristocrat arranging a soirée. He himself, as was his wont, drew a chair into the middle of the room and flashed smiles at them from there, making flattering inquiries about each of them.

They had to admit the actor knew how to entertain.

He offered them nothing else, but from the first to the last moment of their visit he was capable of infusing the occasion with the air of a formal reception. He chattered of distant events, dismissing all objections with a forbearing smile. He praised Tibor's deportment, Ábel's observant eyes, and Ernő's expertise. In what particular field of endeavor Ernő was supposed to be expert he did not specify. He presented Béla with a perfumed necktie.

The one-armed one was enraptured by this and walked around the room with a complacent smile. The actor, whom he had introduced to them, was a roaring success that afternoon. The gang relaxed. By the time the visit had ended they had established an atmosphere almost as free of tension as if they had been by themselves.

They had to wait till dusk so that they could slip away without being noticed. They took their leave one by one, Ábel being the last to go. The actor escorted his guests to the front door and bowed deeply. Having been left alone with Ábel he went over to the window and paid no attention to him. Ábel could see him only in profile. Line by line the mask dropped from the actor's face. First the smile, then the tense attention, the nearsighted helpless look, and the droop of the lips. He stood in silence watching the increasingly dark street, his fingers drumming on the glass.

Ábel didn't move. He was mesmerized by the change in the actor. He waited for him to speak. It was as if he was utterly exhausted. It was some time before he sluggishly turned his head and addressed him in a tired voice.

Still here? he asked sadly and solemnly. What's keeping you, boy?

He stood stock still, his broad back covering the window. Ábel waited a moment, then anxiously made for the door and quickly closed it behind him. He stopped in the stairwell and looked back. He wasn't being followed.

The voice of the actor stayed with him that night and made its way into his dreams.

THEY HAD TO DISCOVER WHAT THE ACTOR WAS doing in their midst. Their delicate ears could tell that the actor's voice was sincere. He, who going by all outward signs must have belonged in the enemy camp, had played it perfectly, never once striking a false chord. He hadn't been patronizing, nor too careful to be impartial, nor indeed too intimate. As far as they could tell it did not tire him to make this infinitely long journey from the shores of his world to theirs; he would undertake it in order to meet them on their own ground. Their sharp ears detected not a single false note. Too much sincerity, confidentiality, and amiability would have seemed as suspicious to them as false intimacy. Had the actor not been sincere, he would have had to juggle halftones and quartertones in their company, and observing such fine distinctions for such a time would have been too exhausting for him. They knew that adults were neither sincere nor trusting with each other. The actor spent his days among adults at rehearsals or at cafés with various local gentlemen of leisure. His regular companions included the short but extremely elegantly dressed editor of the local newspaper who greeted everyone in the most formal manner, the stage prompter of the company whom he had, as he casually declared, "first met abroad," and the man who was his secretary, mailman, and financial consultant, fat Havas, the pawnbroker.

"Havas has money," he indicated with a nervous movement when Ábel asked him something. "Not just money, but articles, possessions. You might not be aware of it yet but it is always advisable to keep on good terms with pawnbrokers. Whenever I arrive at a new town I make it my first business to befriend the editor and the pawnbroker. The two between them can help me achieve that which, alone, I would be incapable of achieving: immortality and sustenance. For a man to attain immortality it is necessary that he first survive."

It was difficult to disagree with him. He had to walk some way to join them, or alternatively, they called over to his place on the afternoons they stayed in town. They kept the secrets of The Peculiar from him until the last possible moment. They weighed every slight shift of his voice on the most delicate of apothecary's balances.

But the actor knew something the others didn't. Was this his true nature or just some instinctive capacity for simulating? He could talk to them as no adult had ever done. Adults made the mistake of trying to talk to them as though they were adults. The actor committed no such crude faux pas. He tried to build no artificial bridges, and neither did he try to pretend he was one of them.

He talked like someone who had come home after a long day, put on his dressing gown, and felt comfortable in his own skin. He used the words they used, feeling no particular need to learn their own thieves' argot. He sat down among them with a nervous dreamy look, his eyes flicking now up, now down, and said:

"How much younger you all are. Strange but you are younger than I thought you were. I was much older than you when I was eighteen. The years dropped off me later."

He was not a giant who squatted down in order to look smaller so the dwarves should not be scared of playing with him; he was an outsize dwarf with a giant's body and a wig whom adults hired for amusement and who, tired and disappointed after a day's work, would go to join his dwarf companions.

Occasionally he smuggled them into the second-tier actors' box at the theater. They sat anxiously at the back of the box while Amadé played to them. He made gestures only they would understand, conveying, with a glance here and phrase there, a complicity whose closeness only they would recognize. The actor performed with pretty much the same imperative as they did, distorting truth by means of a persona, adopting the painful rictus of a mask. To play was as obligatory for him as it was for them. It might be that the actor only ever truly comprehended the shape of his own life when he was acting, much as they sensed the reality of life behind every apparent reality.

It was Tibor's company that mattered most to Ábel now. Tibor, master of the revels, accepted such intimacy with a mild, tolerant indifference, a decent forbearance. He found Ábel tiring but could see no way of avoiding contact.

Ábel would wait for him in front of his house, give the familiar whistle, and they would walk to school together along the river. Tibor had to dine once a week at Ábel's. Ábel's aunt was all in favor of the friendship. The companionship of this gentle, secretive boy seemed to her appropriate to what she imagined and hoped Ábel would be.

Of all Ábel's friends Tibor was the only one of whom she was not jealous. She received the rest of the gang with a certain coolness, catering to them nervously, keeping a close eye on them, trying to translate their incomprehensible conversations into a language she could understand. She followed Ábel around helplessly as if somebody had stolen him from her, no longer daring to enter his room at night to kiss the sleeping boy as she had been used to doing just a year ago. She crept on tiptoe to his door, listening for his breathing as he slept, and her eyes filled with tears. Someone had stolen the contents of her life from her but she didn't know the thief and had no idea just when the crime had taken place, so she slipped back into her room and spent the night sleepless, her heart beating, her thoughts anxious and confused.

Ábel was happy to make an exception of his aunt and hid his indifference and rebellion behind shows of affection. His aunt however sensed that behind this show Ábel was only forgiving her as a favor.

"I'm not taken by that Ernő either," she suddenly announced. "He's after something, my child, I'm sure of it. His father is quite crazy too. Someone must have hammered one of his own hobnails through his head. And I don't like the way Lajos laughs. One should forgive him because he has suffered much, but whenever he grins at me for no reason I feel cold shivers run up my spine. Be careful, my sweet one and only. Think of your father. Your father could get to the bottom of anything and knew the reason for everything. He'd be able to look into the eyes of your friend Zakarka and quickly discover what he was up to. He'd know why young Prockauer has taken to flashing smiles at people. I wouldn't trust Béla either. His face is lined as if he spent his nights up to God knows what, it's as yellow as parchment and full of spots. They're whited sepulchers, all of them, darling. Mark my words. And by the way, where is your father's violin? I've been looking for it for days. When he returns it's the first thing he'll want to find."

Ábel didn't know. He couldn't tell his aunt that the violin had for weeks been resting in their bolt-hole at The

Peculiar and that Béla, who knew not a note of music but could imitate the virtuosos he had never seen to perfection, would entertain them with silent performances on it. He had to pay a forfeit every time he dared touch the strings with the bow.

Now there's your friend, Tibor, his aunt continued. Do you know what I like about him? I like the way he looks at me. Have you noticed how he blushes sometimes? When I address him he raises his eyes and blushes. And it's a good sign when a boy blushes. And he has manners too. His father gave him a strict upbringing.

She would have been prepared to share him, but couldn't bear to admit to herself that there was nothing left to share. Ábel, who had once been hers, was lost to her. The house was big and empty now. The town too seemed emptier without the men. Life no longer had a single comprehensive meaning for her. Ábel lowered his eyes whenever she spoke to him. She had noticed how often, reluctantly, possibly out of pity, he lied to her. He lied to her as if he didn't want the truth to hurt her. And since she dared not investigate the lies she hastened to accept what the boy said.

The scent of Ábel's childhood slowly faded from the rooms. Both of them went round trying to hang on to the lingering trail of it, searching for the life that had gone, the intimacy of the looks they had once cast on each other, the affection once implicit in their gestures. She gave in, and like all those who recognize some major mistake in their lives, found a calm indifference settling on her. The boy had, in some sense, been abducted. Some similar force had taken his father too. The meaning of her life had drifted away from her.

Ábel hovered around Tibor with a bad conscience. Ever since the actor had entered their lives the bond between them was fraught with tension and anxiety. Sometimes he was seized by such fierce jealousy that there were afternoons and nights when he had to slip out of his room, trudge over to Tibor's house, and stand beneath the window to assure himself that Tibor was at home. Other times he would set up watch outside the actor's house when the performances were over. He'd wait for hours for the actor to arrive, his heart in his mouth as he spied on him, feeling ashamed and yet relieved as he sneaked home again.

He endeavored to separate Tibor from the rest of the gang so that he could be alone with him. This experiment was all the more painful as he knew that Tibor found him dull company. Ábel worked with feverish enthusiasm to find amusements for Tibor. He dragged the secrets of home and hearth before him, hastened to bring him gifts, did his homework for him, got his aunt to cook him her special meals. He played the piano for him. He was more than willing to master the secrets of boxing, high jump, and gymnastics in order to amuse Tibor. He found various shy excuses to share his money with him and when, egged on by the gang, Tibor later executed the grand coup of pawning the family silver, he accompanied Tibor the entire length of the hazardous route. Perhaps if he were a direct witness to Tibor's fall from grace he might gain some power over him. Perhaps he could be such a close accomplice in Tibor's fall from grace that, if they had to sin and suffer, at least they might sin and suffer together.

Tibor found his company dull. He was careful to show his boredom nicely, with delicacy and good manners as Ábel noted to his despair. He talked in order to please him and got hold of books in order that Ábel might explain their contents to him.

A copy of Kuprin's *The Duel* lay on Ábel's desk.

"Incomprehensible and dull, isn't it?" Tibor politely remarked. Ábel searched feverishly for an answer but gave up and fell silent, his head bowed.

"Incomprehensible and dull," he said and stared ahead, stricken with guilt.

What did it matter that he had betrayed the spirits of great writers to gain Tibor's favor? A volume of the humor magazine *Fidibus* lay on the shelf. Tibor reached over for it with considerable enthusiasm. Ábel observed and suffered as Tibor leafed slowly through pages of smutty jokes, carefully explaining them to him, feeling nervous in the presence of material of whose existence he had heard only by vague report. What could he give Tibor? Whenever they were separated he felt lost and hurt. He prepared himself for their meetings and tried to invent something new and surprising for each occasion. Meanwhile Tibor yawned discreetly, his hand covering his mouth.

He was distressed to feel so stupid, so inadequate to the honor of being Tibor's companion. He examined himself in front of the mirror. His ginger hair, his myopic eyes, his freckled face, his scrawny body and bad posture made a painful spectacle compared to Tibor, who was fresh-faced, tall, refined yet certain in movement, held his head well, his eyes full of mild haughtiness and self-confidence, his expression conveying a raw yet delicate childishness.

He is my friend, thought Ábel, a hot sweet flush of gratitude running through him. He looks wonderful, he sometimes thought as if for the first time and felt the incomprehensible, agonizing shock of it all over again. He tried to entice Tibor into his own secret world. Tibor gazed with interest at Ábel's house, taking in the courtyard, the garden, the secrets of the hidey-hole, and all the treasures of the vanished kingdom, while Ábel tried to conjure up for him the world of fairy tales and toys he had lived with in the glazed conservatory. Tibor followed him around, courteous and mildly bored. They talked of girls but Ábel sensed they were both lying. They competed in telling each other ever more lewd imagined adventures, not daring to look each other in the eye. They bragged of several lovers, extraordinary, quite remarkable sweethearts with whom—secretly of course—they were still in touch.

They were talking like this in the garden one day when Ábel suddenly fell silent in the middle of a story.

"It's a lie," he said and stood up.

Tibor also stood up, his face pale.

"What do you mean?"

"Every word I have ever spoken about girls was a lie. Not a word of it is true, not one. And you're lying too. Admit it, you're lying. Come on. Own up. Tibor, you are lying, aren't you?"

They were both trembling. Ábel seized Tibor's hand.

"Yes," Tibor reluctantly confessed. "I'm lying."

He freed his hand.

Ábel wanted to share his memories of his father with Tibor. For his father was only a memory now, a confusing figure shrouded in mist, adrift between the concepts of godhead and death. This was the one area where Tibor appeared to follow him with pleasure and enthusiasm. They exchanged memories of their fathers, of their first fears and of every little incident that continued to linger in their minds, glimmering there forever like distant shining myths. Tibor recounted his shock on discovering a fish-bladder condom in his father's bedside-table drawer and described in some confusion—and with evident pain—his despair the first time his father failed to keep a promise and told a lie. He had run away with Lajos that day to hide in the stable at the barracks and felt so desperate he wanted to die.

They had no difficulty talking about their fathers. Their fathers were at the root of every difficulty: they were insincere, they refused to give straight answers, they wouldn't say what they were suffering. The skies around their heavenly thrones had darkened to a gray shower of disappointments. The only way they could make proper peace with their fathers, suggested Ábel, would be eventually to form a pact with them.

I don't think that's possible, shuddered Tibor. Mine might just shoot me. He is in the mood for it. And he'd be perfectly entitled to, I think. If he came home tomorrow and failed to find the silverware or the saddle . . . What do you think it would be like if yours came back?

Ábel closed his eyes. His father's return would be an

extraordinary ceremonial occasion, something between a royal funeral and the emperor's birthday. Bells would no doubt be rung as he marched in, then he'd sit down at the table, deplore the loss of his violin, and look for certain scissors and tweezers. Ábel would enter and stand before him.

"Delighted to see you, sir," he would say and make a low bow. At that point all hell would break loose. Perhaps his father would raise his hand and hurl thunderbolts at him. But it might be that he would walk up to him and there would be an anxious moment while he considered the possibility of taking him in his arms, embracing him, and kissing him. So they would stare at each other, uncertain what to do.

"Maybe he will apologize," ventured Ábel.

"Or else shoot me," Tibor repeated obstinately.

THE CRISIS CAME TO A HEAD AT THE BEGINNING of October. Béla's father conducted an audit and discovered the missing sums. They were small amounts at first and nobody thought to suspect Béla.

The first consequence of the discovery was that a sixteen-year-old apprentice boy was hauled before the court and sentenced to two years in juvenile detention.

The giant buildings of the house of correction rose beside the road that led to The Peculiar and whenever they retired to their hidden empire they were forced to pass by its outer perimeter. The lights of the windows of the correctional institution shone directly at them as they made their way back at night. The enormous red-brick hulks were visible behind high railings where a guard stood sentry at the entrance.

The hearings were concluded and Béla's father sighed with relief that his staff and family members were found to be honest. Only they knew that the avalanche had started. The petty infringements discovered by the father, for which the boy rather than Béla was sent to be institutionalized—the apprentice having, to everyone's surprise, admitted his guilt and spent little time denying anything—were insignificant compared to the "real" crime, Béla's great break-in. These true facts were liable to be discovered any day. Should they be discovered, they would all be lost.

This possibility did not appeal to the actor either, he having been accepted into the gang so recently. Nevertheless he took the news of Béla's crime with equanimity and did not blame any of them since he too had enjoyed a fair share of the money. If it were up to him, he said, he would settle the difference from his own pocket. Unfortunately it wasn't up to him.

Béla had stolen six hundred crowns in one go, six one-hundred-crown bills. His father had sent him down to the post office with the money to post an order to one of his business acquaintances. Béla kept the money and simply told his father that he had sent it but could not find the receipt. The intended recipient, a rice merchant, was bound to claim the money a few days later and then they would all be lost.

What was strange was that Béla had not mentioned

this vast sum to the gang. They had long got used to the fact that he always carried smaller amounts with him. Those hundreds seemed to have melted away in Béla's pocket. When they interrogated him about it, it turned out that the actor who had complained of certain minor inconveniences had received a sum of two hundred crowns in three installments from Béla. The tailor's bill was also rather more substantial than they had thought. Béla had kept the final invoice from the others, and when the tailor turned awkward, threatening to send it to his father, he paid what was owing.

The money had vanished, as Béla calmly declared, every last cent of it. With the last thirty crowns he had purchased, perfectly calmly, a revolver that they took from him by force and entrusted to Ernő's safe keeping. Béla's behavior during all this was perfectly apathetic: he lost weight and his face seemed to collapse. He was preparing to die.

The gang held long extraordinary discussions that went on day and night. They had to produce the money in twenty-four hours and send it by telegram to Béla's father's business partner before irreparable harm was caused. Ábel performed miracles with his aunt, charming and bewitching her, but he could conjure no more than forty crowns from her.

It was at this time that they inducted the actor into the secrets of The Peculiar too. The actor accompanied them with a puzzled yet faintly bored smile, never denying that he had received money from Béla, shrugging his shoulders, for how should he have known where the money was from. I thought you were all rich, he said and gazed straight ahead as if in a dream.

They were not rich but their "warehouse," as Ernő referred to the store at The Peculiar, might possibly offer a few solutions. That was how the actor came to be there at the moment of mortal danger. All hands on deck, said the actor, and pretended to be the captain of a sinking ship giving his last orders. There was a time, somewhere between Naples and Marseille . . . , he said. He was made to swear to keep the secrets of The Peculiar on pain of death.

The actor was happy enough to swear, his only condition being that he should be able to wear a frock coat and that the table should be prepared with four burning candles. He entered the secret room nervously, his face showing no interest, without removing his gloves, his hat still on his head, and stood in the middle of the room, sniffing the air like a connoisseur and declaring in a frostily polite voice and with a stiff, unsmiling expression: Charming! He brightened when he spotted the store of clothes. They had to dress up there and then. He gave tiny cries of delight as he knotted neckties, forgetting the frosty politeness and show of indifference with which he had entered, took a step or two backward, and produced the most exquisite effects with a movement of his eyebrow. They were not going to make any progress with the problem of Béla that afternoon. They were all infected by the actor's enthusiasm. Béla dressed and undressed with a desperate concentration, throwing on one item after another, while the actor delved drunkenly into the store of neckties, silk shirts, and cosmetics that Béla had so thoughtfully and skillfully accumulated. Once they were all strutting around in costumes the actor spread his arms like the conductor of an orchestra, took a step backwards, and with a serious, concerned expression examined each of them in turn, then, his head set back, under half-closed lids, summed up his general impression: "You should all be on stage," he said. And after a short meditative pause: "In an amateur sense, I mean."

They too felt they should be on stage. The utter impossibility of their ambition depressed them. "With an invited audience . . . ," suggested the actor. "Without written parts, of course. Everyone would be free to say whatever came into his head." With the actor to encourage them in their strange costumes they suddenly marveled at their wealth. The problem was that the treasure trove of inestimable value that they had amassed was worth very little in ready cash. They sneaked back into town that evening feeling they were doomed. As they were preparing to part, Lajos waved Tibor over and put his hand on his shoulder.

"The silver," he said.

"The silver?" asked the actor, pricking up his ears. "What silver? If you have silver everything can be fixed."

He pronounced this with such authority that they fell silent, quite awestruck. They knew what silver. The silver that lay in a leather trunk under the bed of the colonel's wife! Only the actor had been ignorant of the silver, and now the solution was perfectly clear to him.

"As long as the silver is really there," he repeated anxiously. "I'll have a word with Havas. He is a friend of mine and knows all about silver."

"What did you think would happen?" Tibor slowly turned to Béla, speaking with childishly clear enunciation, breaking the words up into syllables. His voice was full of infinite wonder. "What did you think you would do? You must have known they would discover the loss."

They stood on the street corner in the light of a gas lamp, forming a tight dark group. It was at this moment that Béla's self-control deserted him.

"Think? Me?!" he declared with great indignation. "I didn't think anything. How could I have thought at all? No. And you?" he hesitated as if he were deeply astounded by something. "Did any of you think at all, at any time?"

And this was exactly what had to be said at that precise moment, in the first moment of sanity they had experienced for months; this was what had to be said in order to set Tibor's question in the real world and expose the unreality of their own actions. It was a question their fathers might have asked, or the mayor, or anyone at all, anyone except Tibor. For the first time they understood that the world they had constructed around themselves, that sheltered them, would collapse about their ears if they broke one single law of the real one.

Conveniently, the colonel's wife had to be taken into the hospital for two days of observation so Ábel and Tibor took the silver and handed it over to Havas. Béla managed to transfer the money to the merchant with a certain regret, as if he could think of better uses for it. Afterwards

Ábel insisted they should visit the apprentice boy who was serving Béla's sentence for him.

Béla had only the faintest memory of the boy. Once they received their visitors' permits and, deeply embarrassed, had laden themselves with fruits and other foodstuffs, they waited for him in the reception room of the correctional institute in a state of ever greater anxiety and restlessness. Through the windows they could see the workshops where other inmates labored—the joinery, the locksmith's, and the bakery—while a detachment of blue-uniformed others puttered about between the long flower beds, attended by a guard. There were quite a few there and each year of the war produced its fresh harvest of them. They gazed at the bars on the dormitory block windows, the bleak hall where they themselves silently loitered, the benches covered with waxed canvas and the single crucifix on the wall. This house of correction was specifically set aside for those who shared their own world and they had never felt so keenly divided from the world and society of adults as they did in the minutes they spent there. They were forced to see that while they played and—half consciously, half unconsciously—built their own society like a cell within adult society, theirs was just one cell of the real world. They understood that there existed not just a cell but a whole world like theirs, a world whose laws, ethics, and structure differed sharply from that of the adults, and that this world had a dynamic that was equal to the one in which adults struggled and perished, that had its own hierarchies and mysterious coherence. They couldn't help feeling that there was a logic behind all that they had done these last few years. It might have been their task, their vocation, to maintain the principle of everything-for-its-own-sake. They huddled closer together and gazed sympathetically through the window at all those unknown others of their kind.

The boy came in somewhat reluctantly, his instructor exhorting him to take more confident steps, his cap in his hand, and approached them with a suspicious look on his face. They gathered round him and spoke to him quietly. The boy had bright passionate eyes, intelligent and stubborn.

"Why did you confess?" asked Béla in a whisper.

The boy cast an anxious glance towards his instructor who was staring out of the window. He gestured for a cigarette and quickly sneaked it into the lining of his cap.

"Because I stole things, you idiot," he scornfully muttered.

They stared at him, uncomprehending. Then, speaking very fast and very quietly, he launched into a speech.

"What do you think? That I was idiot enough to get myself locked up here if they didn't have anything on me? Sure, I stole, and more, more than they know. Lucky for me the gang didn't rat on me. We all stole from the shop, and from the warehouse too."

He fell silent, looked into their eyes suspiciously, then, relaxing, continued. "You stole more than I did, of course, I knew that perfectly well, but what's that to do with me? That's your business. Careful, he's looking this way."

The instructor walked up to them, they handed over

the packages and said their goodbyes with averted eyes. They crossed the big garden without a word while the child prisoners stopped work and watched them go. Once they were far enough away from the gate Ernő was the first to break the silence.

"They had a gang too," he mouthed with amazement.

"And a hiding place," Béla humbly acknowledged.

Lost in thought, they meandered back towards the town where, presumably, there were many gangs just like theirs with hiding places like the room at The Peculiar. They must be there, all over the world, in towns inhabited by adults, among barracks and churches, little robber gangs, millions and millions of them. All there, with their own hiding places, with their own rules, all under the spell of some extraordinary imperative, the imperative to rebel. And they sensed they would not be part of this strange world for much longer, that pretty soon perhaps they too would be classed as enemies by a pre-adult or two. It was painful to be aware of that, to know that something was irretrievable, and they hung their heads.

WHAT THEY COULD NOT BELIEVE, HOWEVER, WAS that all four of them were virgins.

They had lied so much to each other and to others beyond their circle about this, with lies so extraordinarily convoluted, that the truth that seemed, somehow, to pop out in the actor's presence was more shocking to them than to the actor. Their anatomical knowledge of the arts of love had seemed perfect, almost infinitely so. Every single one of their previous companions bragged—and not always untruthfully—that they had crossed the threshold and survived love's ordeal of fire. They had chattered of love and women with such apparent expertise that once the truth was out it sounded quite incredible. Each of them was aware of everyone else's indulgence in the solitary vice, and there was no particular reason to be skeptical about Béla since he had never denied it.

The actor's dark Mississippi-minstrel eyes rolled rapidly under the closed lids.

"You neither?" he turned grandly to Ábel who was chewing his lips and shook his head to confirm.

"Ah!" he spun round to Tibor. "But you, Tibor. Not you? Not once?"

Tibor nodded, his cheeks scarlet, to indicate, Never.

"Béla? You, who for such a long time supplied money to last year's juvenile lead? You told me so yourself!"

The actor fluttered round his room, rubbing his hands. "And you, Ernō?"

Ernō took off his pince-nez as he always did when confused.

"No," he answered dully.

The actor grew solemn.

"This is a very serious matter," he said, frowning. He retreated to a corner of the room, his hands linked behind his back, and was visibly shaken. He talked quietly, walking up and down, taking no notice of them.

"Virgins!" he repeated, and flung his arms up to heaven. "You're not lying?" he turned anxiously towards them. "No, no, of course you're not lying," he reassured himself. "But in that case . . . astonishing, quite astonishing, my friends!" he cried. "How old are you? You've had your birthday? Stout chap! And you? Your birthday is yet to come? Oh, my poor little lamb, my poor dear lambs." He spread his arms wide and brayed with laughter.

"Don't for a moment think," he stopped, suddenly concerned, "that I am laughing at you. It is a beautiful thing being without sin . . . you can have no idea how splendid it is. You must all have guardian angels. If only I had a guardian angel."

He dropped his arms in a tragic manner.

"Unfortunately I have never had one."

Ábel stood up.

"I swear on oath," he said and raised two fingers. "I swear that I have never been with a girl."

"Never?" Béla inquired. "Should we repeat the oath after him?"

"I swear on oath," they all said, Tibor blushing but firmly and loudly, Ernő with bowed head, like someone who had once committed a sin and would never dare repeat the experiment.

They sniffed around each other like dogs. They reminded each other of their old, confused, bombastic lies. Béla had told them he had a child that he visited twice a year. They had spoken of the licensed brothel with such familiarity you would have thought they were practically habitués of it. But now came the revelation that, with the exception of Tibor who had once ventured as far as the door only to recoil from it, not one of them had dared even approach the threshold of the red-light establishment.

"I was in second grade," recounted Tibor in a dreamy, singsong voice, "when one morning in the town where we then lived, I took a roundabout route to pass the brothel. I was perfectly clear about its function, about who lived there and who called on them. I knew it was full of girls and I think I had even heard something about the tariff from someone. There was nothing particular in my head as I passed it, nothing either pleasant or unpleasant. I merely turned my head towards it. I had a school satchel on my back, full of books. It was half past seven and, as I passed, a young man came out of the house. He wore a cap and a shirt open at the neck. As he slammed the door the bell rang and he stopped to tie up his shoelaces, propping his foot on the step. He didn't look round. He didn't care who saw him, he simply continued tying his shoelaces, as if he were at home, sitting on his own bed. There was nothing strange about this and I knew where the young man had come from and, roughly, what he had been doing in there. He had been with the girls. Not that I knew precisely what he would have done with the girls but I suspected it was that about which adults lied to us, that which they had kept a secret. I had learned almost everything from the servants. But what shook me, and shook me so powerfully I had to stop, and with all those books on my back, lean against the wall of some house, wasn't that the young man had been with the girls, but that, inside there, he had taken his shoes off. He had been with a girl and had taken his shoes off . . . What could he have been doing, what kind of thing can anyone do that involves taking off your shoes? It's hard for me to say this.

Perhaps because . . . that was why I didn't really dare go with a girl myself. Because there I was at the threshold of the place, my hand on the doorknob, when the image of the boy came back to me, this boy doing his shoes up. Silly thing of course, he had slept with the girl, he must have taken his shoes off. But as far as I was concerned . . . laugh if you like, but for me there was something terrible about this, as if someone had told me he had killed the girl, or simply committed some indescribably filthy act in there."

"Worse than that," said Ernő solemnly.

"Yes, isn't it?" said Tibor, turning to Ernő with eyes full of wonder, and continuing in that same even singsong voice. "I too think it was far worse. The boy unhurriedly tied up both shoelaces, pulled the cap down over his eyes, and went on his way, whistling blithely. It was early morning and there wasn't anyone else in the street. I could hear the *tap tap* of his shoes as he walked away into the distance. I was still leaning against the wall. What could he have done? What could he have done? He was with a girl, they were both naked . . . without even a shirt perhaps . . . I was all twisted up inside . . . but the shoes, the shoes. Why did he have to take them off? It must be a terrible form of nakedness, I thought, where one person has to take off his shoes in front of someone, and then lie down with her in a bed, shoeless."

The actor kept blinking and was pursing his lips as he waited.

"Well, that tops it all," he said and nodded.

"Indeed it does. The whole of that morning I couldn't help thinking about it. I didn't dare ask anyone. But as always happens, you know, something inevitably comes along to raise the pitch of one's terror . . . That lunchtime when I got home I put my books down still nauseated and disgusted, sick with excitement, and went into the dining room where I found my father sitting on the divan, cursing. I kissed his hand and waited. Father had just returned from the stables. He was wearing a summer jerkin, breeches, and riding boots. He was cursing because he had been calling for the servant. The servant having gone off somewhere, he ordered me to pull off his boots and bring him his slippers. There can't have been anything unusual about this but I don't recall him ever asking us boys to do this kind of thing and it hasn't happened since. And it had to be just that day . . . I stared at my father's dusty boots in despair and I couldn't bring myself to extend my hands towards them. But Father leaned back in the divan and read the paper, paying no attention to me, simply extending his leg towards me. I put out my hand to touch the boots and fainted."

"You started vomiting," the one-armed one recalled without emotion. He was sitting calmly in the corner, his knees drawn up high, his chin propped on his remaining hand, crouched and expectant.

"Yes, I started to throw up. The trouble with that was that once I had come to, my father started beating me with the horsewhip because in his indignation he couldn't imagine any reason for my sickness other than that I found the sight of his feet repulsive. The truth is I had never felt any disgust regarding his feet because I never even considered the possibility that my father had feet."

"And that's why you remained a virgin," the actor declared as if establishing the fact.

"That's why I remained a virgin," Tibor repeated in the same flat singing voice. He opened his eyes wide and gazed calmly around the room.

"There, that wasn't so hard," said Ábel, his voice cracking. "I don't think there's anything particularly strange about the fact that we . . . we haven't been with women. Don't you think there's a reason for that? Perhaps we're together, the four of us, because . . . because not one of us has been with a woman. I don't know. But I don't think there's anything impossible about it."

The one-armed one let go his knees and leapt from his chair.

"But I . . . ," he gabbled, ". . . ever since it was cut off . . . I haven't dared show it to a woman."

The actor stepped over to him and put his arm round his shoulder to console him. But the one-armed one pushed him away, snatched the empty sleeve of his jerkin from his pocket with two fingers, and held it high with a look of contempt. They immediately surrounded him, talking to him. Béla stroked the stump where his arm should have been. Lajos was speaking, leaving words unfinished, his bloodless lips trembling, his whole body shaking. They laid him down on the actor's bed and sat silently at his side. The one-armed one eventually stopped shivering and closed his eyes. They said nothing. Tibor held the one-armed one's hand. A single teardrop ran from under the closed eyelids all the way down his face onto his jerkin. The one-armed one bit his lip. Quietly Tibor stood up and with elegant, light steps went over to Ábel, beck-oning him to follow him to the window recess.

"You won't be in a position to know this," he whis-pered, "but Lajos has never cried before. I beg you to believe me. Not once in his life."

THE ACTOR WAITED UNTIL THEY HAD GONE. Then he ambled out of the apartment, sucking a perfumed mint. The girl with the rickets was playing in the doorway. The actor selected a mint from his pocket and asked the girl to dance a little dance on point for him. He joined her in the dance, and they twirled round in the entrance for a few moments, the actor's arms raised high above his head, the white sweet in his hand glittering temptingly while the rapt child gazed at it like a puppy, her crooked little body finding it hard to twirl and remain on point at the same time. The actor took a few turns with her, then shook his head sadly like a talent scout who had lost faith in his lat-est discovery, and with a tired gesture popped the sweet in the child's mouth. A thin woman in a headscarf had stopped to watch the man and child dancing. She weighed them up with grave, close attention. The actor greeted her amiably and drifted away under the boughs of the wayside trees. He was thinking that he should ask for an advance at the theater where they hated him. He smiled, thinking of that, and looked haughtily in front of him. He was think-ing he should send his light green spring outfit to the cleaners. He was thinking it had become impossible trying to buy a decent American Gillette blade in the monarchy, that German razors were nowhere near as good as American ones. He was thinking he should start dieting next week. He remembered the name of a masseur who once worked on him for a week and who later hanged himself. He might have gone mad while shaving my throat, he thought and wagged his head disapprovingly. He gazed at the light green boughs of the trees and quietly whistled an aria from the new operetta. There were two steps back to make here, and one thing to duck, so . . . He looked around; no, not here, it wouldn't do. He thought he might leave town soon. Once the war was over he would have the hernia operation. He was just passing the pastry shop and he thought of his younger brother who once, for no discernible reason, purchased a box of honey-loaf cakes and brought it over to his place in town where he was working as apprentice to a photographer, as a gift, then, next day, having finished his business, went home. Later he worked as a machinist. He disappeared somewhere in France. He thought he should keep an eye on Ernő. These quiet hangdog types could be dangerous. There was that incident with the one-eyed beggar: he had woken one night to find the man standing over him with a knife in his hand, grinding his teeth. You had to watch everyone, even the one-armed one, but Ernő more than most. He was whistling. He passed the drugstore and spent some time examining the display, being strongly tempted to go in and buy some balls of camphor, not so much as a defense against moths as a fragrance. The strong, sour smell of camphor flooded his senses. He walked on in a bad mood. After all, anyone can afford to buy camphor, even the poorest people. He only had to saunter through the door in an indifferent manner and casually ask for a pinch of camphor. No one would suspect that he wanted the camphor not as moth repellent but to sniff. He didn't have a penny on him. He had to have a word with Havas before he got to the theater. He felt uncomfortable about this. Never, not once in his life, not for a second had he felt certain that he would not have to pack and move on at a moment's notice, in the middle of the night. He felt tense: the air he sniffed was full of menace. It was as if everything in the world were perishing. He wrinkled his nose. He wanted to speak to Havas to tell him that he should take care of his fingers. Nothing more than that he should take care of his fingers. He took a deep breath. The air was dense with the fresh, heavy smell of loam.

The pawnbroker sat behind the barred window. He was alone. The actor entered, whistling and swinging his cane, his hat pushed back to the crown of his head but carefully lest it disturb his wig. The pawnbroker stood up, came out from behind the counter, and propped his elbow against the grille. The actor looked about him dreamily as if it were his first visit, taking in the board that said "Receipt of Goods" and its partner, "Issue of Goods." He leaned against the bars without a word of greeting and stared in front of him.

"Just imagine!" he remarked casually, swiveling his Kentucky minstrel eyes. "They're all virgins."

3

THE PERFORMANCE WAS OVER. THE REVOLVing doors were in full swing and the night regulars were arriving, in dribs and drabs, including members of the company. The bon vivant who had not removed all traces of theatrical makeup passed the booth, stopped, flashed his gold teeth, and dropped some quiet remark to the comic. Both laughed. The actor ignored them. He had delivered his major sketch about the effects of vodka on the human sensitivity to color. Now he was sitting, panting slightly, recovering.

The prima donna took her place among the usual crowd at the bohemian table. The actor fixed his curious eye on the door. The director hadn't yet arrived and the seat on the prima donna's right was unoccupied. The director was like the captain of a sinking ship: he was the last to leave the theater, the night's takings in his pocket. He wouldn't go until the cleaners had swept the auditorium clean.

Let's wait until my assistant reports back, said the actor

cautiously, his hand before his mouth. It would be wiser to wait till then.

He had plans that he had been mysteriously hinting at all evening. They weren't feeling too good. They leaned on the table in desultory fashion, drank their beer, and gazed at the stream of new arrivals. It was the first time in their lives they could sit in the café legally, without anxiety, without fear of being spotted. They had occupied this booth before but for only a half an hour at a time, shivering slightly with the curtains drawn. Tonight was the first occasion on which they could take their place without sneaking in, without embarrassment.

They couldn't help but notice in the first half hour they spent in the adult camp as equals that it was not all gaiety here. Or if gaiety there was, there was less of it than they had imagined the day before. The edgy excitement of the entertainment had quite vanished. A few weeks ago, when such excursions were still counted as a dangerous enterprise, they hadn't noticed the insultingly patronizing manner of the waiter or the servile to-ing and fro-ing of the café manager who had condescended to conceal and shelter them. This confidentiality seemed humiliating to them now and lent a certain tension to the evening. They sat in low spirits, noticing for the first time the dinginess of the décor, breathing in the stale and bitter air.

"What is it?" asked Tibor.

Ábel gave a wry laugh.

"Do you remember how we used to look through the window whenever we came by here?"

Boredom gave way to anxious lassitude. What if everything they had only known from the outside turned out like this? If everything that had been alien and other were now becoming familiar, so that they could relax and take command of the world along with all those secrets that adults fought tooth and nail over—money, freedom, women—and they discovered that it was all quite different and much duller than they had thought?

"I'm bored," said Béla, wrinkling his nose.

He raised his monocle to his eye and glared about him. Other tables smiled back at them. At about eleven their history master appeared in the café. Ernő spoke a quiet word of command and the gang immediately leapt to their feet, made deep bows, and in singsong unison greeted the teacher.

"Your humble servant, sir!"

The chorus rang like music in the room. The elderly man in the pince-nez returned the school greeting, gave a clumsy bow, and muttered in confusion: "Your humble servant." The master hurried away to escape the embarrassing scene. Ábel was of the opinion that he had blushed. Slowly they began to recover their confidence.

"That's the way it has to be," said Ernő. "One has to be careful. Even tomorrow we shall have to hide our cigarettes when anyone approaches us. And we will have to bow deep in greeting, much deeper than we have ever done before. The waiter will have to draw the curtains, and the manager will have to watch that we're not spotted."

They hatched a plan for the following week to confront all their teachers in the afternoon, singly and together, before the staff disappeared on vacation, and ask them to fill in the blanks in their knowledge regarding certain as yet unclear details. They should enter with the utmost humility, stuttering, twisting their hats in their hands, and put their question red-faced, humming and hawing, exactly as they used to do.

Ernő stood up.

"For instance, you go into Gurka and say: 'Your humble servant, sir, I beg your pardon, I do not mean to be a nuisance, forgive me for disturbing you, sir.' He is sitting at his desk, he pushes his glasses up to his forehead, gives a croak, and screws up his eyes. 'Who is that?' he asks in that nasal voice of his. 'A student? What does the student want?' You move closer, you twist your hat in your hands, you can hardly speak for respect, you are so deeply honored. Gurka slowly rises. 'Really,' he says. 'Do my eyes not deceive me? Can it really be Ruzsák? It really is you, Ruzsák.' Then he comes up to you and extends his hand in the greatest embarrassment because he is the master who could have failed you, twice, and has only permitted you to pass now because the army needs you and the commissioner insisted on it. And he is the one who has beaten you time and again right up until fourth grade. He is the one who stood guard on every street corner where girls were to be found and frequently caught the flu because he had been lurking in gateways for hours on end, keeping a sneaky watch on us. He was the one who had his suits made so that the collar covered half his face up to the earlobes, only so that he could creep up on groups of students unnoticed. Gurka. That's your man. He is frowning suspiciously. He doesn't know whether to sit you down or not, so you just stand there, listening, staring at him. He is already regretting offering his hand for you to shake. What can the student be wanting? Whatever it is he can't be up to any good. Perhaps he has brass knuckles in his pocket, or a dagger. 'Now, now, Ruzsák,' he says, gasping for air. 'What brings you here?' You, in the meantime, just stand there, trembling, flushed."

They drew closer together. This they understood. The waiter drew the curtains, concealing them.

"You drop your hat, you cough," said Ábel.

"Maybe. And then you say, 'I have made so bold, sir . . . with your kind permission . . . I make so bold as to disturb you,' shifting from one foot to the other. Gurka relaxes. He puts his hand on your shoulder. 'Speak up, Ruzsák, no need to get in a state about it. I know, my boy. The Creator has not distributed his intellectual gifts equally. In your case, Ruzsák, I have often had to spur you on to greater efforts, indeed, Ruzsák, I may have called you an ass or a numbskull. Don't take it to heart. What's done is done. There are professions, my boy, that make no great intellectual demands, require no sharpness of mind, such as is required by, say, a teacher. Why don't you become a grocer, Ruzsák? There are many professions in the world. The important thing is to carry out whatever duties life imposes on you with honor.'

"But you just continue humming and hawing. And when he claps you on the shoulder the second time you stop. 'The reason I am here, sir, is because I have doubts.' 'Out with them, Ruzsák.' 'The course on Tacitus,' you say.

'What about the course on Tacitus?' Gurka glances at the door, at the window. He clearly doesn't understand. 'That part, that bit about . . . ,' you say and produce a book from your bag. Gurka puts his glasses on, glances this way and that, not quite knowing what to do. What does the student want? But you, by then, are relaxed and modest. At your ease now you explain the matter. 'It's this sentence here, sir, if you'll pardon me,' and you open the book and point to the passage. 'I suspect I haven't understood it properly, sir. I had all kinds of doubt about it afterwards. I do agonize about it as I would not like to have missed the meaning of the detail.' "

Béla leaned forward, his entire face split by a vast grin.

"It's that *plusquam-perfectum,* sir. I just can't see it," he said, beaming and rubbing his hands.

"Yes. That's why you have returned. You tell him you don't want to bother him at all but that you wouldn't want to leave with this doubt gnawing at you. You wouldn't want to find yourself on the battlefield without first having cleared up this passage of Tacitus."

"There are these two verbal prefixes I don't understand," said Béla. "Just these two little ones."

"Gurka sits you down," continued Ernō. "He removes his glasses and looks you over for a while. 'You, Ruzsák?' he says. 'Now, when the exams are over? What am I to make of this, Ruzsák?' 'I beg your pardon, sir,' you answer firmly but respectfully. 'It's just that I have doubts. Having studied under your tutelage, sir, for eight years . . . for eight years, sir . . . I have recognized the importance of such matters. There is Horace for example. And Cicero.

If sir would be so kind . . . just one or two obscure passages . . .' "

The prompter stuck his head through the curtains.

"The place is yours," he said. Only his bald head and brow and his puffy red nose protruded between the drapes, his body remained invisible. He had learned from watching actors at work. He turned his head right and left as if a machine were swiveling it and suddenly vanished. It was like a vision.

Music was playing. The air was thick with the sweet, exciting din of conversation, plates clattering, and a clumsy waltz rhythm. The actor started making preparations to leave. He checked his wig in a pocket mirror, licked his thumb and forefinger, and smoothed his eyebrows. He drew on his gloves slowly, with great care. The actor always put on his gloves as though they were brand new and he was trying them on for the first time: he started with the four fingers, waited a moment, then hastily, with a certain modesty, thrust his thumb into the waiting hole as if it were following its four senior brothers.

"I shall go ahead," said the actor. "You should follow me after a little while, in ones and twos. Lajos, you bring up the rear. I will be waiting for you at the stage door."

He put his index finger to his lips and winked.

"Be quiet. Be tactful," he whispered.

He almost slammed the curtain behind him. They heard his high, singsong voice greeting other customers.

"You must ask Moravecz to explain the real reasons for Joseph II's unpopularity," Ernō continued. " 'This fat horse here is the clergy, your majesty, this one is the aris-

143

tocracy, and this starved blind nag is the people . . . ,' you say. This curious image of history, you feel, has not received the recognition due to it. Here, since you are not in a hurry, is the ideal opportunity for him to expound its virtues . . . 'In Louis the Great's reign, sir, the stars of North, East, and South are in three different seas . . . Why exactly was that?' "

"I don't understand it either," said Tibor solemnly, slightly troubled.

"You have to be very careful about the tone of the questions," said Ernö. "That's the hardest part of it. You must be respectful but firm. After all you are not demanding anything . . . it's nothing more than going back into a shop where you bought something and asking one last time about the worth and quality of the goods you have purchased. Or if you were asking for operating instructions. They are obliged to give you that much. The main thing is that you are simply unable to sleep because your conscience is so troubled by that passage in Tacitus. That's what you have to emphasize. We can rehearse tomorrow."

"There may be other matters we can bring up," said Béla. "Jurák could apologize to the music teacher for his out-of-tune singing. He could even ask for extra lessons, now as a late compensation. We could raise the money."

"What I want to know is what Amadé is up to," said Ábel.

No one knew what Amadé was cooking up, not even Lajos. Béla discreetly part-closed the drapes and they peered through the remaining gap. There they were all sitting: the actress with the director on her right, now arrived and chewing a piece of wurst, the drugstore owner on her left. The editor sat at the end of the table, waiting with bated breath for a crumb of gossip to be tossed his way. Two young officers in dress uniform were sipping champagne. The manager of the café was leaning against the buffet bar. He had a heart problem: his face looked strained, his jaundiced-looking sickly hands hanging by his sides. Why should anyone be here if they were not obliged to be? It was hard to hear themselves talk over the racket. Ábel reflected that even the childhood evenings spent in his father's study with those three gentle buffoons were more fun.

He slowly relaxed and the acute tension to which he had been subject melted away. The shame, the confusion, the sense of shock he had felt after the gang had dispersed at noon gave way to a numb indifference. He was sitting close to Tibor and that was all that mattered. Yesterday he still knew that once he had woken up he would see him in half an hour or an hour and that he would invent some story or an item of unexpected gossip that Tibor would receive with his usual polite, drawling "Really?" but that it wouldn't matter as he would be standing there beside him, listening to him, no one else. But as of noon today, this feeling of assurance, that he would see Tibor at the arranged times and talk to him without anything getting in the way, had vanished forever. He stared at the dirty ceiling, the crumbling walls, and was amazed. He had to bow his head for fear the others would see him crying. He felt the unsettling pain of loss, an apprehension that danger could not be avoided, the kind of thing no one could bear for long. They sat exhausted, gazing at the grimy superior world of adults, this desolate paradise.

"*Intra muros,*" Ábel remarked sourly.

They looked at him, puzzled. Tibor was particularly pale this evening. He sat formal and silent, his head in his hands as if at a funeral. Ábel didn't dare ask him what the matter was. You could never be certain of anything with Tibor for he often surprised you with what he said, things so idiotic sometimes they made you blush. He might perhaps have answered, as he did last Sunday, that it was all the Vasas soccer team's fault: they should have scored with a free kick at the end. Whenever Tibor looked thoughtful it was likely that his mind had wandered into uncharted territory. Ábel was always afraid that he'd eventually say something that lowered his stock in Ernő's eyes. It was only Ernő he feared: Béla and Lajos never criticized Tibor with such severity. He was afraid Tibor would commit some faux pas or say something stupid, and that he would have to be ashamed on his friend's behalf.

How long can it last? he wondered. And what then? The spell that held them together might be broken in a matter of minutes. One word and, like an overloaded fuse, the electricity would snap off and all would be darkness. They had long prepared for this evening. Ábel couldn't say what precisely he was expecting, what form of liberation. The only thing that surprised him was how extraordinarily morose they all felt. It had never occurred to him that the moment of freedom would appear so unattractive.

It was their low stature that made them nervous: they

had suddenly fallen from the highest echelons of their own hierarchy to the rank of second-rate adults.

"We have to start over again, right from the beginning," he said.

Not one of them wanted to set off without Tibor. Who'll go first, asked Ernő. When they remained silent, Tibor made no move: he too waited silently, expectantly, staring at the marble-topped table. He didn't look up, knowing it was him they were waiting for, that they were watching him closely. He was determined to say nothing. The way they competed for his affection, the passionate loyalty they radiated from every side, even more powerfully, more jealously now than before, made him all the more obstinate. He sat like the wounded Paris, biting his lip.

This jealousy radiating from each of them individually, a jealousy whose intensity he could not help but feel, shook and embittered him. He felt anxious, uncertain of himself. Friendship was a burden. It was nice to know that the bonds that had so far united them had now been broken. Thinking this he felt a sense of freedom and lightness. He no longer needed their friendship. It was too much, it weighed him down. Ábel's enthusiasms, Ernő's jealousy, Béla's leech-like clinging, the actor's games and very being: it was all excessive, he could no longer bear it. He felt a great relief contemplating the possibility that, within a month perhaps, the barracks would be his home.

No longer would there be Mother, Lajos, and Ábel constantly asking him to account for his every movement, no longer would he suffer the insufferably critical gaze of Ernō, no longer would he have to endure the presence of Béla, that mincing shadow. He had had enough of them all. He thought fondly of the front of which he knew nothing, only that it would mean a final break with the life he had been leading, a life whose tensions he could no longer bear. His father's face appeared before him out of the chaos, cast in bronze like some heroic statue. There was something certain you could cling to there, though the enormous weight of it oppressed everyone around him. Tibor wanted to settle his bill with Havas. Tomorrow he would speak to his mother and maybe even confess everything, but the important thing was to pay Havas off, to recover the silver, then, with a light heart, to say farewell to Ábel and Ernō, clap Béla on the shoulder, avoid the actor, and, free as a bird, to enter the barracks, maybe the war itself, that great community of adults where he would no longer be responsible for anything, where he would no longer be the idol of a small votary circle all the more burdensome because he was incapable of reciprocating their feelings. Everything would be fine, it would all be all right, a word might be enough and they would all be free of this aching, agonizing spell. He no longer knew who he was. The rules of the game had become confusing, incomprehensible. They were sitting around, waiting for something to happen. What had happened? Whose fault was it? He felt no sense of guilt. He had simply tolerated their loyalty to him. He had been fair: he tolerated them all equally. He felt he had assumed a great burden he could barely support. He had to shake it off with one great effort and move on. He was fed up with the game. He couldn't stand it any longer: it agitated him so keenly that his whole nervous system rejected it.

He thought of Ábel and cast a glance at him. The doctor's son immediately returned his glance with such enthusiasm, such feverish anticipation and readiness to leap to his feet and carry out his orders, that he felt guilty and miserable as he averted his eyes. People were so hard to reject. We think we are free but when we try to tear ourselves away we find we cannot move a muscle. Someone smiles at us heedlessly and immediately we are entangled in that person's friendship. He didn't know what friendship was. He had imagined friendship differently, as taking a lighthearted, pleasant walk, a kind of fellow feeling that imposed no obligations. People spend time with each other, exchanging ideas . . . And for the first time it struck him that such a bond might weigh on one, that it might not be breakable without causing injury.

But it didn't depress him to think that such injury might be inevitable. So what if he hurt someone? Why not punch Ernő in the face and dislodge that pince-nez, why not fetch Ábel a mighty blow or squash Béla's nose, then stride away with head held high? The problem was that he couldn't just walk out, that a man cannot simply abandon a world, a habitation he himself has shaped. They all lived on the same planet and none of them could stop inhabiting it: they were their own sun, their own atmosphere, held together by forces none of them could overcome alone.

I might be able to make my peace with each of them, he thought hopefully. It was not impossible. I'll have a word with Havas, and tomorrow, when Ábel gives that whistle I'll tell him I don't have the time. Perhaps I will write a letter to Father and ask him to come home. If he were here and he forgave me, no one would dare come anywhere near me.

He turned his face away with a proud suffering look. What are they looking at? he strained to think. Perhaps they're waiting for me to stand up so they can form a line behind me, and I won't be able to take a step without them because they're scared I might escape. Oh, to be through with all this! To forget! To play something else, some completely different game! Now, when we are free to play what we like . . . To forget these years, the gang, the thefts, the anxiety, the entire game, this whole crazy painful rebellion . . . Let them feel some pain. Somewhere at the back of his mind he wondered why it hurt when people loved you. Every nerve in his body, every sinew, bristled and protested against the demands that he felt to be radiating from the others. They all wanted him exclusively to themselves, he thought. They're jealous. Filled with pride, he broke into a barely visible smile and raised his head.

One of them has cheated, he thought. The whole game is crooked, has been crooked for a long time. The game was serving someone's interests. He looked straight ahead like a slave owner, disgusted by what he saw. I have to try and find the word, he thought, the word that once pronounced will blow it all to kingdom come, that will explode the whole point of the gang, or lance it like a blister that you only need to touch with a pin, just one word . . . I loathe you all, he thought. If I stood up now and started screaming, that I'd had enough, I can't bear it any longer, they would all think something, their thoughts would be of me, and I want no more of this, I've had enough. I want to be free of them, alone; I want new friends. This friendship is a pain. I can't stand it any more.

He looked up almost as if begging.

We shouldn't have close friendships, he thought. It's not my fault. I didn't ask anyone to be my friend.

He raised his hand and they all looked him right in the eyes. Ernő's eyes shone with a cold and mocking light. They all hate me, he thought and a hot wave of contrariness ran through him.

He stood up and stretched sensuously.

Come on, he said simply, I've had enough.

THEY MADE THEIR WAY THROUGH THE CAFÉ, Tibor at the head, three of them in a single group behind, Lajos bringing up the rear. The bon vivant bowed to the director. People watched them leave. Friends of Amadé, they said at one of the tables. Sniggering laughter followed them out, looks of curiosity. Ábel felt himself blushing. All the tables were talking about them. They stood at the revolving doors. The door was temporarily jammed: someone was pushing the opposite way. There were eyes everywhere. Perhaps books were better after all. They should have stuck to books: people caused you pain, they infected you. I'd never have believed it could hurt so much. I know I've been a burden to him. He's far more stupid than I am. More stupid? What does that mean? He doesn't feel the excitement I feel when I meet someone, when I search through my memories to locate a voice I once heard. Father will be asleep now. Etelka might be awake, she may be sitting in my room. She loves me. Ernő told me she was in love with me. What was the cobbler saying about Tibor's mother? There was no deterioration in her condition overnight. If she should die tonight the colonel would arrive the next day or the day after . . . I must speak to Havas. Why did he call me as well? We will ask him to hand back the silver and we'll give him a signed note to promise that, should we survive and grow to be adults, we will settle the debt. I'll write him a letter and after I'm dead he can give it to Father or to Etelka. Six months or so and I will have forgotten all this. Perhaps I will still be alive and might, one day, write something. That hurts too, but not as much as living with other people does. Here we stand now with everyone staring at us. They look contemptuous: the editor is looking at us, waving us over. Perhaps they know Amadé is waiting for us. There is something disgraceful about going around with Amadé. They don't like Amadé. They smirk when they see him and whisper when his back is turned. Now they're smirking at us too. Perhaps they think we are off to the brothel. That's something of a tradition here. Amadé would lead us. That wouldn't be too bad, actually. Big Jurák, the bodybuilder, visited the brothel last week and said they had a new blond girl down from the capital, and that she showed him her license in which the police specify what streets they may use for soliciting, where they may smile and invite men over, how at the opera and at the National Theater they may only enter the second circle, and how much of the licensed girl's income may be deducted by the landlord for rent. That would make good reading. One should read everything, everything people have written, and see everything they have built and constructed, everything. Some time, perhaps quite soon, I want to write down all I've ever seen or heard, write it down in a great big book, yes, including everything about this town, Tibor, Amadé, Etelka, and them all; everything I see and hear right up to the beginning of my book. Not a bad thing to do. What's up now? Why aren't we moving? Tibor hates me. Ernő hates me too. I think we all hate each other. I loathe Amadé and Lajos gets on my nerves with his stupid questions. He changes subjects all the time without any warning. He gets the wrong idea about everything. I don't want Tibor to hate me. I know he's stupid but I still don't want it. I'm utterly unlike him, and yet his beauty sets him apart. He can't help it that I suffer on his account. If Tibor were my friend I'd go away with him and take great care to discuss everything with him, even if I knew he didn't understand or wasn't so much as listening. Perhaps he would help me if I gave him a present, something special. I've more or less poured out my heart to him. I have nothing I can give him. What would he say if I told him he was beautiful? Maybe he doesn't know. I didn't know it till recently. I must forget the fact that he's beautiful, and once I do that I'll be free of them. Everyone can go his own way and we can forget each other. I should pay a visit to the brothel. If I knew, if everything worked out . . . Perhaps Amadé will take me there now. Get a move on. The prima donna is looking this way too, laughing and beckoning. Maybe she fancies Tibor. What to do if Amadé should introduce us to the prima donna? Tomorrow is free. Everyone finds Tibor attractive. There was an army major in the street yesterday who turned round to look at Tibor. Everyone likes him. Nobody likes me . . . Well, maybe Etelka. It isn't good for a person to love somebody. I shall be alone soon. I feel ill in the afternoons. I must find out who cheated. I must be free of Amadé. And of Ernő and Havas too. I don't want to dream about him any more. I must be free of Tibor as well. When does a person become an adult? The revolving door turned. They stepped out into the street.

THE SQUARE SPREAD OUT BEFORE THEM, FES-tively lit with a thick patina of moonlight, the white walls of a few wide and squat baroque houses swelling and sparkling like the icing on a cake. The music whose rhythm had been swept with them through the revolving doors dissolved and faded in the solemn silence. The church formed one end of the square, oppressing the nearby low houses with its enormous weight. A light was burning behind one of the great casement windows of the bishop's palace. The chestnut trees around the dried-up fountain in the small park in the middle of the square raised their compact little candles.

The air was mild, as heady as on a summer night.

There was not a soul to be seen anywhere. The theater, with its high stage loft and graceless proportions, rose above the park like an abandoned barn, its dark, cob-webbed windows squinting out, half-blind. The town was in the deep first phase of sleep. A train gave a piercing whistle somewhere near the station, as if to remind the populace that it was all very well sleeping and burying your head in the duvet, trains would continue to come and go with their freight of silent passengers. The town was clearly indifferent to such reminders. Before the bar-racks two hard-helmeted guards went on switching posts at the gate.

The bishop sat by the lighted window in a high-backed armchair reading the paper. A glass of water and a box containing a wafer with antipyrine stood on a little table next to him. Occasionally he extended his bony hand towards the glass and wet his lips with a tiny gulp, then read on distractedly. The bishop slept in an iron camp bed, like the kaiser. Above the simple bed hung an ivory crucifix; by the wall a maroon-colored velvet hassock. The drapes of the window were of the same heavy maroon vel-vet. The bishop was a poor sleeper. He went to look for a book in one of the bookcases, running his bony finger along the gilt-lettered spines as if touching the keys of an organ, seeking for a note perfectly fitted to the moment. He tipped a number of volumes forward, then pushed them all back, picking out instead a thick black tome that took some effort to lift. The fragile figure took some time conveying the heavy volume to his bedside table, set it down beside the breviary and the prayer beads, opened it, and examined a few illustrations. The book was by Brehm, about the lives of the animals. The bishop was very old. He sat down on the edge of the iron bed with a soft groan and, with a great sigh, removed his buttoned shoes.

Every window of the hospital was lit: it was like a busy, prosperous factory on an industrial estate where work continued through the night. And at the end of the street, under the bridge, the great steam mill was still pumping. They made their slow way across the square, drawing enormous shadows behind them in the bright light. They stopped in the middle of the park where the harsh raw smell of elder from somewhere in the bushes assaulted their senses: it was as if it were physically touching them. They lit cigarettes and stood quietly, without speaking. That sprinkling of houses, lacquered by the yellow light, had been the backdrop to the theater of their childhood. They knew precisely who lived in which house; they knew the sleepers behind the windows. The gilt lettering on the bookseller's sign had worn away. It was in these shops with their low doors that they had bought pencils, books, collars, hats, sweets, fretsaws, battery-powered flashlights, all on their fathers' accounts, please chalk it up. They never had to pay for anything here, their fathers enjoyed apparently boundless credit, for it seemed to extend throughout their childhood. Behind the lowered blinds of the chemist's window, through a small square-shaped aperture, a sharp beam of light showed the chemist to be awake, probably with company, ladies from the officers' quarters, a few officers, whiling away the small hours with a little *cognac médicinal.* The striking of the clock broke the silence so violently the air was still ringing with its music after it had stopped, as if someone had smashed a very delicate glass. They stood around the elder tree, a cigarette in one hand, the other arranging their clothes as they proceeded about their business. The one-armed one stuck his cigarette between his lips, his hand being required elsewhere.

Tibor started whistling quietly. They walked beside the railings on soft, frail grass. The cobbler was sitting beside a taper in his little hovel, an illustrated almanac in his lap, reading the lives of the generals in a gentle undertone, syllable by syllable. From time to time he stopped reading, looked straight ahead of him, and ran his hand through his beard, moaning quietly. In the civic library, among its thirty thousand volumes, on the moonlit floor of the great hall, the rats were excitedly feasting. The old town had been infested by rats and a rat-catcher was summoned by the council. He locked himself in the theater for a few hours and by the time he had finished there were hundreds of dead rats lying on the stage, in the auditorium, and along the corridors. Ábel could remember the rat-catcher who spent a mere afternoon in town, ridding the main public buildings of rats and mice, then disappeared along with his secrets and the council fee. Someone said he was Italian.

A GOOD SPRING MOON TENDS TO MAGNIFY WHATever it illuminates. It would be very hard to give a proper scientific explanation for this. All objects—houses, public squares, whole towns—puff themselves up with spring moonlight, swelling and bloating like corpses in the river. The river dragged such corpses through town at a run. The corpses swam naked and traveled great distances down from the mountains, down tiny tributaries that flowed into others greater than themselves in the complex system of connections; they floated rapidly down on the spring flood heading towards their ultimate terminus, the sea. The dead were fast swimmers. Sometimes they kept company, arriving in twos and threes, racing each other through town at night; the river being aware of its obligations to the town, going about its business of transporting the dead at night with the utmost speed. The corpse-swimmers had come a long way and spent the winter hibernating under the frozen river until the melting ice in the spring allowed them to continue down the flood towards the plains. There were many of them and they had been there some time. Their toes and bellies protruded from the water, their heads a few inches under the mirroring surface, the wounds on their bodies, their heads, and their chests, growing ever wider. Sometimes they got caught up on the footings of the bridge where millers fished them out the next morning, examining with curiosity the official death certificates enclosed in waterproof tin capsules hung about their necks. There must have been a lot of them because they kept turning up, every week all through spring. If they happened to wind up in town, the editor of the local paper would publish whatever details the millers had managed to glean from the capsules.

The pine woods surrounding the town had been devastated by a storm at the beginning of the war, but the spring wind still wafted the smell of resin into town, and on warm nights it blended with the air to produce an atmosphere thick like pine-scented bath salts. At the corner of fishmongers' alley the butcher and his two daughters slept in a single cubicle, the door to the premises left open, the moonlight lying across the sleeping bodies, and all along the wall the great swelling animal carcasses hanging on hooks. On the marble counter lay a calf's head, its eyes closed, black blood dripping from its nostrils onto the slab. The old solicitor who was the last in town to go to bed each night sat in his study in a cherrywood armchair, the scarlet broadcloth of which was secured at the edges with a speckling of white enameled tacks. He had a clutch of dusty glass cases on his lap and was examining his butterfly collection. Several thousand butterflies lined the walls in similar glass cases, the solicitor himself having captured them with his white butterfly net and put them in a stoppered bottle of potassium cyanide. He carried the cyanide bottle and the butterfly net around with him everywhere, in the back pocket of his long frock coat, into chambers, and into courtrooms too. He had lost two sons in the war. Their photographs stood on his desk in copper frames tied round with black ribbons of mourning. But he did not mourn for them any more because he was old, because it was already two years since they were killed, and because in two years a person can get over everything painful. He was currently examining a row of Cabbage Whites through his magnifying glass, taking great care over the process. A tobacco sieve lay on the table, and a stump pipe. The solicitor had been a lepidopterist for seventy years now: you could see him in the warm seasons of each year at the edge of town, his white beard swaying, the long tails of his frock coat floating behind him as he skipped over furrowed fields holding his net aloft, chasing butterflies.

And there were many others, many thousands of people they knew by sight, by their faces or voices, recalling them all in whatever place the soul develops its photographs, nor could they free themselves of them, the faces of those beggars, priests, and fading women with whom they lived among these pieces of stage scenery, where all who found themselves in the area and remained here through ties of family or work made up a single community whose members knew everything and nothing about each other. But in the moment of their dying perhaps there would flash before them the face of the crippled toy-shop owner in the square by the church who had once explained a new sort of conjuring trick involving a magic cupboard. And indeed there was a professional conjurer in town too who performed every autumn in the culture hall and tuned pianos in his spare time. They were inhabitants of an island from which it was impossible to escape entirely, for when they died the family would bring their remains back and bury them in their native island soil. Ábel threw his cigarette away.

Avanti, pronounced the actor in a flat voice. He was standing at the stage door, his gold tooth glittering in the moonlight. He was smirking.

. . .

He pointed his battery-powered flashlight at the top of the stairs, then ran it inquiringly up the wall where, behind a barred window, hung a notice saying: *9:30. Rigoletto. Rehearsal without script.* The actor led them on tiptoe and having reached the mezzanine threw wide the iron door.

The long corridor was so narrow that feeling their way forward they could touch its facing walls. They proceeded like this in uncertain crocodile fashion, swaying a little, the actor in front almost floating on light feet as he flashed their single source of light first ahead, then behind him. The inside of this theater, as of any other, seemed all stairs and doors. A sweet, musty smell permeated everything, something not quite perfume, damp, or mastic, but a blend of canvas, paint, ninety-proof alcohol, human body odors, dust, dirt, stuffiness, and more than anything that unique theater stench that is a distillation of grand speeches and tirades, stuck together with words, colored lights, and movement, an intensely physical, bombastic stench that clings to actors' clothes and skin and hair, one you can smell even when they're not on stage. For the first time Ábel understood the actor's peculiar need of different, much harsher, broader forms of scent. It was the smell of the stage the actor was trying to mask, for no one likes to smell of work, that was why kitchen maids used patchouli, cobblers crude pomade, greengrocers musk, and why the actor used chypre.

They had never imagined a building with so many corridors. So many stairs, so many doors. They climbed two floors, the actor pushing past ever more iron doors that creaked or swung sharply back at them. The actor was quietly whistling. He was a long way ahead of them with the flashlight. He was whistling a sweet tune in a broken, recurring rhythm. Finally he stopped at a door with a frosted glass panel.

"This is the hairdresser's room!" he announced as he switched on the light. "Sit down."

A bench ran along the wall and one corner of the room was curtained off with a red-and-white striped cloth hanging from the ceiling. A full-length streaky mirror lay on a crude table by a stool. Say hello to the hairdresser! With one hand he drew the curtain aside. Hundreds of human hairpieces hung on long poles beside the wall: blond, brown, gray and curly, wavy and smooth, with all the unspeakable sadness of objects devoid of function. Something of a person remains in hair, even after it has been cut off. A blond female wig with two long plaits dangled in the corner, keeping an eye on the maiden who had relieved herself of it, vainly seeking the shoulder the plaits should be winding over. The black mane that flowed round the neck of the rebel hero was not flowing anywhere, the long fringe falling over the vanished brow in a state of terminal despair beyond all reason. On either side of a bald smoothly peeled scalp some scant white locks covered a pair of old man's ears that must have heard much in their time but were craftily keeping their secrets to themselves. Every hairpiece retained something of the personality of the man or woman from whose head it had been plucked. Hundreds upon hundreds of invisible hanged figures dangled from their hairpieces. They suggested some ancient massacre of hair growers arranged by that most potent of hangmen, time.

"The hairdresser is possessed of supernatural powers," said the actor. "He has something of a force of nature about him."

He paused for breath. "Only he is much more skillful," he added.

He sat down in front of the mirror and examined himself closely.

"There are wigs that more or less play themselves," he said, pulling open a drawer. "This blond one here . . . how often he has done my work for me."

With one violent gesture he tore off his own wig. The action was so sudden, the effect so dramatic they all involuntarily leaned forward on the bench where they had been sitting, huddled and enchanted. Tibor's hands flew to his mouth. They knew the actor himself wore a wig. They knew he changed its color to chime with the passing seasons. There were times it was of a light, dreamlike blondness, sometimes red as fire, at other times pure black. But the movement with which he removed the wig racked them with a sympathetic pain, they could not have been more surprised had the actor with equal suddenness torn off his arm and begun to unscrew his head. The actor's scalp appeared from beneath the wig like a brilliantly waxed snow-white dome that had bubbled into startling view. There was something so naked about the bald head, so physical, so undressed, exposed, and shameless it was as if the actor had ripped off all his clothes with a single movement, cast them on the ground, and stood before them without a stitch. He ran his hand over his bare head, leaned indifferently over to the mirror, and started to examine it with proper professional attention.

You have to be careful, he said, and drew the blond wig over his knuckles, gently stroking its locks with the other hand, careful you don't get water on the hair. That's vital. You're still young so I am telling you this. Unfortunately no one told me until it was too late. There are people who duck under the waves, then try to scrub their hair with soap. It's the most dreadful carelessness anyone can be guilty of. There are others who dip their heads in water after washing. The scalp develops dandruff, the hair dries out, grows pale, and breaks. Never let water come into contact with your hair. There are excellent special washes and dry shampoos . . . One moment! He leaned even closer to the mirror, eyes blinking as he studied his face.

There was a strange indifference, a lifelessness about his face as he sat bare-skulled before the mirror. Only his eyes were alive, every other feature dropped into a mask of death, as if, having ripped off his wig and revealed himself naked, the actor had wiped from his face every mark that time and life had posted there, all expression, every crow's-foot of individuality: he was naked now, empty and dead, mere matter with which he could work as he wanted. Grasping his nose between two fingers he turned his head this way and that, like a foreign object. It was a stranger they saw sitting in front of them, mere raw material that its proprietor could shape as he liked. He rubbed his face with infinite care as if he were alone. He pulled his lids down, rolled his eyes, covered his ample jowls with his hands, and like a painter in the middle of a portrait leaned back in his chair and examined himself through half-closed lids.

"I have approximately thirty-four faces," he mentioned as if in passing. "Thirty-four, or it may be thirty-six, it's a long time since I counted them. I can do a Negro priest, darlings . . . I have a Cyrano. I have a Caesar that is without a wig, genuinely bald, it only needs two lines here by the mouth . . . Watch!"

He picked up a stick of charcoal and drew two lines by his cheekbones. His face looked markedly thinner. Every aspect of his face suddenly assumed a sharp angular look, somehow cruel, and his baldness took on a life of its own, like some symbol of fate, such a clear mark of a man's secret suffering that no amount of successes, victories, or triumphs could compensate for it.

"My Caesar does not wear a laurel crown," he said. "He thrusts his shame in your face. Let them note it and tremble. The fate of entire worlds is contained in this bald head."

Slowly he settled the blond wig over it.

"And here we discover the problem of whether to be or not to be."

He paraded before them, bowing from the waist.

"And I tell you, Polonius . . ."

He stared before him in his Hamlet frenzy. He pulled one lock of blond hair over his brow, pouted and took a few trance-like steps. Now he was someone whose part he did not know: a man who had once passed him in the street of whom all he could retain was his supercilious smile.

"He has been me in various parts," he said meditatively. He sat back down in front of the mirror and removed the wig so he was bald again. He dragged half a dozen wigs out of the drawer, threw them on the table, trying first one then the other. He stuck a little goatee under his chin and sideburns on his cheekbones, and coughing and puffing with gout raised his foot, put on a faint voice, and ordered hot wine. He toyed with faces and patches of hair as if taking them from a mold. He brought the well-known features of the long dead to life without even seeming to try employing a few vocal modulations, all immediately identifiable. Then he pushed all the props to the side.

"Perhaps, one day," he said, "I will discover a mask that I can use for a long time, for the rest of my life. It's not so easy. Shreds, patches, hair, and paint are of little help. This stuff here," he tapped his face with two fingers, "is pliable material, but you have to know how to use it. Naturally, it shrivels and hardens. Flesh has a life of its own, my friends, as has the soul. You have to command it, tame it. This body of mine," he cast his eyes over his entire length and gestured dismissively, "is all used up and I'm bored with it. I want to appear in public in another town next time, in different outward form. Like a ruddy-cheeked youth, perhaps. But I can't. Maybe I will go away and become an old man, the wrinkles that much more firmly set, more intractable. I am aging."

Frustrated, he slapped at his double chin.

"Here's one I really like," he said, drawing forth a scrap of hair. "And this. And this," he threw the wigs up in the air. "Believe me, if I were to put on this scarlet head of Titus no one would know me."

And he put on the Titus head. The shimmering copper locks flopped over his brow right down to the bridge of his nose. With a few delicate touches he applied rouge to his lips until they looked young and full, emphasized his eyes with a matchstick, and suddenly the lifeless pupils were full of light. His face was radiant, red, alive with sin, full of shameless arrogance. His voice too had changed. He spoke in the resounding tone of command.

"I have thirty-four faces," he shouted and blew out his cheeks. "Or is it thirty-six? Who can recognize me? I shall disappear, like the invisible man, I shall slip between people's fingers. My realm is the world of immortals because I slip between death's fingers too. He won't know my face. Even if I am alone he won't find the real me at home."

He hesitated, looked around, and dropped his voice.

"Everyone has many faces. Sometimes I no longer know which is the last one, the one under which there is nothing but bone."

He peeled off the Titus head and wiped the paint from his face with a napkin. Once more he fell to examining the raw material and relapsed into depression.

"Can this fat, toothless pig be me? Nonsense. The devil take it and consign it to hell."

He removed his dentures and shoved them aside next to his hair as though they had nothing to do with him, then he wiped them clean with a cloth and carefully put them back in his mouth.

Ernō stood and crept up behind him. The actor looked

for a cigarette, threw a towel around his neck, and, cigarette in mouth, examined himself suspiciously. With an unexpected movement he twisted the towel tightly around his neck.

"In Paris," he said, "this is how the waiters sit and dine after they have finished their shifts. They twist their napkins into a rope and wrap them round their necks like scarves."

"I'm sure you're right," said Ábel.

They soon forgot everything else. There was a reason the actor was with them tonight. He was preparing something that was bigger and more amusing than the idiotic postgraduation larks that usually ended in drunken fist-fights at the brothel. They could rely on the actor. They were enchanted by his transformations. Lajos watched him with fascination as he fussed with wigs, face paints, patches, and boxes of rice powder. Ábel was wondering whether the actor had a hidden face that he himself might not have seen, one that he would put on just for tonight. He remembered that half minute or so when the actor had remained alone in his room by the window. A cold shiver ran down his spine, but he knew that he could not leave the room now, not for any price. He would see this last night through with the gang and the actor and would not move until the actor discarded his final mask. The way he sat in front of the mirror now, with the napkin around his neck, unshaven, bald, a cigarette in his mouth, his legs crossed, his hands carelessly on his hips, he looked entirely foreign, like someone who spoke a strange language, practiced a mysterious trade. You couldn't tell where he came from, what skills he possessed, or what he was doing here at all. He sat back, he drew on his cigarette, he dangled his feet. He was a complete stranger. So unfamiliar was he that they felt shy and fell silent. This was entirely the actor's territory. All those hairpieces by the wall, all those destinies and personalities hanging in the shadows, all were part of his domain. At one gesture of his, whole armies might come to life, figures with terrifying faces might emerge. The actor gave a haughty, confident, self-satisfied smile. The cigarette butt shifted from one corner of his mouth to the other.

Ernő alone harbored reservations.

"What are you up to?" he asked in a flat voice.

The actor threw the cigarette butt away. "Now to business," he said and sprang to his feet.

HE SAT ÁBEL DOWN AT THE MIRROR, LEANED back, crossed his arms, one finger to his lips, and examined him carefully. He went over to the window, leaned against the sill, and thought about it a little more. He indicated with a gesture, as a painter might, that Ábel should turn his profile towards him. Then, finally having solved the problem, he leapt over to the table, tore off a tuft of black hemp and held it next to Ábel's face, shook his head, gave a whistle, and with two fingers turned the boy's head this way and that in a deeply contemplative mood, sighing *aah* every so often.

"You ask what I'm up to," he chattered, vaguely distracted. "I'm coming to grips with things, preparing a little party. We do what we can!"

He picked out a grayish wig with a side parting and ran a brush through it.

"You have aged, my child. You have distinctly aged recently. Suffering adds years."

He carefully brushed the wig into a center parting.

"I thought it might be appropriate as a kind of valedictory gesture," he said. "We could, of course, go and visit the girls too. Or make our way over to the Petőfi café."

He wound a little cotton wool round the end of a match and looked for some glasses.

"Now face the mirror. I'm beginning to see what you will look like in thirty years' time. Remember me then."

With a sudden movement he clapped the wig onto Ábel's head the way a hypnotist might put to sleep some volunteer from the audience using no more than a simple hand gesture. Ábel was immediately transformed. An old man stared back at him and the rest of the gang from the mirror. Aged brows clouded over startled eyes. The actor began to attend to the eye region with his stick of charcoal.

"What I've imagined is a little celebration . . . a celebration of us all that you won't forget. We did once talk of appearing on stage together in full costume, and everyone would say whatever came into his head. A kind of show for art lovers only . . . with everyone taking responsibility for himself. We'll give them a proper show all right."

So saying he stuck a small graying goatee on Ábel's

chin, tore it off again, and tried muttonchop whiskers instead.

"The moment is here. You can have the run of the entire costume cupboard. We have the stage complete with scenery. The auditorium is empty. We are performing only for ourselves. I have ensured that we will be left in peace till the morning."

He gave a smile of mild amusement. He settled on the muttonchops and stuck two gray streaks of hair next to the ears. The sweet smell of mastic filled the room.

"Well, one could do worse," he said examining his work on Ábel with satisfaction. "The lips are narrow . . . let's add a little disappointment. And some doubt. And here . . . do excuse me, darling, I'm almost done . . . a little pride, a little canniness."

Each time his hand moved Ábel changed a little more, becoming ever less recognizable. They stood behind him and watched.

"It's not magic, it's not witchcraft," the actor declared as with a few very rapid strokes of the brush and the charcoal he emphasized one or two features and blurred some sharp lines.

"We haven't sold our souls to the devil . . ."

He ran a brush right through the eyebrows.

"It's just manual skill and expertise. Wind the clock forward thirty years and . . . here we are!"

He stuck the towel under his arm and the comb by his ear and made a great bow, like Figaro in the opera.

"My compliments to you, gentlemen. Next please."

Ábel stood up uncertainly. The little circle behind him backed away. The actor was already considering Ernő.

"Cold heart, green bile," he chanted. "Sting of conspirator, serpent's tongue, you can already see the vague trace of a hump on his back. You will always be freckled."

He pressed Ernő into the chair in front of the mirror. Ábel stood in a corner, his arms folded. He felt a great calm. He was wearing a mask and that was reassuring. A man could live behind a mask and think what he liked. Tibor watched him with a superior smile. They laughed and surrounded him, the one-armed one sniffing curiously at Ábel, taking a tour of him. The mask looked solid and reliable. Tibor stared at him with round eyes. Ábel laughed and he could see from his friends' faces that his laugh had changed too: they were looking at him with serious expressions, with genuine admiration.

"Let us hurry nature on a bit," said the actor, who was giving his full attention to Ernő now. "Let us correct her. That's all it is. I merely bring out what is mature in you," he said, fitting a red wig on Ernő's head. "If he looks like an adult, well, let him be an adult," and so saying he covered the freckled band above Ernő's upper lip with a deepred mustache.

"Let him bear the consequences of his adulthood. The brush in a master's hand is led by instinct, but he has his three advisers: Learning, Observation, and Experience. You are a hunchback, I tell you." With both hands he seized Ernő's temples, bent his head back, and stared deep into his eyes.

"The head of a monster. I shall now strip you of your

skin and replace it with a new one, the shed skin of a snake." He pressed down Ernő's eyelids with his thumbs and gave the rest of the gang a wink in the mirror.

As one after another the actors retired to the "dressing room," they examined each other suspiciously, but not one stood in front of the mirror. It is extraordinary how quickly people get used to their new appearances. It was a shame the costumes didn't quite fit them: some were too big and their hands and feet were lost in the folds of their garments. But within a few moments they had grown taller and fatter. Ernő stood at the table, leaning on his stick. His sharp hump rose under his ample old-fashioned cloak; his red hair fell in straggly locks across his brow from beneath his tall top hat; his old-fashioned frock coat and silk knee breeches hung awkwardly on his thin frame. Next to his nose a thick, hairy wart sprouted. His heavily ringed tiny eyes danced nervously, blending confusion, resentment, and obstinacy, and his mouth was twisted into a bitter grimace of suffering.

"Life has taught me to prize truth, the truth above all," said Ábel, his voice low and severe.

"Button your trousers," replied Ernő.

They had dressed somewhat carelessly in their hurry. Ábel drew the red robe close around him. Béla, a half-naked Spanish sailor with a headscarf and locks flirtatiously plastered next to his ears, sat on the windowsill, hands on hips. The one-armed one was lost in the folds of his toga. He sat on the table, dangling his bare sandaled feet, a band round his head. He stared straight ahead, with a haughty, wounded look, and the pride of Mucius Scaevola who had sacrificed one arm for the state but had his own independent opinion on everything.

"To me, Rome is . . . ," he was saying.

They paced restlessly up and down in their narrow cage. They were puzzling out their as yet unknown roles and trying hard not to notice Tibor.

Colonel Prockauer's son was leaning into the mirror, as charmed by what he saw there as Narcissus had once been. Two long blond bunches of hair hung in front of his shoulders, the high-waisted silk dress tight around him as he raised the long loose train skirt with one hand and crossed his silk-stockinged legs with their lacquer-shod feet. Under the deep décolletage his well-formed breasts, created by the actor out of two towels, heaved and rose with each breath he took. His arms, his neck, and chest were sticky with thick white powder. The actor's fingers had magically elongated his eyelashes, and his adolescent spots were masked by a pink blusher the actor had gently brushed and puffed across his cheeks.

You couldn't really tell, not at a glance anyway, whether he was woman or girl. Ernő circled him warily, raising his top hat and muttering incomprehensible compliments to him. Tibor responded with a smile, then immediately turned back to re-enter the spell of the mirror. He tried a few steps, holding his skirt high. The wig was hot and smelled foul.

"I'm sweating like a pig," he declared in a deep voice that was not his own.

Ernō offered his arm. The one-armed one cut in.

"I have only one arm, sweet damsel," he said, "but it is strong and you can cling to it."

Ábel opened the window. Hot air poured in along with the heavy milky scent of earth. They stood silently, the open window reminding them of reality, of the houses in the square, and of people who might be spying on them from afar. They looked at each other and couldn't bring themselves to laugh. They were overwhelmed by the consciousness of their utter complicity, the tremulous joy of belonging, the delight of pulling a huge ridiculous face at the sleeping world, behind its unsuspecting back, perhaps for the last time. For the last time perhaps the actor held together the ropes that bound them. Their shared memories, the spirit of rebellion, everything that united them: their common hatred of a world as incomprehensible and unlikely as their own, as ignorant of itself and as false, all flashed before their eyes. And the ties of friendship too: its anxieties and longings, the sad effects of such anxiety still evident in their eyes. Tibor raised his skirt and spun round, astonished at himself.

"You know," he said in genuine surprise, "a skirt is not really as uncomfortable as you'd think."

A sailor entered the room, a fat man whose stomach bulged beneath his striped sleeveless vest, over his wide blue canvas trousers, his shoes of Muscovy leather, and blocked the doorway with his girth. A pipe dangled from his lips and his waxed hair, brushed forward under his loose-fitting cap, was plastered greasily across his forehead. He was squinting. He stood there awkwardly, took the pipe out of his mouth, and waved to them to follow him, then turned off the light.

He clunked about on the echoing boards in his noisy shoes and turned on the spots. Light exploded in their eyes, both from below and from the side, and behind the light a deep dense darkness bulged towards them, the impenetrable cavernous darkness of the auditorium accompanied by the funereal mothball smell of canvas sheeting. The actor went here and there, entirely at home, an engineer attending to business, barely noticing them, operating handles, checking resistors, subtly, fascinatingly, modifying the light until eventually it was all concentrated in one area of the stage, merging in a pool of heat and color, a gentle glow at the edges of which ends of ropes, canvases, lighting boards, and stage flats faded into the murk. He tugged one rope and a clutch of other ropes collapsed towards him, of which he grabbed one. Enormous colored sails turned slowly with lazy flaps while the sailor, pipe in mouth again, set about the ropes and colored sails in preparation for the coming storm. A wide terrace complete with palms and steps leading up to it descended before them, blocking their view, and some faded rose bowers followed, swirling with dust. Wait for the storm, the sailor muttered indifferently, then hurried off into the wings, setting a distant wind to screech and whinny through the bowers. A few harsh claps of thunder rang out over the howling storm. The actor solemnly stepped out from behind a dusty cactus, rubbed his hands, lit his pipe, and looked about him shaking his head.

"I don't think this is quite right either," he said, and waved away the Riviera scene. "Stand center stage, would you?"

The scenery swam aloft, disappearing in the heights, and the rose bowers jealously followed the sunlit landscape. Plain white walls appeared as if from nowhere. The conjurer threw his rope up towards the ceiling and the stage miraculously narrowed. Suddenly they found themselves prisoners in the cabin of a ship. Behind portholes the wind was still buzzing, but was now joined by the slap of waves. Two low lights appeared in the wall and a narrow door opened beside one of the portholes. A lamp with a faded shade dropped like a stone from above. The sailor dragged at a knot of ropes with both hands and a rhomboid ceiling lowered over the cabin. The shaded lamp came on. Then they were all working, the only sounds being the actor's brief words of command and the wailing of the wind that Ábel now controlled. It did not take as much skill to whip up a storm as people tended to think. A single movement was enough to induct Ábel into the secret.

"Drive them on, Aeolus!" he said as he pushed a claw-footed table center stage. "You are master of the four great planetary winds."

It was a surprisingly easy task mastering the four great planetary winds. The one-armed one rolled a barrel up against the wall. They carried sea chests, most probably containing ship biscuits and water. Aeolus whipped his servants on, their painful howling extending over the ocean.

"All hands on deck!" the actor bellowed. "Ladies first! The sea chests go round the table. Secure the portholes!"

He stopped.

"One time the Negroes leapt into the sea . . . ," he began. "No, I've already told you that."

He kicked a rosebush left over from the previous scene through the cabin door. Loud thunder shook the air, the boards trembled under their feet. Ábel was laying the storm on mercilessly.

"That was a close one," the actor pronounced after the latest bolt, and spat. "Take a breather, Aeolus. Relax a moment."

There was a strange silence. The lights, the walls, the furniture, everything was in its place, unlikely yet unmistakable, so that Ábel's entrance was a little unsteady, his steps uncertain, counterbalancing the swell of the sea. With the minimum fuss they took control of their new realm. Ernő made a formal gesture of taking Tibor by the hand and ceremoniously leading him over to the table. The one-armed one stood on the barrel, absorbed in watching the storm with its roof-high waves through a porthole. Ábel clapped an arm round his shoulder.

"A sublime scene," he said with awe. "One cannot help but feel one's insignificance."

A trapdoor opened in the floor and a tray laden with glasses rose through it, the naked arm of the actor supporting it and rising with it until his head appeared. He made a formal show of climbing through, then let the trapdoor clap shut behind him. He raised the tray high in the air and, leaning forward at a sharp angle, moved around with all the weathered skill of a ship's waiter in a storm, his body seeming to collapse after the tray with its glasses that he eventually deposited unbroken on the table.

"The two most important things," he gasped, "alcohol and a cool head. There are people who panic in a storm: some lose their heads, others the contents of their stomachs. We are making eight knots full speed, the temperature is falling. One good draught of brandy, gentlemen, a mouthful of ship biscuit, a bit of refrigerated meat, and we feel readier to face the following hours with equanimity. The captain is at his post and the passengers are inclined to trust him."

The tray was piled high with ship biscuits covered with meat and flasks of water-colored brandy. The actor gave a modest smile. He sat down, tapped his pipe against the tabletop, adjusted his belt, and stuffed a great hunk of meat into his mouth.

"Creation is hungry work," he said. He wiped the rim of the bottle with his hand and took a long draught.

"Burns your mouth!" He turned to Tibor. "A snifter for you, my lovely incognito?"

THE LOVELY INCOGNITO ADMITTED THAT AFTER the first glass she felt like throwing up. The actor knew a cure for seasickness that you should take an hour before the storm set in. They laid the lady out across the chest, fanned her, and tried to entertain her. The cabin darkened somewhat. The cabin boy left them every five minutes to increase the roar of the four winds and to provide a weather report.

Danger draws people together. No longer sturdy and Spartan, the actor fell ravenously to eating and drinking. He was the first to wilt. They had never seen him so drunk. Ernő, who drank cautiously, taking little sips, kept an eye on him as he wasn't convinced the actor was genuinely drunk. The actor meanwhile pulled a barrel up to the porthole, sat down on it, and stretching his arms wide pretended to play an accordion while singing in a harsh nasal tone.

"The Negroes sang this one," he remarked. "That was before they leapt into the water."

The monotonous melancholy air swirled and faded in the high auditorium. The actor rose to his feet and tirelessly continuing to play on the imaginary accordion walked up and down, undergoing a curious series of metamorphoses. He sang and played, but a few minutes later seemed to have vanished to be replaced by a fat drunk sailor sitting on the edge of the table, this time with a real accordion, his song full of the sadness of docks, harbors, and stagnant water, his face quite transformed, his eyes asquint, awkward in body, good-tempered, with a brandy-sodden joviality, somehow ponderous. He hadn't actually done anything, merely transformed himself. They couldn't understand what he was saying as he mixed words from English, Spanish, and other languages unknown to them, in a kind of incomprehensible macaronic, then he gave a croak and fell to praising distant skies and climes while radiating regret for years of pointless roaming.

The actor certainly knew his trade. It was a fat, drunk sailor that sat at the edge of the stage singing into the dark auditorium. The rest of them wandered up and down behind him, humming along with the hypnotic rhythm while the storm continued unabated outside and the vessel with all its passengers lurched towards an unknown harbor. The heady smell of brandy floated through the cabin as the sense of danger and a mood of mutual reliance took hold of them. In any case, there was going to be no escaping each other's company until the ship was safely docked. Tibor was feeling better and fell to eating with an appetite that belied his seeming sex. Béla was sitting at the actor's feet, his chin propped on his palms, observing him. They waltzed round each other, the actor setting the rhythm for the dance, his voice overflowing with melancholy.

It was the first time any of them had set foot on stage. The strange thing was that they felt perfectly at home there. They took possession of this world composed of three walls and a few boards as if nature had intended them for it. Ábel stood by the footlights and quietly recited something for the benefit of the invisible audience. As for the actor, he was absorbed in his acting and was growing ever more remote, ever less like the figure they had known, already recalling Le Havre, relating tales of amorous nights in various harbors, gazing around him as if they were all strangers. His vast half-naked body shook with every gesture. He was no longer sucking in his stomach and his flesh bulged through his vest, and as he passed before the spotlights Ábel spotted tattoos that served as tickets, some on his arms, some on his chest.

"Beware! A man with a tattoo! Take care, I say!" the one-armed one cried out.

Ernő was wearing his top hat. His hump weighed heavily on his back, pressing down his upper body.

"My intentions are honorable," he said frostily. The one-armed one threw himself on Ernő and Tibor leapt between the combatants, giving a faint shriek. Ábel had the impression that there were too many of them, too many strangers and newcomers, and miscounted their numbers. The actor was dancing in a corner, stubbornly, insistently alone, his accordion constantly moving, not to be forgotten for a second, while his heel stamped out a stiff, nervous rhythm. The gang sat down around the table and Ábel took out his pack of cards.

"I refuse to play with cheats," the one-armed one mumbled, clearly drunk.

But the sight of the pack enticed the actor over too. He examined each card carefully, slowly appraising it, drinking, rattling his change, then getting into arguments, using strange offensive-sounding phrases. They smacked their cards down, propped themselves on their elbows, pulled a lamp closer, Béla once again offering himself to be searched. There was silence for a while. The ship was clearly in calmer waters now, the wind abated. While they were dealing the cards again the actor left the cabin to return with a fresh bottle of brandy and declared with satisfaction:

"It's a starry night. Wind southeasterly. By morning we shall be in Piraeus."

Ábel wanted to know how long they had been here. Even experienced sailors tend to lose track of time. But what does it matter, he thought with dizzy delight. It's a fine ship and we're making good progress somewhere between sky and water. We will have arrived somewhere by morning. He clambered down into the prompter's box and watched the proceedings from there. Béla had one arm round the actor's neck, his legs crossed, the smoldering remains of a cigarette in his mouth, his body slightly bowed as he stood, slender and boyish, with a gentle, somewhat decadent smile on his yellow face, an unconscious picture of lecherous, bovine self-satisfaction. Tibor threw off his long wig with its bunches, and Ábel was pained and surprised to note that he remained as effeminate, as girlish, and as much the ingénue without it as he had been with, his beauty spot still fixed above his upper lip, his arms still white, and his bosom still in place. He was sitting between Ernő and the one-armed one, chin propped on two fingers, holding his cards with a feminine, grande-dame-ish, almost woman-of-the-world air. Ernő cut him a fan from a cardboard box and Tibor employed it, fanning himself slowly and easily.

Ábel leaned on his elbows in the prompter's box. It was more interesting watching than taking part, he thought. He felt dizzy. Only the actor seemed to behave as naturally as you might expect of someone who had spent his whole life on this very ship, wearing a striped vest, with a pipe in his mouth, never stepping out of his role, not one voice, not one glance out of place. He was scanning the company, looking for something, and when he discovered Ábel in the prompter's box he began to protest.

"You cheat!" he bellowed in a tremendous voice. "You scoundrel! Have you no manners? You spend your time on shore observing where the tide is sweeping us! Fancy spying on others, eh? Get back to your place among the rest. Push his head under the water!"

They rushed Ábel, grabbed his arms, and dragged him from his nook. Ábel put up no resistance. He lay flat on the boards, his arms spread wide. The actor took a contemptuous tour of him, as if he regarded him as no more than a corpse. He poked at him with his toes, then turned away.

"There are people who are utterly corrupt," he declared with plain disgust. "People addicted to the most depraved passions. But the worst of them are the voyeurs who derive their satisfaction from observing other people indulge their passions. I have always loathed them. There was a time in Rio when I smashed in the teeth of one. These are the kind of people who drill holes in walls. They are pimps, purveyors of pomade. Beware of such. People in the act itself are inevitably innocent. Sin begins the moment you leave the circle and watch from outside."

He circled the cabin and put a bottle down next to Ábel.

"Drink!" he ordered, then slumped down at Ábel's side as if exhausted. "Over here, Madonna!" He laid Tibor's head in his lap with gentle paternal solicitude. The boy lay down compliantly beside him. He filled his pipe and puffed at it in the manner of an old salt or an ancient gold-miner about to tell far-fetched yarns.

"You must be very careful on board ship," he said, nodding. "Nowhere else do people live in conditions of such ruthless servitude. And I know what I'm talking about when I say that. There was a time . . . what I mean to say is that you need strict discipline on board. Just imagine: year after year, locked up together like prisoners in one small cell. A sailor quickly loses his sense of all that is fine and lovely in the natural world. He is constantly under surveillance, never alone. It's the most terrible thing that can happen to a man. Mutinies, when they occur on a ship, burst on you with a sudden fury: the men go about their ordinary jobs for years without a word of complaint, without a voice raised in anger. Should one of them express a contrary opinion he is simply booted off at the next port of call, and you can't expect the ship's judge and jury to see the joke. Then something happens, something utterly insignificant, and a line is crossed. This sort of thing happens with exceptional suddenness and later you can't determine what really caused it, because it seems so very stupid: a row over a cake of soap or a drop of grog, it's all beyond understanding."

Béla stood at the edge of the stage laughing.

"That was the box we used to reserve!" he cried. He stretched his arms out towards the dark auditorium. "Box three on the left!" he shouted with boundless delight. "That's where we had to sit every Sunday afternoon, our hair neatly combed, forbidden to lean on the balustrade. We wouldn't get any sweets either because Father said peo-

ple would laugh if they saw the grocer's children sucking sweets." He leaned forward and bellowed into the
auditorium.

"My father has principles! I have none!" He was reeling
with laughter. "If only he could see me here . . ."

"Box two was better," said Ábel. "That was our box,
number two on the right. Tibor, if only your father could
see you now! Careful, your skirt is riding up."

Tibor sat up and smoothed his skirt down. Ábel
addressed him most solemnly.

"Have you ever read poems with cotton wool in your
ears? Or prose, for that matter . . . . It's quite different, you
know. You should try it some time . . ."

The actor fished in his pocket for a contraption that
looked a little like a pocket watch and splashed perfume
on his palms and cheeks. The cloud of sickening chypre
enveloped Tibor too.

"A proper sailor likes his scents," said the actor. "His
pockets and his chest are full of gifts for his friends and
brides."

So saying he dipped in his pocket again and brought
out a small hand-mirror, a comb, some cakes of soap, and
ceremoniously handed them round. What was left of the
chypre he poured all over Tibor.

THERE WERE CONTRARY STORIES AS TO WHAT
happened later. Ernő asserted that everyone, with the
exception of the actor, who had in fact drunk the most,
was drunk. The actor was only pretending. The one-

armed one obstinately maintained that the actor was genuinely and helplessly drunk because there was that embarrassing moment when he touched him with his fingertip and the actor collapsed like a sack.

What they all remembered was that round about dawn the actor made an interminable torrent of a speech and behaved most strangely. He walked up and down waving his arms and told ridiculous stories in a mixture of languages. No one the next day could remember what he actually said. He kept mentioning the names of foreign cities, made grandiloquent gestures at the dark auditorium, and shouted obscene remarks into it. There was one time when they were all speaking at once. The one-armed one was weeping and staggering around. He went from person to person, tapping each on the arm and pointing to the space where his missing arm should have been. "There's yours," he said, "but where is mine?" He wept, sat down on the ground, and felt about himself. "There must be a mistake," he pleaded. "Help me look for it. It must be here somewhere." They stood around not knowing what to do. They tried whispering soothing things into his ear. He was impossible to console or calm. He screamed and shouted and started vomiting. They washed his face. Tibor sat down with him and laid his brother's head in his lap. The one-armed one was twitching, his whole body racked with tears.

"More," advised the actor. "Give him more drink. Crying is just a stage you go through. Let's see where this leads!"

They drank straight from the bottle, the actor disappearing from time to time, returning with more bottles.

He obviously had a supply at hand. Ernő bellowed over the chaos:

"Where did you get the money?"

They stared at each other in the unexpected silence. True enough. How could he afford all this? The actor was known to be stingy with money. Now he grinned.

"You're my friends . . . ," he said. "What does it matter? Think of me as your patron . . ." He lurched over to the prompter's box. "Ladies and gentlemen . . . Behold Maecenas . . . patron of the arts . . . for my little friends . . ."

He reeled about, laughing.

"Let there be music!" he declared.

He pulled a gramophone from one of the trunks and with uncertain fingers put a record on.

"Hush, needle," he cajoled. "Hush. Let's dance."

He stood up straight, stepped over to Tibor, and made a bow. The one-armed one scrambled to his feet.

"Look in the trunk," he said. "The trunk."

The record was playing so quietly that at first they did not hear it. The actor swept Tibor into his arms and began to dance with him.

Ábel followed them, somewhat ill at ease. The actor was dancing properly, as if he hadn't drunk anything, dancing as if it were the most natural form of locomotion for him, as if his heavy body were rendered weightless, mercilessly dragging Tibor along with him, barely perceptibly lifting him with both arms. The music was so quiet and slow that for some time the two caught up in the dance were the only ones to hear it. It was a mewling, self-pitying kind of tune, with much rubato, the rhythm broken up, and the actor was performing a hitherto unknown kind of dance to it, improvising sweeping gestures, taking Tibor with him. His face was solemn now, almost pious. It seemed to Ábel as he trailed them that the actor was staring deep into Tibor's eyes. Both of them were highly serious as they danced, disciplined in opposition, staring each other out, not turning away their heads, not even for a second. The two pairs of eyes were watching each other with such anxiety, such close attention it seemed to be vital not to let the other out of sight as their feet and bodies swayed. They kept their necks stiff, head and neck indifferent to the dipping and rising of the torso. How does Tibor know how to dance? thought Ábel. Perhaps he was simply allowing his helpless body to be guided by the actor who had caught him up in his own orbit, Tibor following wherever he was led. Where was this dance leading? They were moving slowly in constant, calm, even patterns as the record wound down. The actor released Tibor and the boy put his hand to his forehead, staggering and grasping at the air before him as if he needed something to hold on to. He stood there, his hand raised, waiting for the actor to return, and it seemed to Ábel that he was not entirely in control of himself. The actor meanwhile was back at the gramophone, putting on another record.

This one was louder. The one-armed one stopped whimpering. The actor seized Tibor and swept him into an ever faster rhythm, occasionally slowing and hesitating, holding back. Ábel felt the pair were stating oppositions in their dance, resisting its true momentum. The actor held

Tibor at such a great, precise distance from himself, he was like someone fastidiously carrying a weight over a deep crevice, a feat of considerable strength but one that clearly showed the effort required. In both music and dance there was a latent progress towards some rapidly approaching, desired, irresistible event, a restrained intensification as the actor danced into a circle of light and remained there, not moving out of it, not for a second. Béla stood beside the gramophone, adjusting the needle, winding the mechanism. They did not change the record. The actor stopped between two bars, stopped for a second, let go of Tibor, and in a single movement pulled off his vest and disposed of his wig, throwing it high into the catwalk.

He danced on half-naked. His heavy breasts shook with each maneuver and his bare back shimmered like pale bacon in the spotlight. The actor now tried a new movement, drawing almost imperceptibly closer to Tibor so that without actually touching they were still dancing body-to-body, with an all-but-invisible synchronicity that seemed to join them ever more firmly with each step. It was as if a veil were winding about them, one that tightened with each turn, becoming so tight it was impossible to push against. It was as if it were dictating the pace of the music, so that it was the record that was speeding up with them, growing more tense and excited, clicking over the grooves.

The one-armed one scrambled to his feet again and stole up behind Ábel, craning forward, gazing at the dance. Ábel felt uncomfortable like that and stepped away, but the one-armed one reached for him, squeezed his shoulder, and whispered: "Turn off the music!"

But before Ábel could respond something happened, something that struck them as so sudden and unexpected that for a moment they could do no more than stare without moving, as if they were witnessing some extraordinary natural phenomenon.

The music had finished and the needle continued scraping at the still-turning record but no one paid attention to that. The actor took one more turn with his partner, then he too stopped still, leaning over a little to one side, then freezing like a statue depicting a figure caught in movement. They stood there, both of them, tipping to one side, unmoving in the glare of the lights, a tableau vivant, an allegorical embodiment of "The Dance," clear and appropriate. The actor had one foot off the ground, his upper body strongly leaning the way the momentum of the dance had taken him. The statue slowly came to life, balancing itself by spreading its feet, moving its arms to raise and support Tibor whose head was cocked back as if he were looking up. The actor's vast equine head fell forward, his mouth hovered over Tibor's. Very slowly, as if having to overcome an invisible resistance, as if reluctantly and yet inevitably, the mouth moved with due care and regard to cover Tibor's. The boy's head fell back under the weight. Their lips were joined and did not part as the actor with one hand supported the head that had collapsed beneath his, the head powerless, the eyes closed.

Ábel and the one-armed one both leapt on them at once. Béla made a kind of barking noise and attacked the actor's feet, using both his hands to try and topple the colossus, but the enormous body stood so firm on the great pillars of its legs that for a while they were incapable of shifting it. Ábel got hold of Tibor's neck and pulled it back with such force that they both fell. They rolled over and over, ending up under the table and remaining there for a second tangled in each other without moving. Tibor was torn from the actor helpless and corpselike, as if released from a powerful magnetic force field, falling weightless, ejected from its ambit. Béla kept tugging at the actor's legs like an angry dog, whining and grunting. The one-armed one let go of the actor, leapt forward, and smashed his fist into the back of his head. The figure slowly collapsed. It was like downing an enormous effigy.

Ernő stood at the edge of the stage shielding his eyes with his hands, straining to look into the dark.

There's someone out there, he cried.

They froze in their places. The one-armed one was the first to crawl slowly across the body of the fallen actor, joining Ernő. The cobbler's son leaned far out into the auditorium and pointed his trembling stick to a dark and distant box at top balcony level. There was someone sitting at the back of the box. Béla approached, his teeth chattering. Ernő's voice resounded in a high screech through the hall.

There's someone out there! Look! And he's been there for some time!

But no one was capable of moving. Out of the silence, in the impenetrable dark, at the back of the box, a chair toppled over and a door slammed shut.

4

THE COLONEL'S WIFE STOPPED BETWEEN THE two beds. She was carrying Tibor's black uniform on her arm, and held the brilliantly polished black lace-up shoes in her hand. She came on tiptoe and, still on tiptoe, stopped on swollen, unsteady feet in the half-dark. The square window glimmered between the beds. She gave both beds a furious, feral glance, shifting her attention from one to the other and back.

Lajos lay propped high on his pillow, as stiff and unmoving as a corpse. His remaining hand rested on his chest, the sleeve of the missing arm hanging off the edge of the bed, his face calm, serious, smooth. Tibor lay slightly across his bed, one foot sticking out from beneath the covers, his hand gripping the bolster.

The colonel's wife raised the clothes to her face with difficulty and took a good sniff. The boy's smell was detectable through that of the broadcloth and the cheap perfume that had lingered round him on his return that night. So there it is, she thought. The boy has spent the night with some woman.

Incontrovertible proof, she thought. The boy has been with a woman, doing what all men do. That was the odor he brought back with him, on his body and his clothes, while she was stuck at home, waiting up in her bed, with her straggly hair let down over her skinny shoulders, in her nightgown, imagining the most terrible things, weeping and sobbing because she could just see him as a man, his angular head nestling between an unknown woman's breasts, his groin rubbing against the woman's groin, the woman who was robbing her of her motherhood, disputing her ownership of the family. That was what really mattered, what she should never forget: that she had been robbed. They are all thieves, she reflected with contempt. That's how it was in her most agonizingly jealous years too: she was being robbed. This furtive miserliness that had held the family together, a family that was continually straining to break apart, whose members were always set on wandering off, always resented and coveted anything her menfolk took from the house, every farthing, each drop of blood. Everything here belonged to her because it was she who kept guard over the family, indeed *was* the family, an island in the greater world outside, an island on which they built houses and settled people—all of this was hers, everything that grew here grew out of her flesh and blood. But the men went straying after other women. They were robbing her, so she was jealous of every word the three men took with them when they left the house. They gave money to other women, fed them with endearments that were hers by right: their very movements, their blood and sweat, were offered up to them. One day they all deserted her, left the island, gave false, conniving excuses for their absence, citing the call of duty, the needs of the nation, the binding oaths they had made, and when they came back they were never the same again. One came back without an arm. She looked at the empty dangling sleeve. That arm was unquestionably hers: she had given birth to it. That was her flesh the boy had squandered somewhere. He said it was the war, but she knew these were just words, that men made war just to escape their homes, because they didn't want to fulfill their obligations and earn a proper living.

The little one had slept with a woman last night. She leaned forward carefully and her eyes sought out her son's mouth in the half-dark of the bolsters. The mouth was open, the lips swollen with blood. His father had just such a mouth. That's how it goes, how it always goes, one is left alone on a sinking island.

She arranged the clothes on the chair. She knew she was nearing the end of her life, and was quite aware she had to die. It might be a year, it might be tomorrow. Her foot was swollen and dropsical. There were nights she couldn't hear her own heart beat. She was accustomed to the thought of death and spoke of it as she might speak of a much-loved, intimate family occasion. She had no difficulty accepting the thought of death, she was only concerned that her sons would come in, call for the doctor and Mrs. Budenyik, the woman who washed corpses, and Mrs. Budenyik would strip her and wash her wasted body and swollen dead legs, those legs that had died before her sensations and reason did, with acidic water. She had no intention whatever of intruding upon Mrs. Budenyik and her business with the dead. Mrs. Budenyik had been a midwife once, and had seen her naked and more than naked when she gave birth to her sons. She was part of the family, first as an associate member of the great family of woman, secondly as a member of Colonel Prockauer's family. She was the last to wash Granny and the first to wash little Tibor. It's laughable, she thought, that Mrs. Budenyik should complete her work here, prepare her nice and clean for her final journey, wipe the death sweat off her with a cloth soaked in acidic water, not allowing the boys to remain in the room as she did so. The thought that tortured her was that the boys would be allowed to remain, maybe out of pity, or for lack of a firm hand, while Mrs. Budenyik washed her down. This fear never left her during the period of her illness while she lay helpless in bed. She knew why the boys should not look upon her naked body, alive or dead, it made no difference. She wore high-necked nightgowns that buttoned to the chin. The boys had never seen her while she was washing or lightly clad. She knew that if a look of theirs should burn a hole in the wall that had, for decades, divided her from them, everything would fall apart. The boys would only see the mother in her, and nothing but the mother, the guardian of the majority of the laws of behavior, as long as it never occurred to them to look upon her flesh, to notice that their mother was a woman too, someone her husband might take in his arms, into whose ear he might whisper endearments, a person whose body his fingers might explore. Whenever she thought of this on her sickbed she gave a groan. She must discuss the business with Mrs. Budenyik before it happened. Now that the youngest had taken leave of the house and spent the night with a strange woman she felt she could abandon her resistance, that her death was very close.

Making a great effort, she returned to her room and lay down once more in the bed she had only stolen from at night when everyone else was asleep. There was no need for the boys to know that she was still capable of moving about. For years now the boys had believed her to be bed-bound. And that was how it should be: there were certain advantages in the strategy she had developed for holding the family together. She kept the keys under her pillow along with the letter of credit from the pawnbroker for eight thousand crowns. Her few items of jewelry—her diamond-encrusted black enamel medallions, her earrings, her long gold necklace, and her little gold watch—she stored under the bolster. The silver, the antique beaten silver, the remaining glitter of her once glittering family, she kept in a leather trunk under the bed, and across her chest, in a small deerskin pouch, she hoarded the ready cash her husband sent her back from the front. That was all. The longer she existed in this state of pretended helplessness the better she understood the advantages of central control, of keeping everything hidden but close to hand. It was indeed a considerable advantage and a vital element of her strategy that she should be lying helpless in bed. Her bed was the epicenter of the entire family, the heart through and around which the blood flowed. She had been lying there for three years, apparently without moving. She knew there was a war on but in her heart of hearts thought it a mere excuse, a quibble that enabled her husband to go philandering and prevented him sitting at her bed. The older boy had made off with much the same excuse a year before. Now it was the younger one's turn. What a fraud it all is, she thought, exhausted.

She lay in the bed unmoving, dreaming of teeth. She dreamt all her teeth had vanished. She knew this meant death: her lifelong experience and her various books of dreams told her as much. She was going to die: the boys would search her room, find the silver, the valuable papers, the jewels. She was planning to set up some kind of trust that the orphans' court would handle, something that would allow the father and the sons the quarterly install- ment of a silver spoon or fork. She lay in bed with her eyes wide open, listening to the first sounds of morning. Every so often she tired and dropped off. In bed she always wore an old and not entirely clean mantilla shawl as if she were expecting visitors. She thought it natural that the wife of Colonel Prockauer should have plenty of callers. She had long been oblivious to the fact that no one visited her. All her life she had dreamed vainly of a soirée that she, the wife of Colonel Prockauer, would organize, opening up all three rooms of the apartment as well as the garden where there would be lanterns and items of improvised furniture, and small tables laden with wine, cold meats, and pastries; a soirée with perhaps a Gypsy band, with all the officers of the garrison present and even the commander dropping in for half an hour, not to mention various local dignitaries, with the mayor at the helm. She had often calculated whether the rooms would be big enough and tried to estimate the cost of the evening. She would stand at the garden gate in the gray silk dress made for her on the occasion of their silver anniversary, the dress she had never worn since, with her two sons by her side welcoming the guests. The colonel would wear all his decorations for the occasion. Whenever this frequently imagined but never realized dream came back to haunt her she began to cry, but no one was aware of this.

The boys woke. There was the sound of running water. They were washing and talking quietly between themselves. The maid was searching for something in the kitchen. The work of the day was beginning, that curious, complex struggle in which she took part despite her immobility, not relaxing for a second but directing the affairs of the household as well as every stage of her sons' lives from her bed. The sideboard opposite the bed contained the food. She had arranged it in such a position that she could keep an eye on the girl's every movement, so that not a cupful of flour, no slice of bacon, no single egg should leave the sideboard without her observing before the girl closed it and deposited the key back under her pillow. She willed herself upright in bed when the boys went out of the house, gazing after them through the walls, mentally escorting them, watching them all the way. There were times she could swear she could see them hanging about some street corner in town as clearly as if they had been standing in front of her and could even hear their voices as they chatted with this or that person. In the evening when they returned she would interrogate them about their movements and sometimes their accounts tallied with what she had imagined.

The maid came in, kissed her hand, and set the breakfast, drawing open the blinds. The mother handed over the key and watched anxiously as the maid searched out items in the sideboard. She held the box of sugar in her lap and counted out five cubes. The boys received one and a half, she and the girl one each. The hot sun poured in through the window with the full strength of summer.

"Get some meat for dinner today," she told the maid. "Open a jar of cherries. Use the old plum jam to make some jam pockets, it's there next to the soap."

She closed her eyes. Let everything be as though it were his birthday.

She should give him something today. She took mental note of her valuables, but every gift presented a risk and could lead to temptation. If she gave him the gold necklace he might sell it or give it away to some woman. Lajos once sold his watch. Her husband had once taken out three thousand crowns and gone off to a spa where he went through it all while she stayed at home struggling to bring up the boys. She had to make up the three thousand from the household budget and it took eight years, taking out ever more loans, saving pennies out of his captain's and then his major's salary. Prockauer needed white gloves every day of the week. In summer he changed shirts every other day. When time allowed he would blend cologne with the water he washed his face with while she, the mother, had to wash herself with crude soap.

"He said I smelled of tallow," she said quietly to herself.

The maid's hand hesitated in the act of laying out the food, but she didn't look up, being familiar with the invalid's habit of occasionally making strange comments without introduction or indeed any connection in the same low voice, some statement that did not require an answer. Mother looked sideways at the maid to detect whether she had heard. She didn't mind being heard, in fact it gave her a certain satisfaction that under the cover of her illness she could time and again give voice to whatever incurable state of affairs preoccupied or tortured her. Prockauer had once admonished her for not using scented soap or perfumes. Her hands, like those of many officers' wives, carried the permanent smell of paraffin since Prockauer's gloves needed daily washing. These slights were a constant pain to her. Photographs of Prockauer hung on the wall opposite, above the bed, showing him at the various monotonous stages of a military career from second lieutenant to colonel in full dress and on horseback at his last frontline post. She had been talking to the pictures for the last three years, conversing with them through long nights and endless afternoons, silently or in a muttering whisper. Prockauer had made off to the front where he was undoubtedly carousing and getting into debt. It gave her a certain pleasure to think that Prockauer would have to be dealing with his creditors by himself. She sought out the colonel's face in the picture and glared at it from under furrowed brows, mocking and ironic.

THE BOYS KISSED HER HAND AND SAT DOWN TO breakfast. Lajos had been wearing civilian clothes for a while now. He put on old summer outfits that he had slightly outgrown, whose waists were now a little tight so he looked like a schoolboy in them. He tucked his armless sleeve into his coat pocket. Ever since the amputation he had grown fatter and more suspicious. He complained of the small portions provided for him. He accepted offers of extra helpings from his mother and brother at dinner, put on a wheedling voice to plead for the tastiest parts, offered to swap things, and the maid sometimes complained that he had eaten the leftovers from dinner that she had put away for supper. Just as well that I keep the pantry in my room, thought Mother. In the few months since Lajos had returned from the hospital he had grown a belly and his mother suspected he was eating in secret somewhere. His mouth and his eyebrows had stopped twitching but the glazed, indifferent look in his eyes persisted, relieved only by the odd flash of curiosity or malevolence.

He is still handsome, thought the mother, his hair and brow reminiscent of the colonel. But his suddenly plump body and the awkward, uncertain movements of his remaining hand seemed grotesque. His voice too was strange: slow, drawling, singsong, faintly babyish and complaining, just as he did as a child when he wanted something and was not given it. He was sluggish and gluttonous. She did not dare send him out to work. She had to tolerate her twenty-year-old son idling away the day with his younger brother's friends. There were times he put on his ensign's uniform, pinned his medals on his chest, and stood staring at himself in the mirror in his mother's room, turning round like a model, talking to himself as he used to do in childhood, completely ignoring his mother's presence, as if he were playing at soldiers. He felt no shame before his mother nor did he answer her questions once he was deeply immersed in what he was doing.

It's money they ask for, she thought and closed her eyes. It was morning and battle was about to commence, the battle that never ended, not at night, not even in her dreams. She tightened her thin bloodless lips. She had calculated last night how much she would give Tibor: five crowns for the photograph and ten for the banquet. She wanted to give him an icon too, the picture of St. Louis, the patron saint of the family, because the elder Prockauer was named Louis, after him. She wasn't sure whether her gift of St. Louis would delight Tibor. All the same she extracted it from her prayerbook and put it out ready on the bedside table.

"Mother," Lajos wheedled in his singsong voice. "Tibor needs some money."

They had discussed this final two-pronged attack at dawn while they were washing. No one else could help them now. Mother would give them the money so they could pay Havas off in the afternoon, then they could smuggle the silver back into its proper place. Tibor would volunteer for military service and the gang would break up in the evening. No one mentioned the night that had just passed. Lajos had taken Tibor home, laid him down on the bed, pulled off his shoes as though he were an invalid, covered him up, and sat at his bedside until he fell asleep. Tibor surrendered himself entirely, offering no resistance. At night he woke, went over to Lajos's bed, and, when he saw the one-armed one's eyes were closed in sleep, quietly stole over to the basin and gave his face a good wash with soap and brushed his teeth. He rubbed at his face a long time, then went back to bed.

He lay restless and wide awake, occasionally raising his hands to his mouth to rub his lips. The bed was slowly spinning with him but there was something reassuring about the dizziness: he felt he had stopped dancing, in a moment the record would stop turning and it would be quiet, and they would be standing perfectly still, the sun would rise and there would be light. I'll go to the swimming pool in the morning, he thought. He felt he had plummeted from a great height to a deep, very deep place, the kind where one could lie flat out, quite calm, because nothing more could happen and it was only that he did not dare to move in case he discovered he had broken his arm or his leg. From time to time he would put his fingers to his lips and smile in relief. No more harm could befall him now: he was over it all. Mother would give him the money and they could all go on living their own lives. I could recover, he thought. Once I'm away from here I will be well again.

"I don't know anything," said Mother instead of

answering. "No one tells me anything. I lie here, helpless, I might not even make it through to morning, but you come home at dawn, climbing through that damned window. Tibor, my baby, I don't even know whether you passed your exams."

The fact that Tibor had failed, and the consequences of that failure, had completely slipped their minds since yesterday so now they quickly had to think of something to say.

"Where's the certificate, my dear?" asked Mother.

The one-armed one looked around as if their mother were quite elsewhere and said encouragingly:

"They'll give you one, you'll see. Trust me. They have to give you one, no question about it."

Tears began to roll down Mother's cheeks. She could cry at will. Tibor watched her with a desperate indifference. He had got used these last three years to his mother crying each time he was asked something.

"They haven't given them out yet," he assured her. Mother continued crying exactly as before, her tears neither more nor less copious, as if some engine had been turned on and now had to run its course before switching itself off. Once she had dried her tears she picked up the icon and presented it to Tibor.

"This will protect you," she said, sniffing. "I daren't even ask where you were last night. I know you need money today, Tibor, my baby. I have already made inquiries. The photographer will cost five crowns. How much is the banquet?"

"They're not giving a banquet," Lajos answered. "They are arranging a May picnic."

"A picnic? What a strange idea," she said disapprovingly. "You'll only catch a chill in the end. Lajos, be sure to take your coat."

"Mother," pleaded Lajos, "I spent four months bivouacking by the Isonzo, in a trench, in the rain. There's nothing I don't know about cold and damp."

He stood up and put his hand behind his back, standing as the Prockauers tended to do, and walked up and down the room. Mother watched him timidly. It had been Lajos's habit, as it was his father's, to put his hands together behind his back and crack his fingers. Of course he can't do that now, she thought with forbearance. She was frightened because there was no discipline now. Any moment now they might rebel, come over, and gently, without any violence, lift her from the bed, deposit her elsewhere, and fall to searching the mattress and the bolster, and there, before her very eyes, seize the silver, the jewels, and the money, her cries and entreaties falling on deaf ears, the boys triumphantly ransacking the whole apartment—and should she scream for help they might even stuff a napkin in her mouth to shut her up. Something had happened. She had lost her authority over the boys. She gazed at the various photographic images of Colonel Prockauer's military career as if beseeching his help. It was, when you came down to it, easier with Prockauer. She understood that what wrecked a life were those unpredictable moments when a person loses courage, remains silent, fails to open his or her mouth, and allows events to take control. Maybe she should have asked Prockauer not to go to the front. Being a high-ranking officer he could, presumably, have stopped the war.

Every nook and cranny of the long room was stuffed with unnecessary furniture, objects to which the foul smell of the sickroom clung, the smell of isolation and neglect. This, the room in which Mother lay, was where they had to eat. Once, in a circus, she had seen a woman in an evening dress control two wild wolves with no more than a look and a whip. She felt she had to engage her sons' eyes, and that once she had done so order might be restored: one flash of her own eyes would draw the boys back into her magic circle. But the boys avoided her eyes. The contact was broken. She no longer had power over them. They were silent when they entered her room nowadays. She knew this silence spelled danger. They had been silent for months. She was wholly ignorant of the reason for their peculiar absences: they did not share their thoughts with her. They were preparing for something. Maybe their plans had already come to fruition and they were only waiting for the opportune moment when they could rise in rebellion, they might even have accomplices, the maid, or some other person. Maybe they had already agreed that on some given signal they should seize her and pick up her thin body, though maybe Tibor could do that by himself while Lajos searched the mattress and the bed with his remaining hand. But they wouldn't dare touch the ready cash she carried on her own body, she quickly thought. She clenched her hands. She felt the onset of fear and started shivering.

Suddenly she sat up and pushed the bolster under her back.

"Get out," she said. "I'll give you money. Now out with you!"

The one-armed one shrugged, gestured to Tibor, and they returned to their room. Mother listened carefully, her hands on her chest. They're on the alert now, she thought. They might even be spying. Fortunately she had positioned her bed so it could not be seen through the keyhole. Whenever she was obliged to give them money she sent them out of the room. Her hand tightened on her breast and she wondered what she would feel at the very end. She thought back to the moment of Tibor's conception, in the eighth year of their marriage, after several months of sleeping apart. Prockauer returned one afternoon from the training ground wearing his riding boots, dusty, whip in hand, his brow lightly perspiring, and threw his military cap on the table. They were alone in the room. Little Lajos was outside, playing in the garden. They had hardly exchanged a word for several months. Prockauer slept in the dining room on a divan, while she slept with little Lajos in the double bed in the bedroom. They were past the stage of looking for excuses to loathe one another. They struggled with it for a long time, but by the eighth year all loathing had faded, as had the times they had fallen back into each other's arms. The constant battle that was consuming both their souls, the war they were fighting with and against each other, had run out of steam. For the past few months they had silently, calmly, almost forbearingly, as if out of a common sympathy, settled down to simply hating each other. She was sitting in the rocking chair by the window attempting to remove a grease spot from Prockauer's yellow breeches, a particularly fine pair of twill breeches, the grease spot presumably caused by the oiled saddle, somewhere near the knee. This spot, which was larger and eye-catching, much like everything else in Prockauer's life, seemed more than usually vivid to her now as she recalled it. She felt peculiarly compelled to remove such spots. Prockauer came up to her, quite calmly, and without saying a word, put out a hand and grabbed the scruff of her neck, raising her some way from the chair the way he would have lifted a sleeping dog, gripping it where it was least likely to hurt. While struggling in Prockauer's embrace her body was infused by a delicious pain that told her she was alive, that she was still living, inhabiting this specific moment, and that what would follow would be a downward slope that led, possibly, to death. She thought back to that moment now, to that one moment of perfect consciousness, struggling in Prockauer's arms and, somewhere between sleeping and waking, felt alive, quite alive for a moment. Never again was she to experience such a feeling. Tibor was the product of that moment. Prockauer had touched her a few more times later, but she couldn't remember those occasions. Gently, with some trepidation, she opened her nightshirt and brought out the pouch: this was what she now had to attend to. The pouch was attached to her nightshirt with a safety pin. She sought out fifteen crowns, deposited the coins on the icon on the bedside table, then, somewhat assured, leaned back on her pillows.

She called to them in a weak voice and timidly pointed to the money. Lajos stared at her without saying anything, then sat down in a chair opposite her bed. Tibor counted the fifteen crowns, nodded, and pocketed the coins.

"I know we have no money, Mother," he addressed her cordially. "I wouldn't in fact ask you for any. I have to go out now. When I return this evening I would like you to provide me with the sum of six hundred crowns. Do you understand? Six hundred."

"Six hundred crowns," said Mother rather fast, as if addressing a natural request in a perfectly relaxed manner.

"Will you give it to me?"

"Six hundred crowns," she repeated. Her hand grasped the air. Six hundred. She collapsed back onto her pillow and stared straight ahead of her with a frozen smile. Their father is fighting on the front. Six hundred. She let out a few faint shrieks and vigorously shook her head.

Tibor sat on the bed next to her, put his hands together, and waited for her to calm down. "Don't excite yourself, Mother," he said. "I see you don't understand. But don't get overexcited."

He stood up.

"Something will come along."

"Six hundred crowns," Mother repeated. "Six hundred silver crowns. Good lord. St. Louis."

She had to be laid down on the pillow again. Incomprehensible sounds bubbled from her lips. Tibor put his hands on his mother's brow and indicated to the one-armed one that it was hopeless.

"There's one hope left," he said and leaned close to Lajos. "I'll speak with him this afternoon."

The one-armed one solemnly nodded but never took his eyes off their mother who was gasping quietly now, her closed eyes mimicking sleep. Just as solemnly, he leaned forward with an expression of utmost curiosity and carefully examined his mother, as if he had discovered some new feature on her. Curiosity and confusion mingled in his smile: he was wholly absorbed in her.

"In The Peculiar tonight," said Tibor quietly by way of farewell, and tiptoed towards the door.

"Tonight," echoed the one-armed one, but his eyes never left his mother and he placed a finger to his lips, demanding silence. Once Tibor had closed the door he stood up silently to look down on her. He gazed at her for a few seconds, listening for any noise, his curiosity taking on an officious air. Suddenly Mother looked right at him and the two pairs of eyes met with hardly any distance between them. They regarded each other, round-eyed, the way people stare at each other for the first or the last time. A sudden rigid horror blazed in Mother's eyes, like two safety lamps, and her dull eyes started to burn. She raised a hand to her breast in defense. The one-armed one sat down again, as if determined not to move from here until he had discovered something.

The maid entered and cleared the table. Mother wanted to give some instructions, she wanted to sit up, to say something. Her eyes followed the girl with undisguised anxiety but the one-armed one raised his finger to his lips and indicated that she should be silent. Mother began to shiver, her teeth were chattering. Once the maid had gone out he pulled his chair closer to her and leaned forward.

You have to give us the money, Mother, he said, his voice calm and quiet.

There was no severity in his voice, no hint of threat, but Mother immediately closed her eyes as if in a faint. From time to time she opened them to find the boy still there, still calm, insistent, his gaze never leaving her, and she closed her eyes again. They remained like this for a long time, unmoving. Mother stopped trembling as the odd sidelong glance assured her that the boy was still at his post. Time passed infinitely slowly. Mother drew the nightshirt tightly about her chest, closed her eyes, seeing nothing, hearing nothing. She knew there was no longer any point in doing anything, but before surrendering herself she would stiffen, play dead as a termite does when it senses danger. The one-armed one drew the chair still closer, propped himself on the edge of the bed, and made himself comfortable.

ÁBEL SLEPT AT THE PECULIAR. THERE WERE NO curtains so he woke early. Through the glass the mountain and the pine forest had just emerged from their covers in the warmth, their shapes lazy and rounded, like a plump girl's. He sat down at the window in shirtsleeves and held his face up to the sun. One could get drunk on the sun on an empty stomach. He had slept deep and remembered nothing. Such giddy happiness flooded through him that he didn't dare move in case the giddiness vanished. His body warmed through, his frozen limbs relaxed.

He had to be in town by ten. The class photograph that was to join the others in the gallery, the gallery that included their fathers, was to be taken in the yard of the institution. He picked up his clothes. The building was deserted: the owner was hanging lanterns in the garden. Aimlessly he walked up and down the room among the accumulated hoard of things. It was all junk, boring, rubbish. He spun the globe and waited for it to stop. He carefully put his finger on Central Africa. Good heavens, he thought. What does it matter that the actor has kissed Tibor Prockauer?

He hadn't gone home that night. When they parted in front of the theater he took a few steps homeward then turned and took the route leading to The Peculiar. He ran part of the way to get out of town as fast as he could, then slowed by the river. The night was warm and bright. He never considered going home. Perhaps I shall never go home again, he thought vaguely. There's a change coming, something different from everything up till now, something other than Etelka or Papa or the teachers or Tibor or the actor, perhaps something much simpler and nicer, everything's up for grabs, the whole thing needs careful, independent, rational thought. But that's just a feeble consolation, he thought. The various buildings of The Peculiar glimmered white in the moonlight, picturesque, improbable. He crept quietly up to the room, the musty closeted smell mingling with the scent of rum, choking him. He opened the window, threw himself across the bed, and immediately fell asleep. The actor was coming towards him, his chest bare, his wig crooked. Tibor's head fell back. Ábel was tugging at the actor's arm. It's cooled down! It's a starry night! He was bellowing.

The dream faded. He slept deeply, his body still.

He put on his clothes and set off for town. He was hot in his black formal garments. A tuft of hair was sticking from his pocket. He drew out the wig, then, looking round to make sure no one could see, threw it away. The hairpiece lay on the road like a squashed furry animal. He raised it with his toe and gave it a disgusted kick. Whoever once grew this tuft of hair, he said to himself, is, from this moment, dead forever. He hurried past the repairman's fence. He had lost his hat somewhere the previous night. The air was pure and clean, the sound of bells swam in it. May eighteenth. Friday. The photographer. He wanted to have a word with Tibor afterwards. Then it's Havas at two. He might look in on his aunt. In the evening they would come out to The Peculiar. None of this was of particular interest really. He stopped, looked round, and for a moment considered going back to The Peculiar and waiting for them till evening. But then he thought he had to speak to Tibor. He lengthened his stride.

Over the fences peeped the branches of various fruit trees. The previous afternoon's rain had beaten down the flowers. He passed the swimming pool, then stopped on the bridge to look at the yellow-colored river of his childhood, now in flood, the long grass bending over it into the water, his nose crinkling to the sharp sour smell.

Judge Kikinday, the man the mandarin had condemned to death, was just crossing the bridge.

Ábel leaned over the rails. If there was any justice Kikinday would have died long ago because it was three years now since the mandarin had sentenced him, in the belief that that would be the simplest course to take. Kikinday had himself sentenced several men to death, and hanged seven, overseeing the executions personally. The last was a Gypsy.

The mandarin was Ábel's first friend, his own private discovery, the only mythical figure he had not found in old tales, but had personally invented. Maybe somebody once said something about what might happen if a mandarin in China were to press a button. Soon after Ábel rebelled against the town he found what remained of an old, dysfunctional bell, and whenever his enemies got him down he pressed the button and arranged their execution. Say he told a lie, for example, and his lie had been discovered: the accuser had to perish. In three short years he had been obliged to order four persons' executions and in three cases the order had been carried out. Szikár was the first, the biology master who had hit him in fifth grade. The second was Canon Lingen, who had spied on them in the park. The third was Fiala, his classmate in sixth grade, who had betrayed a secret Ábel had entrusted to him. And the fourth was Kikinday, Colonel Prockauer's friend, who had threatened to write a letter about their doings to his father when he came across them in a bar.

The mandarin was Ábel's personal secret, someone he never spoke about, not even to the gang. The mandarin lived somewhere in China in a room with yellow wallpaper and had long sharp fingernails, a two-foot-long pigtail, and sat at a lacquered table with the mechanism on top of it. He had but to touch the button with one of those fingernails and someone somewhere in the world would perish. The mandarin was neither good nor evil: he administered justice disinterestedly. If someone in San Francisco looked askance at somebody, or spoke roughly, the mandarin would frown and examine the matter and, having done so, take action. His power extended over the whole planet. He touched the button with those refined long fingernails of his, a button that was no different in Ábel's opinion from the button on a common doorbell, and someone in a distant corner of the world dropped dead, his head flopping over. Very few people knew this. People in general believed that Szikár, the biology master, drank himself to death, that Canon Lingen died of hardening of the arteries, and that Fiala's early death was due to tuberculosis. Ábel, however, knew that all this was beside the point: the true cause of death was the mandarin. Ábel regarded himself as the mandarin's local representative and that it was incumbent on him to act in a disinterested yet, of course, more conscientious spirit in such matters of judgment. The mandarin was Ábel's most closely guarded secret. Everyone is happy to play the hangman in their imagination. Of the four sentences handed out by Ábel, judgments conducted in utmost secrecy under conditions of emergency in a form of martial law, three were approved by the mandarin and carried out with remarkable expedition. Kikinday, on the other hand, who had been sentenced some years ago, was clearly in a state of conspicuous health, and crossed the bridge now, panting a little but with the greatest possible dignity. Ábel knew the mandarin was simply delaying the execution. The game had long been imbued with a greater significance than he had earlier thought possible. He had recently sought out the instrument of execution, the dysfunctional hall doorbell that had been gathering dust in a drawer. After the resolution of the Fiala case Ábel felt tortured by uncertainty. The judgment, though not in itself unjust, might have been a touch severe, and maybe it would have been enough to commute it to lifelong hard labor, condemning Fiala to work out his time in a bank or the tax office. One can be wrong, thought Ábel. Now here was this Kikinday character . . .

"Nebulo nebulorum," the condemned addresses him with the impeccable courtesy so often remarked in town. "And how do we like being an adult?"

Ábel looks up at Kikinday's swollen face, the black teeth grimly glimmering under the Kaiser Wilhelm mustache, the whey-colored eyes swimming in the air above Ábel's head. They cross the bridge together on their way to town. Kikinday asks after Ábel's father and inquires in due patriarchal manner when Ábel and his friends hope to join up and move to the front. It was the way he questioned Lajos too before he went out. There is no malice in the question, for Kikinday stops every young man between seventeen and nineteen years of age and makes the same inquiry concerning their military plans.

They make their way slowly past the line of poplars,

ever closer to town. A thin fog hangs over the river, the kind of early fog expected on very hot days.

Kikinday observes encouragingly that military training takes much less time now than it did in his day.

"You are lucky not to know the meaning of real training," he sighs. "How would you know? You haven't hung about in barracks, followed by three or four weeks of drill, no, you can go straight to the front. In my time," he stretched his arms wide as he always did when talking about "his time," a time he did not describe in any precise detail but indicated with a gesture that spoke of some half-forgotten, never-to-return golden age of mankind, "in my time we had to squat, lie on our stomachs, and march in the baking heat. Your generation? Three weeks and you're off."

Kikinday had wasted few opportunities in recent years to wave his hat at the younger generation as they departed in cattle trucks. He was always first among the local dignitaries at the station bidding farewell to the troops: this role befitted his social standing and established him as a friend to youth.

They took leave of each other by the courtroom. Kikinday made Ábel promise to inform him when he was about to set off on his travels. With the greatest tact Kikinday always referred to such military leave-takings as "setting off on one's travels." Tower-like he made his way up the cool steps. Ábel watched him reach one of the landings. He began to feel sick. He himself ascended the three steps that formed the entrance to the school with great care. The class was standing in a semicircle under the linden tree. He squeezed himself in at the end of a line, the form master sitting at the center with an expression of the greatest historical gravity while Béla and Tibor lay like two chained mastiffs couchant at his feet. The photographer had set up his equipment complete with black cloth and was barking out a few words of instruction, the last words of instruction they would ever hear in this yard. At the very last moment, just as the camera was about to click, he quickly spun around and turned his back to it. Ernő noticed and did the same. And so the class ceremonially entered the school gallery's version of eternity.

"Future generations may well scratch their heads," said Ábel, "wondering who they were, those two figures turning their backs on immortality."

The various groups dispersed while they hung back, loafing in the sunshine, sleepless and shivering. Béla's teeth were chattering from exhaustion.

"I must sleep," he said. "I can't go on now. Till tonight then."

"Till tonight."

Ernő suddenly butted in.

"I went by his place this morning," he whispered.

They stopped and listened with downcast eyes, somewhat coldly and against their wills, as he quickly continued.

"He wouldn't let me in. He spoke through the door, saying he was all right, he felt fine. He said not to wait for him."

A deep silence followed his words and he himself suddenly fell silent. Tibor lit a cigarette and offered a light to the others.

"Then we don't wait," he shrugged, perfectly courteous. He stood there for a while, then extended his hand for them to shake. "Very well then, tonight."

Then he linked arms with Ábel.

They had to wait at the swimming pool. It was still the hour set aside for women. They sat down on a bench by the ticket office. The smell of rotting boards, damp sludge, and the familiar stench of stale underwear hit them. They could hear the women's cries.

"Hairdressers," said Tibor.

The leaden weight of the heat smoothed the water and gave it a metallic sheen. The heat was sticky, dense, almost tangible. Tibor leaned back and started whistling.

"Please stop whistling," said Ábel.

Tibor examined his nails. In a distracted singsong voice he declared: "I don't like the look of Mother. Her behavior was distinctly odd this morning. But what I meant to say was . . . we're seeing Havas at two."

He whistled a few more bars and blinked at the river, his mind elsewhere.

"What I really meant to say," he continued, "was that half an hour ago I walked into the local recruiting office. The commanding officer there is a reliable officer of my father's. I volunteered. He in turn gave me permission to enlist as a volunteer. I start tomorrow morning, first thing."

When Ábel did not respond he put his hand on his knee.

"Don't be angry, Ábel. I just can't go on like this." He raised his arm and indicated everything around him. "I can't go on like this," he repeated. "There's nothing I can do about it."

He rolled a cigarette, sat down on the wooden railings of the bridge, and dangled his feet over it.

"What do you think we should do? I think everyone could take away whatever was important to them from The Peculiar tonight . . . I must return the saddle whatever happens."

He licked the cigarette, lit it, and when he had waited for some time in vain for a response, he repeated uncertainly:

"What do you think?"

Ábel stood up, leaned against the boards of the cabin. His skin looked gray and pale but his voice was calm.

"So it's over."

"I think so."

"The gang, The Peculiar, are all over?"

"I think so."

"In that case there's something I must tell you," he said and took a deep breath. "I should have told you long ago, I wanted to tell you. Please don't be cross, Tibor, there's nothing I can do about it."

He rested his head against the wall. In a plain, almost chatty way he said: "I had to tell you this just once. I love you. Does that surprise you?" He stretched out his arms, and quickly, feverishly continued, his voice reassuring. "Don't be angry, but I've suffered a great deal on your account. More than a year now. I myself can't explain what it is I love about you. I had to tell you sometime. Maybe it's because you are beautiful. You're not, if I may say, particularly bright. You must forgive me saying so because I'm an unhappy creature. I would give you everything I own, whatever I am likely to own in the future. Do you believe me?"

Tibor leapt off the railings, threw away his cigarette, seized Ábel's arm, and tugged at it frantically.

"You must swear!"

He was shaking Ábel with all his power in sheer desperation.

"I swear . . ."

"You must swear that you'll never mention this again."

"I'll never mention it again."

"You want to remain friends?"

"Yes."

"So not another word about it, all right?"

"Not a word."

They were breathing hard. Tibor let go of Ábel's arm, sat down on the bench, and put his head in his hands. Ábel slowly crossed the bridge, stopped, leaned against the railing and out over the water. Someone's feet were tapping on the bridge behind them. Tibor waited until the steps died away, then moved over to Ábel, leaned on his elbows beside him, and put an arm around his shoulder. He had tears in his eyes.

"Do you believe in God?"

"I don't know."

"What do you think?" he asked timidly. "I think we will survive."

They looked at each other. Tibor leaned towards him carefully and, very gently, touched his face with his hands, first on the left side, then on the right. For a moment they stared at each other, then Ábel threw himself to the ground, facedown in the earth. He was shaken by wild uncontrollable sobs, his hands scrabbling in the mud as he pressed his face into the softness, his whole body racking and tossing. He wept quietly, at the back of his throat, with a slight wheeze. Then he stopped moving and lay there a long time while his weeping subsided. When he sat up he wiped his face with his muddy hands and looked wearily around him.

"It's finished, I think," he said slowly, with surprise. "I'm quite certain now that we will survive."

He looked straight ahead and gave a shiver.

"I wasn't so sure of it before."

AT PRECISELY TWO O'CLOCK THEY STOPPED OUT-side the pawnbroker's. It was the only two-story house in the passage. The gray heat spread everywhere, thick as glue. Metal shutters covered the entrance. They rang at the side door and waited, and when no one answered, Tibor turned the door handle and led the way in. The damp sour smell of cabbages greeted them in the dim stairwell, where narrow wooden steps led up to the pawn-broker's apartment.

Plaster was peeling from the wall. Dirt, cobwebs, a squalid sense of neglect enveloped them.

"Are you scared?" asked Ábel.

Tibor stopped and looked around.

"No," he said uncertainly. "Not exactly. What I feel is

loathing, just as the actor said I would. And the air is foul."

He turned round.

"Leave it to me and don't say anything," he said quietly.

They had dined at the riverside café, having spent the remainder of the morning in silence. Only occasionally did Tibor emerge from the water and venture onto the shore to lie on his back, gently rocking. They had undressed in the same cabin, their talk general and louder than usual, Ábel laughing a lot, rather nervously, and once outside they shouted ribaldries at each other across the banks. They seized every chance of rendering the memory of what had earlier passed between them as uninteresting as possible. They talked of things that were of no great consequence, of their plans, of what the future might have to offer should things work out well, providing that the insignificant event that was waiting for them—the enlisting and what Kikinday had tactfully referred to as "setting off on their travels"—did not prevent them. Tibor wanted to set up a stud farm in the lowlands. Why specifically a stud farm he could not say, but he confessed that he had been reading up on the subject and had secretly struck up acquaintance with horse dealers. Having dwelt on this for a while he suddenly stopped as if he had just woken up and courteously asked: And you?

Ábel shrugged. "Might go abroad," he said.

The sky was gradually clouding up. There was a distant rumbling but the rain couldn't quite rouse itself to fall. They were helpless. They couldn't think of anything more to say. Ábel went into the cabin first, then waited in the street while Tibor got dressed.

There were two doors along the upstairs corridor and they looked and wondered what to do. But before they could knock one of the doors opened and Havas stepped out.

Later, when Ábel thought back to this afternoon, to these days generally but specifically to this afternoon and this night, it was, above all, to the shock he experienced the moment he saw the pawnbroker emerge through the door of his apartment. Havas is standing in the doorway, wiping his walrus mustache with the back of his hand, smiling, he bows a little, and, using one hand only, fusses with the unbuttoned collar of his shirt. As he smiles his eyes are almost entirely obscured by the rings of fat that surround them. He makes a welcoming gesture towards the door and allows them to pass through it ahead of him. His breath reminds Ábel of kitchens, of washing-up and cold lard. That might be because the hall too smells strongly of stale food and the table of the room into which they are ushered is covered with the neglected remains of food in bowls, on plates, and in cups. None of this would strike him as shocking were it not for some glimmering memory, larger than life, that he has seen all this and experienced it before. But at the same time he knows for a fact that he has never been here. It was a dream, a dream in which he had met Havas, who had appeared, exactly as he has just done, in his doorway, wiping his walrus mustache with the back of his hand, buttoning up his collar with the very same smile. It is as if he has experienced it all: the smell of cold food, everything down to the last detail, the smell, the quality of light, the sounds, all exactly the same. He knows that this is the only possible way for the pawnbroker to appear, smoothing his mustache, fussing with his collar, but never before has he been quite so shaken by a sense of déjà vu, to the extent that he takes a startled step back. But the pawnbroker fails to notice his shock, bows low before them and ushers them into the room, then closes the door.

"Please be so good as to take a seat," said Havas, pushing two chairs up to the table. "I assume the young gentlemen have had their dinner. I would be greatly obliged if they would permit me to continue mine."

He waited courteously while Tibor indicated that they did not mind, then sat down, tied the napkin around his neck, and took a brief survey of the pots and plates.

"I do believe I had got this far," he eventually said and pulled a dish of what looked like pâté towards him, dipped into it with a soup spoon, and pushed the spoon into his mouth. "Do not be astonished that I eat meat without bread," he said, chomping with what seemed like a modest smile. "Bread is fattening. Meat is not. I have got used to doing without bread altogether as you can see. May I offer the gentlemen something?"

"Please do not trouble yourself, Mr. Havas," said Tibor.

"A nip of *kontusovka*? No?"

The uncorked earthenware bottle lay on the table within easy reach.

"A sickly overweight person like me has to be very careful what he eats," he said, taking a swig from the bottle. "I have to maintain a diet of sorts."

He waved his enormous hand over the table with its bowls, plates, cups, and salvers where slices of meat, pâtés, and various kinds of sausage lay in cold melted fat. There was no fresh food anywhere. The pawnbroker was clearly a carnivore, and kept every small remnant of meat.

"I'm a lonely old widower and must watch what I eat," he repeated, cutting a slice of beef, picking it up, and biting substantial chunks out of it.

"So I have worked out my own diet. Flesh is the most easily digestible material, gentlemen. It breaks down so readily. I only have to cook twice a week, on Saturday and Wednesday. Nothing but meat. I can't eat in restaurants," he said closing his eyes, "because the portions I allow myself there are so minuscule they attract too much attention. You get to an age when you don't want to draw too much attention to yourself. In my case," he hesitated as he licked a finger shining with grease, "I have to eat two pounds of meat at any single sitting."

He picked up a hunk of half-chewed ham on the bone, raised it to the light and took a bite out of what was left on it.

"I feel positively ill otherwise," he declared. "I must have precisely two pounds of flesh, without bread, once at dinner, once at supper. I cook such meat as will keep for a few days. I have to watch that there is some variety too. I have an extraordinary digestion. It will accommodate four or five kinds of meat, and indeed desires two pounds of it, but if I eat only one kind, say for instance two pounds of beef at dinner, my stomach demands attention by the afternoon. Pâté is my chief source of nourishment. I keep a constant supply of various pâtés because they keep best without going bad. Sometimes I have to eat in the afternoon too. May I offer you a slice?"

He pushed the gray pâté in front of them.

"Ah well, as you please."

He took a big bite out of the ham, his teeth tugging at an obstinate shred of meat, and tore some gristle from the bone.

"I take the odd sip of *kontusovka* between bites. This is genuine, pure, Polish *kontusovka*. It keeps your stomach in order. One's intestines are constantly in rebellion, gentlemen, and *kontusovka* works through the system like a hose, like a fireman's hose, a squirt or two puts out the fire, brings peace. I commend it to you."

He put his head back, raised the bottle to his lips, and took a few gulps. He looked round with red eyes.

"I believe," he said uncertainly, "that with the gentlemen's kind permission, I might finish now. Please allow me to put the food away."

He stood up with difficulty, picked up several dishes at once, put his thumb through the handle of a bowl, opened the doors of an old shelved cupboard in the corner, and put the food back there in precise order, one dish at a time, throwing the chewed ham bone into a box by the stove. Once he had put everything away he carefully turned the key in the cupboard.

"I am a lonely widower with family troubles," he complained, "and I cannot allow myself the luxury of servants.

My habitation is cluttered with objects whose care I cannot leave to strangers. In any case I like being at home by myself."

He dropped the key into his trouser pocket and stood at the window so the room suddenly darkened for a moment. He searched for a cigar, lit it ceremonially, then sat back in his chair, and made himself comfortable, skillfully adjusting his stomach. With elbows on the table he blew the smoke in the general direction of the lamp and focusing on a spot above their heads asked:

"What can I do for the young gentlemen?"

The smell of decaying rancid fat was so intense Ábel felt as though he were choking in the room. They sat for several long minutes, silent and unmoving. Havas's manner of eating, his sheer being, had overwhelmed them: it had the power of some inflated natural phenomenon. They could not have been more surprised if he had dragged a live kid into the room, dismembered it in front of them, and proceeded enthusiastically to consume it. The room was full of blackflies. The smell of the food had attracted them through the half-open window and they fell furiously to stinging legs and faces.

"There'll be a storm," said Havas, scratching the back of his hand. "The blackflies are acting up."

He smoked his cigar patiently, prepared to wait. The room was full of curious objects. Three chandeliers hung from the ceiling but not one had a light in it. A huge camera was propped on a tripod by the wall. A crowd of tin tankards jostled dustily on top of a cupboard. There was a row of seven-branched candelabra ranged on a table as for an exhibition and various musical clocks were fixed to the wall, not one of them with moving hands.

"A first-class piece of machinery," said Havas, who had followed their glance to the camera. "Nothing I could do. It was never redeemed: I was stuck with it. There are so many articles on my hands. Are the gentlemen acquainted with Vizi the photographer? He specialized in baby portraits. Now he's abroad. His wife brought it in. She was left without a penny. She knew nothing about photography. I'm looking after it for the time being. Should Vizi return he can have it back. Its estimated value is two hundred crowns. He can go back to photographing new babies and their firstborn siblings. Do you remember him? He took your pictures too, gentlemen. He stood behind the box, wiggled his hand for your amusement, and said: watch the birdie! A ridiculous profession. Once I had a picture of that sort taken too. I lay naked on a bearskin, my strong little legs kicking in the air. Who would ever think that was me? Imagine me lying naked on a bearskin now like a well-behaved infant, kicking my legs . . . But Vizi can have his camera back. Havas has a heart."

"It's a fine collection you have here, Mr. Havas," said Tibor, quietly clearing his throat.

They ran their eyes politely and admiringly round the room as if that had been the sole object of their visit, as if they wanted no more than to inspect the private collection of a genuine aesthete. There was a decided orderliness in the room, though not one you could detect at first glance. A casual visitor might have thought he had strayed into the chaos of an overcrowded junk shop, but once his eyes had gotten used to the half-light and had adjusted to the mess before him, he would have noticed how everything was in its proper place. A stuffed fox stood on top of an American traveling trunk. An empty birdcage hung on the wall. Ábel's attention was caught by the birdcage. It seemed such an unlikely object for Havas to possess that he couldn't help asking if Mr. Havas was fond of birds.

The pawnbroker was busy with his bottle of *kontusovka,* sniffing the top of it.

"Dear God," he muttered with distaste. "They're making cheap imitations of this now. It comes from Poland, so the fakes must be made there too. Genuine *kontusovka* burns your throat . . . Birds?" He turned to face Tibor. "We get what we get. It was pawned like the rest if you please. It was offered to me though I cannot think why I accepted it. I'm not a pet shop. But it was such a tiny singing sort of bird . . . a siskin, if you know the species, gentlemen. A person gets lonely. It sang when I woke in the morning. You wouldn't believe, gentlemen, how quickly a lonely person such as I can get used to a singing bird. Trouble was, he couldn't get used to meat. He only sang for two days."

He looked straight ahead, seemingly lost in a sad memory.

"Why should I buy him seeds and millet, I thought, when I have so much meat? Swallows eat flies. Why shouldn't a siskin eat meat too? The cupboard is always full of meat. I gave him tiny snippets of the finest veal. He couldn't get used to it."

He waved the matter away.

"I couldn't keep him long. I am not, I repeat, a pet shop. This was a piece of speculative business, you understand, gentlemen? I never take animals as surety. But Havas has a heart and one day a lady comes in, a lady of mature years who has seen some troubles in her time, and pushes this cage over the counter. What is your ladyship thinking of? I ask her. What is the value of a siskin? Now I really have seen everything. Tears and words. It was this thing and that thing. She desperately needed four crowns. She was expecting some money in three days' time and she swore by all she loved that she would bring it in because this bird was everything in the world to her. Call this business! I said to myself. But she wouldn't go away and the bird started singing. Three days, I said, fine, because I was in a good mood and I have a heart. The young gentlemen cannot begin to imagine what people bring in. People of the utmost refinement . . . the entire town. Naturally, I don't say anything. But the bird kept singing. It's hungry, I thought. But it didn't eat the meat and then it stopped singing. I knew it would remain on my hands. What would a lonely widower want with a caged bird?"

He propped his heavy brow on his hands and stuffed the cigar into a cigar-holder.

"Now imagine, gentlemen. On the third day the lady returns. She stands at the counter. Here are the four crowns, my dear sweet Mr. Havas, may God reward you for your kindness. May I please have my bird back? What bird? I say. She begins to tremble and stands there, her mouth wide open. The bird, Mr. Havas, she says, my bird, the siskin you kindly agreed to take for a couple of days, my darling little siskin? And she grips the bars on my counter. I look at her and think, yes indeed you should return that bird. The problem was that it was no longer singing."

He indicated the litter basket full of bones and leftover food in front of the stove.

"Fortunately the cleaner only comes in last thing in the evening. So I let down the shutters, go up to the apartment, search through the litter basket, and find the little creature. It was already rather stiff. Lucky I still had it, I thought, now Havas, go out and show the client that you don't lose anything through carelessness in this business. I picked the little bird up, and placed it in a box, properly packaged as the contract regarding all returned articles requires. It was no bigger than a pocket watch. I tie the box round with string, as is proper, and seal it precisely as required by the contract. I pass it back over the counter to her and wait for her to say something. What is this, Mr. Havas? she asks and turns the box round in her hand. For God's sake, what is it? You should have seen the lady, gentlemen. She was wearing a pair of knitted gloves that only half covered her hands. She had a little black straw hat on her head, worn high like this. One siskin, I answer. I wait. She breaks the seals, tears the string, and there's the siskin. She lifts it out, holds it in her palm, and gazes at it. I thought she was going to make a scene. But just imagine. There was no shouting, all she said was: oh, oh."

"What did she say?" asked Ábel and leaned forward.

Havas gave him a glance. "She said: oh, oh," he repeated. "Nothing else. Nor did she go away but just stood there with the bird in her hand, the tears dropping from her eyes. Then I grew angry because isn't this just the kind of thing that happens when a man listens to his heart? Why cry for the bird, your ladyship? It wouldn't touch meat. Are you not ashamed of yourself, all this fuss about a bird? Ashamed, Mr. Havas? she asks. Then I got really angry, as I always do when I pay too much attention to my heart, then have to bear the consequences. Does your ladyship not know there is a war on? I said. Are you not ashamed to weep over a bird when so many are dying day after day? You should be ashamed of yourself, I said, and slammed the shutter down. I am not an evil man but my heart wasn't up to it. Do you know what she said? Who should I cry for? she asked. Then I started shouting: You scarecrow, you bird fancier! Millions die and you have no one to weep for? No one, she answers. Then weep for those millions, I tell her, and by this time I don't know whether to shout or laugh. Can you imagine what she said to me then? I don't know those people."

He half filled a glass with water and drank a long draught.

"I don't deal in birds. Imagine, gentlemen!" He smashed his fist down on the table. "I'm sorry. But I get into such a temper each time I think of that old woman and her siskin. One should pay no attention to one's heart. I accept everything: silver, binoculars, slightly used clothes, but birds, no." He raised his head defiantly and blew out a dense cloud of smoke that he dispersed with his hand. "No, and again no."

The room grew darker. The wind was whipping the dust off the road and the first shimmering twilight of the storm settled on the room and on the scene through the window. The blackflies were mercilessly stinging Ábel's face and the mixed odors of the room were making his stomach heave. He glanced pleadingly at Tibor. The pawnbroker was taking regular sips of water: the thought of the bird that had so excited him was still bothering him. His fingers drummed on the table and he kept grunting. The acrid, almost refreshing smell of mothballs triumphantly overcame the smell of rotting food.

"We've come about the silver, Mr. Havas," Tibor said in the sultry silence.

They waited with bated breath. The pawnbroker ran his eyes over the room as if seeking a fulcrum, some familiar landmark to help him understand what they were talking about.

"The silver?" he asked. "What silver?"

Tibor took out his wallet and handed him the ticket.

"It's the family silver, Mr. Havas," he said quickly. "I have to tell you Father is rather fond of it. That's why we have come."

"But this ticket is long out-of-date, gentlemen," the pawnbroker said. "The contract is perfectly clear. It expired a month ago."

"But we thought . . . ," said Tibor, then got stuck. "Didn't Amadé explain?"

Havas stood up with the ticket in his hand.

"Amadé?" he pondered. "Do the gentlemen mean the

dancing master? No, he said nothing. But perhaps the gentlemen don't know."

"Don't know what?" asked Tibor. He too stood up, and took a step towards Havas.

"Oh!" said Havas, surprised. "I thought you knew. He went away at noon. He's gone for good. He was here this morning to say goodbye. It's usually the way with actors," he said shaking his head, then went over to the window and carefully reread the details on the ticket.

"I'm sorry to say it's out-of-date. Was it family silver? An old much-loved heirloom? Generally we only lend according to the value of silver, pure and simple. We can't take sentimental value into account. But I am surprised to hear he didn't take his leave of you gentlemen. For, as far as I am aware, it was specifically the gentlemen, his friendship with the gentlemen, that is, that was the occasion of his departure."

He carefully closed the window.

"We shall have a hurricane. Just look. Once it's over we'll have a nice cool evening. But no, it's a real surprise . . . the young gentlemen should certainly have been aware of his departure."

They were so tense they were ready to leap. Ábel was unable to speak. The pawnbroker sat back down at the table. Second by second the room was growing darker. They couldn't see each other's faces in the gloom. With his back to the window the pawnbroker was indistinct, a large dark shapeless mass.

"May I suggest the young gentlemen sit down?" he addressed them courteously. "Let's talk this over."

He waited, then continued with the odd pause for breath.

"He was here this morning. He came in a carriage laden with trunks. He came for money, of course. They're real characters, those actors. Not all the wealth of Darius is enough for them. Being a foolish man with a foolish heart I naturally gave him some, especially once he explained why he had to leave town. I couldn't remain indifferent to his plight . . . He was, I had to admit, in serious danger."

He gave a dull, flat laugh.

"How extraordinarily mobile these people are," he remarked in acknowledgment. "It's nothing to them to pack everything in a few hours and move on. I'm not the sort of person who could make such sudden decisions. Look around you. Then try to imagine the storeroom below, the real thing. Because all you see here is the stuff people have abandoned. People are extraordinary. They find themselves in a spot, pick up the nearest valuable thing, be it silver, a clock, or a pair of earrings, and over they come to Havas. They think six months is a long time. But most of them haven't a clue what is likely to happen in six months' time. Then one day there they are in front of me, begging."

He looked over the ticket again, holding it slightly away from him as though he were nearsighted.

"Six hundred crowns. A pretty sum. Many people could live for six months on that. A silver dinner service for twenty-four . . ." He stood up, went over to the bed, groaned as he bent down, and drew out a worn old green leather trunk. "Was this the item?"

He opened the trunk and the Prockauers' family silver lay pale and glimmering before them. Tibor seized Havas's arm.

"I knew it would still be here, Mr. Havas. You couldn't have done that to us! You have no idea how terrible it would have been! But everything will be all right, Mr. Havas. You will have our bond."

The pawnbroker removed Tibor's arm and, without a word, closed the trunk and pushed it back under the bed with his foot.

"The customer offering items for pawn is not obliged to give his name," he said. "Please to consider that I cannot know who the silver belongs to. This ticket," he sat back down at the table and handed the ticket over, "has expired. The customer failed to extend the term of the agreement. The pawned item was auctioned off at a public auction."

"Who bought it?" Tibor asked.

"I did," said Havas calmly. "I made the highest bid. Auctions are publicly advertised well in advance."

"But in that case, Mr. Havas," said Tibor in his singsong astonished voice, "everything is all right. You give us the silver and we give our bond that the money will be repaid in the shortest possible time. You know us, know who we are. You must understand. Please don't think ill of us, Mr. Havas. But back then . . . Didn't Amadé say anything about it?"

"Whether he said or did not say anything, gentlemen, by law and by right the silver is no longer yours."

"By law and by right, Mr. Havas?" asked Tibor.

"By law and by right. I go strictly by the terms of the contract. The young gentlemen will not understand: it is a delicate matter. I am not permitted to ask anyone's name."

"We graduated yesterday, Mr. Havas," Tibor exclaimed. "Please understand. We are no longer schoolboys. That which was, is in the past. Please think it over . . . We will recover the money in no time . . . Amadé was your friend too."

"Actors are such peculiar people," said Havas pleasantly, considering the matter. "They come, they go. People like me are like rocks, we sit firm. That man seemed to have been born with wings. No ties bind him. But he really should have taken his leave of the gentlemen . . ."

The gale shook the window.

"It's starting," he said calmly. "Don't the young gentlemen understand? Amazing. A detective was asking after him in the morning."

He made a movement with his hand.

"He was advised, in strictest confidence, to leave the town immediately. Or be kicked out."

He leaned on the table.

"Someone had made a complaint against him. It's an ugly business, gentlemen. The complaint was that his behavior regarding a certain circle was drawing attention to him. He suspected his fellow actors. But the point was that a complaint had been lodged. That's a very unpleasant business, gentlemen."

Ábel held on to the table. The question he asked was so quiet they could hardly hear him.

"What was the complaint?"

"Allegedly, the corruption of certain young people. There are such folk. It's a bad business. Bad for the young people's future too. It's a small town."

"But it isn't true," said Tibor in a cracked voice.

The pawnbroker nodded.

"I know, I know. Allegedly there are witnesses. It's a small town and a whisper quickly spreads, gentlemen. People in small towns have time for such things. Scandals blow up quickly. It is hard to imagine what might happen if witnesses actually appeared."

"Witnesses to what, Mr. Havas?" asked Ábel. "What did they witness?"

"The corruption. Be so good as to think it over. The actor, they say, was himself corrupt to the core. I take a different view. The charge is that he corrupted young boys. They say he organized orgies. The complaint has it that he dragged a lot of boys off to the theater, boys from good families, and set up an orgy there."

"That's not true," screamed Tibor.

"That's what the complaint alleges," the pawnbroker went on unrelentingly. "The young gentlemen would no doubt know better. There must be something in it, though, or he wouldn't have left in such a hurry. He shot off as if pursued by the four winds, gentlemen. There is only ever destruction in the wake of such a man. According to the complaint one witness saw, strange to say, the actor kissing the son of a prominent family."

Ábel stepped up to him.

"It was you in the box, Havas. You . . . you were

watching us. You arranged it all. You put the actor up to it . . . O God!" He swayed. His lips were white. "What do you want? . . . Tibor, ask him! . . . What's going on here? . . . Let's go!"

"Unfortunately the rain has started," said Havas. "Perhaps the young gentlemen may care to sit the storm out here."

HE WATCHED THE STORM. THUNDER SHOOK THE window and the rain swept in waves over the pavement. He gently wagged his head.

"The young gentlemen know nothing about life," he said in a quiet, even voice. "We are very slow to learn anything. I myself was ignorant for a long time. Please be so good as to hear me out. It's pouring out there and you have nothing better to do. I come from a humble family with no pretensions, but perhaps I may help to enlighten the young gentlemen. Things are not so simple as people imagine. I was forty before I learned anything. It is impossible to say one man is like this, another like that. Be so good as to consider that. I once had a family, a wife, and a daughter: I know life. Nobody can know what awaits him the next morning."

He was breathing heavily, asthmatically.

"I eat heartily and I drink heartily, gentlemen, but I have a heart and no one can say I haven't one. I understand the delicate situation in which the young gentlemen find themselves very well. I will do what I can to help.

Given certain conditions, if the young gentlemen can produce the appropriate amount by, say, tomorrow night, the original loan and the interest owing, I am prepared to return the items previously pawned. No one can force me to do that of course, but Havas says to himself: these are young gentlemen of good breeding, or rather, excuse me, children. Extraordinary children. Help them if you can. Havas is listening to his foolish heart again. Deep down he has qualities of which the world knows nothing."

"Tomorrow night?" queried Tibor. "It'll be there, Mr. Havas. One way or the other you'll have the money by tomorrow night. But for heaven's sake, what are you talking about here? What do you mean Amadé corrupted us? What do you mean that we were observed? It was only a game, Mr. Havas. There was nothing I could do about it. There was nothing I could do about anything."

He began to tremble.

"For God's sake, Mr. Havas. What kind of complaint? What are they saying? What has happened?"

"I beg the young gentleman not to ask me questions I cannot answer. Please be kind enough to agree that I should give you explanations for such matters as I deem right. What I consider right is that I inform the young gentlemen of the situation in which they find themselves. What the actor did? Are the young gentlemen to blame? I cannot answer questions like that. And even if all happened as the complaint has it, it is still an open question for me whether they were actually guilty or not."

They could no longer see his face. Only his voice

emerged out of the murk, grave, stumbling with a dull resonance, sometimes like the warning growl of some animal.

"You never know how the devil gets into a man. Allow me to furnish you with an example. The young gentlemen will keep quiet. They will have every reason for keeping quiet. And I am glad to offer them this example because it is important that they should understand something of life. As I said before, it is not so simple. Take a man. Let us say he is married, with a daughter. He goes about his work. He has a thriving pawnbroker's business in some town, but the devil gets into him, he eats a lot, drinks a lot, and chases every skirt he sees. He needs money and it is as if the devil himself were guiding his hand, for everything succeeds, whatever he touches turns to gold, so much so that he grows overconfident. He travels to Lemberg, ready to supply the regiment with soap, when, there in Lemberg, he makes a mistake. It is all too possible, alas, to make mistakes in the course of business. The devil gets into him. Four months. He sleeps on the prison mattress for four months, his diet reduced to that fit only for an invalid. Two rolls and two pints of milk a day. This for a man who needs meat, who must have his meat. He is a number, number 137. He sits, he sleeps in a cell for four months, debating with the devil. He doesn't understand. Kindly consider that the bucket that is put aside for such purposes as are necessary is there in the cell with him. However much milk he drinks he longs for a little slice of bacon. So he lies there and dreams and doesn't understand why he should have to be number 137 in Lemberg, and the thought tortures him, as he is a big man with big appetites. He is a widower. His daughter is running the business and he writes to her: My dear daughter, pressing business has unexpectedly delayed me here, look after yourself, *Mein gutes Kind,* write to me care of Poste Restante, Lemberg, Central Post Office, 137. Four months. Such things happen."

He was struggling for breath. He relit his cigar.

"As I understand it the young gentlemen are not yet acquainted with the lives of adult men. So a little bird tells me. Never mind. I must stress that the man we are talking about is a big man with big appetites. Give him a decent meal and a nip of brandy and he can't pass a skirt without chasing after it. He spends four months practically in cramp. I once saw a hunting dog out in the yard. It was in a crate that had been misdirected so the dog had arrived a day late, but it never once messed the crate where it slept, if I may so put it, it would rather suffer cramps, and that was how it arrived. The doctor had to lift it from the box and give it a dose of salts. Now imagine a human being. At long last he goes out into the street, it's the end of October, afternoon, he is a little unsteady on his feet, he waves a carriage down and says, take me to the best brothel, the nearest brothel, and be quick about it. The rain is falling. He takes his hat off and sits like that in the open carriage, his face up to the rain, wishing for more rain, heavier rain, let it pour, he thinks, his tongue licking at the rain, never having realized before just how good rain tasted. The carriage rolls along the cobbles, a woman has stopped at the side of the road, she holds an umbrella, she wears brown shoes and black stockings, in four months hers is the first female face he has looked on, the woman laughs and shouts out: Hey, *meshugener.* Do the young gentlemen find this difficult to understand? He is taken to a high-quality house. There are palms in the salon. Yes, madame, he says, one, two, whatever you have available; the ladies only arrive in the evening, will a brunette do? The woman is indeed brunette, she has gold teeth and a mole at the side of her nose, but she's quite pretty. He doesn't even see her. He takes his coat off and sees that prison leaves a man with a certain smell on his skin. On the mirror is written *Happy New Year,* in gold.

"Now please to imagine," he continued and raised his hand as if for attention, "that after all these preliminaries nothing happens. I am not sure if I am making myself clear. Nothing. He slowly gets dressed, his clothes are almost dry by then, the warm smell of rain and the smell of prison emanating from them. What's going on? he thinks. The girl is sitting at the mirror in her nightdress, smoking a cigarette, looking at him over her shoulder. Ahem, he says. Pardon. It can all be explained, the man has come a long way. A long, long way. Next time then. He is already standing by the door. Idiot, he thinks. You are forty-two years old, what's this to you? Can't you dance on the billiard table till six in the morning, drink two or three bottles of bubbly by yourself, and top it with half a bottle of cognac, plus a stick of dry salami and four or five hard-boiled eggs? He turns his hat round and round in his hands. He doesn't understand. He can't find it in himself to leave. He can neither leave nor stay, he is worried that he'll make a nuisance of himself, that he is going to hit somebody. The girl moves towards him, every part of her body swaying as she approaches, looks at him with desire, throws her cigarette away, puts both hands behind his neck, rises on tiptoe, closes her eyes, and kisses him, very gently. Come here, she says quietly. They move back into the room, the girl with her arm round his neck, keeping close to him. He sits down and looks around. He feels like a fool. He understands nothing. The girl silently goes about her business, flitting here and there in the room, puts on some perfume, adjusts her hair, applies some powder, takes off her nightdress. She is wearing black stockings and red suspenders. She is very attractive. Drink has ravaged her face a little but she is still attractive. Her body has a yellow tinge, is very cold to the touch, her body hard, in fact just as you like them, he thinks, not an ounce of fat. She comes up to him, close your eyes, she says. He closes his eyes, the girl leans over him and kisses him: flesh is simply a kind of mechanism, he thinks, and she is a good mechanic. Think of something, he tells himself. Something cheerful. The patriarchs. David. Solomon. Solomon had a thousand wives. No, that's not a particularly cheerful subject, he thinks. He reaches for the girl's neck."

He held his hand out. They backed away. His arm described a circle in the air.

"The girl throws herself on him, all of her. That's the kind of girl she is. She embraces him, kisses him while he continues shaking his head like an idiot. The girl's body is seized by a cramp: the smell of mouthwash, cigarettes, and something a touch sour emanates from her mouth, she hasn't eaten a thing all day, she's working on an empty stomach. He will never forget that. The girl kisses his eyes, throws herself this way and that. Time passes. He removes the girl's hands from his neck, he must sit up, he feels he is drowning. The girl slowly withdraws. She is wearing lacquered shoes, little half shoes. She pulls at her stockings and sits at the edge of the bed, and never stops staring at him. How long haven't you been able to do it? asks the girl. He shrugs. It is always somehow comical when a supine figure tries to shrug. I don't know whether the gentlemen have noticed that?"

He waited anxiously for them to answer for a moment as if it were a matter of the utmost importance to him.

"Somewhere along the line you have made a mistake, he thinks. But when? Where? It occurs to him that his mother used to have a black brooch that she wore on a black ribbon round her neck and when she leaned over him the brooch swung to and fro. Isn't it strange, gentlemen, how at the most important moments of life a person thinks of the most irrelevant things? For example, how they made a party coat for him out of his father's black coat, and how the sleeves were too long for him. The girl keeps her eyes on him, never looking away. That's the kind of girl she is, he thinks, she's a living creature like him. She is sitting at the head of the brass bed, wrapped in a piece of scarlet silk, her hair over her forehead, slowly raising the long cigarette-holder to her lips, solemnly watching his every movement, saying nothing, only staring. What are you looking at? he asks her. You want me to give you a smack? The girl just continues staring, her two elbows propped on the brass bed frame.

"You're impotent, she says.

"He moves in her direction and raises his hand but she is already at the door, and says it again, loudly, just imagine it, gentlemen, as if she were passing sentence: You're impotent.

"Then she's through the door. The madame is waiting, it's a top-notch house, we hope you may favor us with another visit, she says. We offer an unparalleled range of girls. He goes down the steps, why of course, he's sure to come back. The rain is beating on the pavement. Nice town. A little dull perhaps for a longer stay. He calls in at a café to drink a glass of tea. The place is full of Polish Jews. He drinks his tea with brandy and eats a meat pancake. In the evening he returns to the brothel. He is going nowhere for a week yet. He returns every night, calling for different girls, for the same girl. By now they are all laughing at him. The girls stand in the hallway in their chemises, waiting for him, pointing and laughing at him. He can't bear to leave. He grinds his teeth, beats his head against the ground, weeps, gets more money. He stalks the streets like a maniac during the day, looking round, perhaps even talking to himself. He doesn't understand. It is as if suddenly, for no reason at all, he were utterly paralyzed. It is like suddenly going blind. Like losing an arm. I hope I am not boring the young gentlemen?"

Rain beat against the glass and thunderclaps continued

to shake the window. He spoke more loudly, as if wanting to outshout the thunder, not moving.

"Lemberg is bad for his nerves, he thinks. One night he steals out to the railway station. You had a home once, he thinks. Frida cried a lot when she was alive, because you led a riotous life, a big man with big appetites, but at least you had a home, you were somebody, you used to have visitors on winter evenings. You could have been on the town council. Now you are nobody, you are less than a flea. Why? He doesn't understand. He feels like dying. The dead find a home in the bosom of Abraham. I don't know whether the young gentlemen are acquainted with the scriptures? The train moves forward in the rain, two Polish peasants at his feet, they smell of garlic and cheap spirits. He looks down and shakes his head like someone who has been knocked down, he mumbles. People look at him. A pity his daughter ran away two weeks ago. The young gentlemen might not be aware how far everything is connected. Trouble never travels alone, they say. His only daughter has run off with a crippled Uhlan lieutenant. He tears up her clothes, won't say a word about her to anyone. You're only human, he tells himself, you only want to enjoy your brief time on earth. No, you are a louse, a flea, he says to himself, a nobody, nothing. A piece of dirt under God's foot. What did the girl in Lemberg say? Just thinking of her he begins to tremble, he feels dizzy, he sees the girls sitting on the stairs in their chemises, pointing at him and laughing. Months go by like this, he comes and goes, says nothing to anyone, but he won't visit the girls any more. When he thinks of that specific Lemberg girl he sees red, the blood pounds in his temples, he wants to smash and break things, and wants nothing more than to get on a train again, go back to Lemberg, find the girl, and beat her head against the wall. When he is alone he prays or drinks or curses. You'd hardly recognize him. You didn't have a good word to say to your Frida while she was alive, he tells himself: God gave you the cell as punishment, he has bound your strength, you feel the curse of your fathers on you when you remember what the girl in Lemberg said. Nothing is as it was. He goes to the rabbi, gives him money, talks with him. Rabbi, he says, God has punished me, I can't make love any more. The rabbi looks at him, saintly man that he is, what does he know of life? Be patient, he says. God is putting you to the test for your sins, be patient and wait. Yes, God, I am waiting, he says. You were an impulsive man, says the rabbi. You didn't keep the feasts or the laws, you cheated and chased skirts and drank as if there were no tomorrow, you were a lush, a coxcomb, what do you want of God now? There is a season for all things in life, says the rabbi. There are ups, there are downs, there's plenty and starvation, do you think the scriptures and the law mean nothing? Go to the temple and pray. So he goes to the temple and prays. He feels so miserable that he can't look anyone in the eye, he just stands by the pillar like a leper. And he doesn't understand the prayers, he just stands and bends this way and that, and mumbles to himself, but he is no longer capable of crying or wailing, and there's no improvement. He spends a whole year like this. He doesn't talk to anybody. He goes around town but once he is on the street he fears that he might suddenly start running and knock over anyone in his way. He says nothing, is silent, he bites his tongue, that's how he goes round. A year of this. A whole year."

He fell silent, nodded, and grasped the table with both hands. A thunderclap.

"That was a close one," he said respectfully, but did not turn his face to the window.

"The gentlemen would do well to realize that things are never simple," he said slowly, his voice loud now. "You never know what you will find the next morning. He no longer wants to wander around the town. The fury builds in him until he is like a walking bomb, an explosive device in his chest, and he is afraid, afraid of being alone with another man because he fears he might strangle him, fears he might be a danger to people, to the town generally; he feels such fury and power he thinks he could set the town on fire, to cover it in salt and plow it all up. The girl in Lemberg, he thinks, she told him. How could such a girl know something he himself didn't know until fairly recently? Does someone like him bear a visible mark? Can others see it too? God, oh God. It's impossible to live like this, he thinks. He walks the street with his eyes on the ground, he dare not look young girls in the face, no, not the young men either. He hates young gentlemen, the healthy vigorous ones who can go with girls. One day I shall have them in the palm of my hand, he thinks. He weeps like an old woman, blaming himself. One can live neither by the stomach nor by any other appetite, he thinks. The patriarchs were right to lay down the law, but you, you laughed at their laws. You were a lecher, a lush, a glutton, you wronged your friends and acquaintances, that is why God is punishing you. That's how he talked to himself. Impossible to live like this, he thinks. The Lord rained fire on Sodom and Gomorrah, he burned both flesh and bone. We are all sinners, he thinks, and God has sent his rain of fire on me too for my sins."

He raised the bottle, put it to his mouth, and drank as if choking, in loud gulps.

"One day he is sitting in the shop and a cripple comes in, a man with a great long false-looking beard. He wants to pawn a cuckoo clock with a chain. Rejected, he slowly hobbles to the door where he stops and says: We are all sinners. The very thing you said a moment ago, he thinks. He calls the other back. The man comes over to the counter and starts preaching. Only sinners may be cleansed, he says, and mutters something about the brazen serpent. He listens, a fool at last after all those clever people. Miss, he says, write down *one cuckoo clock,* but secretly he thinks, another thing connected with birds, a bad sign. The bearded man goes away but not before leaving his name and address and offering his friendship. When it comes to money he is not such a fool. Meanwhile the man goes on living but he can't taste his food, his drink is bitter, sometimes he has trouble with his vision, and whenever he sees a woman he turns away and hangs his head. It is the hand of God that smites you, he thinks. One afternoon he picks up an old pair of shoes and thinks of the fool down fishmongers' alley. He calls in. The man immediately rises from his three-legged stool and as soon as he sees him hobbles over and begins a rant about the exodus from Israel and about sitting by the fleshpots in the land of Egypt. How does this man know I am a lover of flesh? he wonders. The bearded man sits down on the stool, continues his oration, his speech somewhat confused but perfectly amusing. A little boy is sitting in the corner reading by candlelight, paying no attention to them; my son, says the bearded man, one day he will be one of the gentry, stand up, Ernő, say hello to the gentleman."

He leaned right over the table, his chin propped on his hands, his face glimmering close to the boys' own faces. He was speaking more quietly now, in broken sentences, panting slightly. Ábel sat back, his hands grasping the legs of his chair, not moving a muscle.

"A very bright little boy," said Havas almost whispering. "A scrawny little sparrow of a boy, but very bright. Next day he brought the shoes over. You could have the most remarkable conversations with him. He came often, always at the same time, after dinner, I could talk to him for hours. Oh, he was so bright, he knew everything. He listened very attentively when the talk turned to serious matters. He was an ideal listener for a serious person to talk to, to reveal his innermost thoughts and troubles to. He was a very poor boy but with a lively sense of ambition. He had plans. He wanted to travel abroad. It was a delight spending time with him. His clothes were so ragged that any sensitive man's heart would have gone out to him. He wanted to be rich when he grew up, a scholar, a powerful man. He wanted to live in town, in the town where he had been poor, where he had had to carry books for his better-off classmates, to teach so he could eat and drink, to polish, on occasion, his classmates' shoes. That was because his better-off friends often took pity on him and, wanting to help him and his family, sent their shoes to his father to be resoled. He had much to learn because his lot was harsh, because he could not afford to pay school fees, and because his very body was frail and awkward, like his father's. You couldn't even begin to compare him to his better-off classmates. He was vastly ambitious. There was a time when he would come every afternoon, dine here, not scorning the fleshpots served up by his lonely widower friend. He would take gifts home to his father, who would also call sometimes but never when the boy was here, and would bow and scrape and say: only sinners may be cleansed, and, I am most grateful to the noble gentleman for his kindness to my son. Meanwhile the little boy continues to call and there are many things a growing boy like him requires, clothes, books, underwear, because he is preparing to study abroad, and he has gone to the post office to open a savings account where he puts whatever money he occasionally earns. He talks about everything under the sun, particularly about his friends. He has three friends, he says, and a fourth one too who is not at school but hangs around with them."

It seemed the thunder had stopped for a moment, that they were utterly frozen in the sudden silence, as if they had fainted away or simply couldn't move. Then a single great gust of wind tore the window open, knocking things over, sweeping the rain in. The pawnbroker did not move so much as a muscle. It was as though he had lost the powers of both seeing and hearing.

"They have so much to talk about. One day he tells him what well-brought-up boys they are. Everything is different with them, even now when their fathers are away. The way they greet each other, the way they talk, it is all so different from the way we do such things. Because that is how intimate the talk is now. He talks about their games. They have decided to tell lies, he says. Then, another day, that now they are stealing. One day soon they'll be coming over. The actor is a fascinating man. Even on the basis of such a brief acquaintance they can tell he's a fellow spirit. There is something sorrowful about him. And when the actor calls in he tells me what interesting and well-brought-up boys he has befriended. Rebels, all of them, he says. They are in rebellion for some reason or other. One day young Ernő fails to call. He is only to be seen together with the three other young gentlemen, something has happened to him, he is constantly tracking one of the other young gentlemen. One day the actor says: now's the time, what if we arranged a little private performance with the boys? Absolutely private. You sit up there in one of the boxes and watch. No one will know. It will cost, of course. The actor offers to arrange it."

He went over to the window and closed it. The water was lying in puddles on the floor.

"What a storm!" he said, shaking his head. He feared it might wash away whatever entertainment the young gentlemen had been planning for tonight.

He gazed at the empty bottle, pushed it away with disgust, and walked round the table.

"Unfortunately by that time the actor has a bad reputation," he said, stopping in front of them and crossing his arms. "He is being watched. Someone from the theater might be keeping an eye on him. Or maybe someone else. They report him and the young gentlemen would be ruined if there proved to be a witness to that private—should we call it—performance. The young gentlemen continue to be subject to the authority of their parents and others senior to them. A witness, someone who knows the problematic affairs of the young gentlemen, could bring about a situation of the utmost unpleasantness. The young gentlemen would never be able to face their kind parents and relations again."

Tibor was slowly backing away towards the door. He hadn't said a single word throughout the pawnbroker's speech, but now he swallowed and stuttered.

"What do you want?"

Silence.

"Ábel!" He leapt over to him, seized him, and shook his arm. "Speak! . . . What's going on? . . . What does the man want?"

Ábel put his finger to his neck as if adjusting his collar before saying anything. The pawnbroker smiled.

"Havas has a heart. The position is clear to the young gentlemen now. Extraordinary boys like these, thought Havas, were certain to call at your den sometime. You must amuse them as best you can. Now here they are."

He surveyed them, still smiling.

"Havas is ready to oblige the young gentlemen. Until, let us say, tomorrow night. Master Prockauer can put the pawn ticket related to the family silver back in his pocket.

Tomorrow, at this time, shall we say, I would be pleased to see the young gentlemen with or without the money. In the meantime I wouldn't want to spoil tonight's entertainment. The young gentlemen should think the matter over and do what seems sensible to them. Havas is not going anywhere, he is not to be moved, he sits here like a rock. His financial circumstances, his physical condition, tie him to the place. One at least of the young gentlemen's friends can reassure them that Havas is always friendly and generous. His personal relationships are, as ever, first rate. The young gentlemen should act according to their perception of the situation. Havas doesn't like shady deals. He is perfectly open, has nothing up his sleeve. It is up to the young gentlemen to decide."

He looked around.

"You can't hear the rain now. If the young gentlemen would like to take their leave now . . ."

He opened the door.

"I bid you a pleasant evening. Till tomorrow, at the same time."

He courteously ushered them through, bowed a little stiffly and painfully. They heard him turn the key in his door as they stood in the stairwell.

THEY WAVE DOWN A CARRIAGE AND ASK TO BE taken to The Peculiar. They draw up the carriage hood and sit in the cabin that smells of mice, not too close to each other, hearing the rain's gentle pitter-patter on the leather above them. Ábel is shivering. It has just occurred to him that he has not had a proper wash for twenty-four hours, has not changed his underwear or eaten hot food. His teeth are chattering as he sits in the corner, the carriage bumping over the uneven cobbles, opening his eyes whenever there is a particularly violent jerk to see the wall of some house, a pile of stones, the trunk of poplar, a garden fence. It seems to him that this is the longest journey he has ever made. They are just passing the cobbler's wall when he feels Tibor's hand on his. Ábel, croaks the colonel's son. What is this? Are we dreaming? The wheels of the carriage rumble on. Ábel would like to answer but hasn't the strength to shout over the noise of their passage. He weakly raises his hand to indicate that he wants to say something but can't find his voice. Do you believe it? asks Tibor. Ábel mouths silently back at him. What? He is cold and shivering, yet is seized by hot flushes. His teeth continue to chatter. He feels feverish. Do I believe what he says about Ernő? About us? Is it true? He can't answer. He closes his eyes.

They stop the carriage near The Peculiar and walk over swollen muddy fields. Everywhere there are fruit trees devastated by the storm. In the plowed furrows there is the delicately sprinkled sparkle of ice. They make their way across the field, muddy themselves, reeling a little, pass the fence, avoid the garden by entering through the back door, and steal up the stairs to their room.

The room is still as Ábel had left it that morning. He walks uncertainly to the window, closes the shutters, and collapses on the bed. Tibor sits down at the table. There's no one in the garden. Lanterns, painted scraps of paper, hang soaked and useless on wires. Overturned tables. A shroud of mist descends from the pines. But there is a rumble and a clatter from the hall below: conversation, the clinking of glasses rise through the floorboards. The picnic crowd must already be here, sheltering in the dim-lit restaurant. The damp fog settles and darkens into evening. Tibor glances at his wristwatch. Half past six. They spent over four hours with Havas.

"Answer me now, Ábel," he says, his elbows on his knees, leaning forward. "What did you know of all this? What's this about? Did you know about Havas, the actor, and Ernő? . . ."

Ábel hears the question as from a vast distance, his eyes are closed, his arms and legs spread wide. It takes a great effort to sit up, then he feels about on the bedside table and lights what's left of the candle he had used the previous night. The room is dark by now.

"I knew nothing," he says slowly, his tongue heavy in his head, half-asleep. "I told you all I know this morning. There are no secrets. There's nothing in any of this that we should keep quiet about." Nevertheless, he falls quiet for a while. Then, uncertainly but more animatedly he continues.

"Did it never occur to the rest of you that Ernő was always talking about something else? It's hard to describe, but whenever I said 'tonight,' or 'pen,' or 'person' and he repeated the words 'tonight' and 'pen' and 'person' he meant something else by it. I often feel this way when I'm with strangers. I never felt it with you, not even when you didn't understand what I was saying. With Ernő I felt it all the time. Something separated him from us."

The colonel's son reached over for the tin of tobacco lying on the table, rolled a cigarette in his trembling fingers, leaned over to the candle, and lit up.

"So you knew nothing?" he asked, his mouth dry.

"Nothing."

"And what you said to me this morning? . . ."

Ábel props himself on his elbows and with a new kind of carelessness, with a curious joy and sense of liberation, answers: "That I loved you? But of course I love you. But wait, Tibor. I am just beginning to understand. I love you, I like looking at you, there were secrets we shared, and so we told each other more or less everything we could tell. Or at least I did . . . I don't have anyone else. Auntie, poor thing, the servant, and Father, and, well, you know all about him. One day perhaps, if we are still alive, once I have forgotten everything, he and I will be friends. I don't know. Wait, maybe I can explain it to you now. I was jealous of you too. I wanted you to be my friend, mine alone, not Ernő's or Béla's or the actor's, none of whom were worthy of you. Of course I loved you. It's not what Havas was talking about though, Tibor, not at all. I know that now. And I prayed for you. I have a special friend you don't know about, the mandarin, who is disinterested and fair. I prayed that you should remain young, handsome, graceful, light in spirit, and that you should escape the filthy struggle in which our brothers and fathers are currently engaged. I prayed you should always be as elegant

260

and refined as you are now, that you should suffer no crisis of doubt, that nothing should trouble your conscience; that you should always blush when someone addressed you. And loving you was a painful feeling, agony and humiliation, but there was nothing sly about it. Nothing. Do you believe me? And now, after all this, I no longer know if at bottom—that is, at some depth I cannot see—everything was in fact as simple, pure, and well-meant as I had thought it to be. But I knew nothing about any such arrangement, Tibor, believe me. You and I, we had to be together because something was drawing us that way. To me you were beauty and friendship, the ideal if you like, but never fear, I never thought of you that way. Maybe I would have liked to touch your hair, but that was all. No, no, no!" he cried and stood up. "Oh, Tibor, what has happened? Why is this happening to us? Look round this room, these things we stole, the things we said, all the games we played here. Can't you see what it was all about?"

His voice was feverish, his passion high, his hands squeezing his narrow face.

"It really was intolerable the way they lied and tortured and hid everything from us, as by right, as if their world were the only one that was wise, mature, and decent. It was they who dragged Lajos away and tore his arm off, I don't even know where, and so they went on torturing us with foreign languages, with the higher mathematics, and with rules of ethical conduct, while all the time they were sharpening their knives against us . . . I know you're joining up tomorrow, Tibor, but I want no part of them, I want nothing of Havas's world or Kikinday's world or your father's world . . . I would sooner die. We rebelled, Tibor. We defied their laws. That's what this was all about. That was behind the games, the pretense, this room at The Peculiar. We had to escape, we had to be revenged on them somewhere, hence this room, and look, the saddle and the globe . . . ! I love you, but I know now that my love is quite different from what Havas was talking about. I am your friend because you are more beautiful, because there is something in you I shall never possess . . . some lightness, some crucial difference in the way you move and speak . . . I don't know. And it was all beautiful, The Peculiar, the secrecy, everything . . . But someone cheated, and that changed everything. Do you understand? Someone has cheated and now everything is foul. Are you as sick as I am? I can't bear it . . ."

He bowed his head and rested it on the bedpost, as if about to throw up. The door opened without knocking. Ernő and Béla stepped in and quickly slid the bolt in place. Béla was already drunk.

"After the rain stopped," he said, his tongue heavy in his mouth, "our superiors, our mentors got drunk as quickly as they could."

ERNŐ STOOD BY THE BOLTED DOOR, LEANING against it.

"Have you seen Havas?" he asked. He was without his pince-nez, his hands in his pockets. His voice was sharp, aggressive, shrill. Tibor took a step towards him.

"You stay where you are," Ernő ordered in a commanding tone, extending one arm. "And you too," he said to Béla who was looking around, puzzled. "Stay on the bed," he advised Ábel. "We're listening. Go ahead, speak freely. What did he tell you? Everything?" And when Tibor moved he repeated: "I told you to stay where you are. If you attack me I will defend myself. I've had enough of punishments. It had to come out sometime. I've waited a year for this. No more superciliousness, Prockauer."

He half withdrew his other hand from his pocket, then quickly slid it away again.

"Go on, Prockauer. Speak."

His voice sounded quite different. It was as if a stranger were speaking.

"Have you gone mad?" asked Tibor quietly, mesmerized in the stillness.

"Ask me something else," said Ernő. "Out with it. Did he tell you everything?"

His eyes were constantly challenging theirs, seeking out now one, now another.

"You entered his den, did you? And was it interesting, Prockauer? And my delicate Ábel? How did you like it?"

When they remained quiet he continued.

"I have warned you once. It's all the same to me. You can scream and shout, you can spit in my face, it's all the same to me now."

The silence disturbed him. He went on a little less certainly.

"I was there this morning, begging him to listen, to

give up the whole thing . . . You don't believe me? But he's not human . . ."

He was thinking. Suddenly the flow seemed to have stopped in him.

"I don't know . . . there are such people. That's just the way it is."

He immediately recovered.

"I will not allow myself to be insulted, I warn you, not even if he told you everything. I will defend myself, against all three of you, even if you bring the whole school, the whole town and the army, I insist on defending myself. If you don't lay off me I will tell them everything. You can learn one or two things from Havas. He's not alone, you don't know this yet, but there is a considerable power ranged behind him and within certain limits he can do what he likes. If he takes against someone, that person is done for. He probably lied to you. Did he tell you some pathetic story? No? And what about me? What did he say about me?"

In his terrible impatience he was stamping on the floor and screaming.

"Why don't you say something?"

"Is it true?" asked Tibor. The cobbler's son threw back his head.

"It depends on what he said."

"That you, and Havas, and the actor . . . ?"

"What?"

Tibor sat down at the table, put his head in his hands, and spoke quite gently.

"It seems to me that everything I see here has only served to put us to sleep. Doesn't it seem that way to you?"

There was no answer. He quietly turned to Ernő.

"Havas claims that you used to visit him."

"I have nothing to say about that," said the cobbler's son.

"But this is a very important matter," Tibor continued quietly but intensely. "If you don't want to answer, that's up to you. What concerns us is your betrayal. Is it true that you told Havas what we were doing? Is it true that you told him everything, all we said, all we planned, about this secret life of ours about which no one else knew anything?"

"Yes," he answered sharply.

"Good. And is it true that you and the actor . . . that you worked together against us in some way, and that Havas put you up to this?"

"Claptrap!" he declared vehemently. "The actor was a vain monkey. What did he know? Havas had him in his grasp, but in quite a different way from me. The actor was working entirely for himself."

"But then it was—you?"

"Yes, me."

"But why? What did you want? What was it all about? What did you think would happen once we got mixed up in this mess? What's the point of it for you? Were we not your friends?"

"No," he said very loudly.

They fell silent. They listened.

"Are you not one of us?" asked Tibor quietly.

"No," he repeated.

He too was speaking quietly now, as quickly and deliberately as if he had prepared for just this speech, every word of it ordered long ago.

"You were not my friend, Prockauer. You were not my friend, wealthy Ruzsák. Nor you, you genteel beggar," he turned with a contemptuous flick of his head to Ábel. "I would have been happy to be your friend, Prockauer, delighted in fact, like the others here. Now I can tell you because I myself haven't been aware of it for long, that there's something about you that will be a source of much trouble to you throughout your life . . . something you can't help that draws people to you. A particular set of people. But I couldn't be your friend because you are who you are and I am who I am, my father's son, and I cannot simply wriggle out of that. I would like to have been your friend. Your mother was generous enough to give me a pair of shoes for repair that first afternoon when I visited you, years ago, because she wanted to help my poor sickly father. You gave me coffee, Béla's father gave me bread and cheese, and Ábel's ancient aunt stuck a jar of preserves into my pocket each time I left you. No one had to stick jars of preserves into your pockets when you visited somebody. Shall I tell you everything? A thousand days, a thousand minutes per day, you hurt me in such ways. No, there was nothing you could do about it. Nobody can ever do anything about it. You were all sensitivity and goodness."

He spat.

"I loathed your sensitivity. I loathed your goodness. I

loathed you each time you took a knife and fork in your hands. When you greeted someone. When you smiled. When you thanked someone for some object or a piece of information. I loathed your movements, the way you looked, the way you stood up and sat down. It isn't true to say that one can learn such things. I learned that there was no money, no power, no strength, no knowledge that could produce the same results. I learned that I could live a hundred years, that I could be a millionaire, that you might all be rotting in your graves, in your crypts I should say, since even in death you would have your private mansions, not like us, we dogs who live in cellars and kennels all our lives, that even then I would have no luck because I would recall how Tibor Prockauer could simply give a wave, smile, and say 'Sorry' when he unintentionally upset someone . . . Whenever I thought of this I would groan in my dreams, scream and groan 'Tibor,' and it would sometimes happen that I would turn and see my father who had been sleeping at the foot of my bed, and he would sit up and nod and say: 'You are suffering on account of the young well-born gentleman. One must be cleansed.' Cleansed, yes. I cannot cleanse myself, but I feel a little more cleansed when I think how you too are in the mud now. And that you too will die. I live in misery, I set out from another shore and there is no way over to your world from there, there never has been and never will be, not ever! Locusts and bears, says my father. I loathe you all. May you all drop dead, but let me first torture you a little. You may deny the world I set aside for your torture but it matters to you. I cheated. I lied. I betrayed you. I cheated at cards too, I cheated at everything. Every word of mine was a cheat."

He drew a greasy pack of cards from his pocket and threw it on the table.

"Tomorrow Prockauer goes to Havas. You'll go whether you want to or not. The chains that hold you are strong. Don't bother struggling. May God have mercy on you."

He stopped. The words stuck in his throat. He looked around, frightened. His voice was quite different now, almost tremulous.

"I would have liked to be your friend. But I was always afraid that you'd tell me off for something. I mean, you did once. On account of the knife and fork."

"That's something you can learn," Béla retorted furiously.

It was the first time he had said anything. They stared at him. He was embarrassed and looked down at his feet. The candle had burned right down. They could only see outlines in the darkness. Tibor silently stood up.

"Well, then," he said, somewhat at a loss. "We could go now, I suppose. I can't think why we should carry on sitting here. We know everything now. And the candle has almost gone out," he added as if that sealed the matter.

"You go ahead," croaked Ernō. "I want everyone in front of me. I don't want any of you behind me."

He kept his hand in his pocket and moved away from the door. Tibor raised the candle and held it up to his face. He gave a silent cry. Ernō's face was so twisted, it spoke of such unknown, unbearable sorrow that Tibor had to take a step back.

"We should tidy up here, of course," he muttered uncertainly as he stood on the threshold. "We should all take what belongs to us before we go. We can leave the costumes here," he said, pointing to the pile of clothes. "I don't suppose any of us will need them again. In any case the game is over."

"What a pity, Tibor," said Ábel, almost weeping and feverish. He hadn't said a word until now. "Look around you. It will never be like this again."

They descended the stairs on tiptoe, Ernő bringing up the rear. He followed them down the short way to the ground-level guest room in a state of inexplicable terror, as if he were in the gravest danger, almost fearing for his life. His elbows were tight against his waist, his hands never leaving his pockets. Not one of the others said anything to him on this short journey, not then, nor later in the night. It was a considerable surprise to all of them when, later, they had to look for him.

IN THE LONG, ALE-SMELLING, FRESHLY LIME-washed bar all done up for the picnic, they discovered a surprisingly lively atmosphere. Considering the early hour, the party must have been in full swing for a while.

At a folding table set up in the corner, at its narrower, upper end, sat Moravecz, Gurka, and the headmaster. The new arrivals hadn't expected to see Kikinday sitting on the headmaster's right. The town clerk was sitting between the gym teacher and the art master, while his son, who had been their classmate, was seated opposite him, silent and nervous, out of place. Now and then he would stand up, go over to the counter, and throw back a glass of *pálinka,* so that finally, much to the father's surprise—for as far as he could see his son had not touched a drop of alcohol all evening—he suddenly collapsed about midnight, showing every sign of alcohol poisoning. In the succeeding chaos somebody indicated that they should be on their way. Laying the boy on an improvised stretcher, the majority of them departed.

Those who remained, Kikinday, Gurka—the master of festivities, who employed formal courtesy to maintain a proper distance between himself and his ex-students despite the intimate atmosphere of the occasion—and Moravecz, drew closer together at the head of the table and permitted such students as still kept company with them in these late hours to join them. Ernő spent the whole evening sitting silently beside the tight-lipped Gurka. When the gang and a few other hardy partying souls somewhat reluctantly accepted Moravecz's invitation and the tipsy group moved closer to him, Ernő stood up and left the bar.

Memories of this May picnic survived for several years, not only in the unwritten annals of the school but in the town at large. The general opinion was that it was one of the most successful graduation parties the venerable institution had ever organized.

Because of the unusual heat the assembled gentlemen had left the town in the early morning and, together with their students, had settled down in the shady, lantern-lit garden of The Peculiar before being sent running into the bar by the storm. Considering the airless and damp hall, the company, including the more moderate among them, rather surprisingly succeeded in drinking themselves into a party mood in the time the rain continued to fall, so much so that the various courses of the banquet, together with its customary toasts, tended to dissolve in a spirit of universal good humor. The effects of alcohol were amplified to an extraordinary degree by the intense heat. Feeling decidedly jolly, Kikinday beckoned over every young man who was liable for military service, felt his muscles, and addressed words of encouragement to them all regarding their shortened period of training, referring particularly to the one-armed one.

"It was Prockauer's idea," he kept repeating. "Where's the one-armed Prockauer?"

Tibor, who represented the two-armed branch of the Prockauer family, politely informed him, more than once, that his elder brother was probably at their sick mother's bedside. When this information failed to register on the well-oiled Kikinday's consciousness, and when, within a few minutes, he began to call again for the one-armed Prockauer, Tibor fell silent. The gang was secretly of the opinion that Lajos had been delayed by the bad weather. The one-armed one tended to lie in bed during storms with a pillow over his head.

"There might be other reasons," Ábel suggested anxiously.

Tibor pretended not to hear. After midnight when the hall emptied they set about serious drinking. They hadn't had much real practice with drink and Ábel, who had a high fever, behaved out of character, speaking loudly, banging the table, and demanding to be heard. Tibor listened broodily, casting occasional dark looks here and there as if seeking someone, then bent over his glass. Béla tried to annoy Gurka. He sat down opposite him and would now and then lean over the table, screw up his eyes, and like an underprepared student hungry for knowledge demand to know the significance of this or that quotation from Tacitus. Ábel stood up with the glass in his hand and began to make a long feverish speech. No one paid any attention to him.

Round about three o'clock they went out into the yard. A shadowy figure stood there with a lantern in one hand and a big hooked stick in the other, a stick far taller than himself. He was in quiet conversation with the landlord. He approached them slowly, holding the lantern above his head, raising the enormous stick high with each step.

"Here they are," he said and shone the light in their faces. "I was just looking for the young gentlemen. My comrade at the front, young Mr. Prockauer, asked me to look for you tonight."

Now they recognized him and stood amazed. It was the cobbler.

. . .

"IT IS IN FACT THE YOUNGER MR. PROCKAUER I want," said the cobbler in his normal steady manner despite the strangeness of the meeting. "Though if I understand the nature of the message correctly, it is addressed to all the young gentlemen."

Tibor stepped forward.

"What news of my mother, Mr. Zakarka?"

The cobbler turned the lantern and the stick slowly towards him and gave a nod as he might to anyone asking an intelligent question.

"The noble lady," he declared with satisfaction, "is as well as can be expected in the circumstances. There was a decided improvement in her condition tonight. Sometime during the afternoon she had appeared to weaken to the point that at about five o'clock young Mr. Prockauer called me over to the house of the honorable gentleman, me being his fellow soldier at the front, so that I should be nearby in case I could be of use. I should mention that young Mr. Prockauer had been tending his sick mother with remarkable selflessness the whole day, literally not shifting from her bedside, watching over her. By the afternoon things had proceeded so far that her heart had almost stopped. There was a moment when Mr. Prockauer came to me in the next room with his finger to his lips indicating that the unhappy event was at hand. But a fortunate turn in the evening suddenly rendered the lady back to health."

He hesitated. "Praise be to God," he added. He put the lantern down beside him on the ground and leaned on the stick with both hands.

"It is a fine night, though walking is difficult for me nowadays, alas. But young Mr. Prockauer's request was so heartfelt I couldn't refuse him. He told me to take a cab at his expense, but I chose to come on foot as walking is more appropriate to my humble station. The disciples went on foot. So the message is a little late in arriving but a few minutes is as nothing in eternity."

"What message, Mr. Zakarka?" asked Tibor, trembling. "Do tell us."

"Of course," he replied slowly, like a machine that once started could not be stopped by any human intervention. "There has been a wondrous turn of events. The hour of cleansing is nigh. Especially for the young gentlemen. My benefactor, the colonel, has come home."

"The colonel?" asked Tibor, gasping for air. "What colonel? You mean my father?"

The cobbler kept nodding, deep in thought, as though he hadn't heard the question.

"God has been merciful to me," he declared with satisfaction. "When the colonel entered the room in full battle order, escorted by his batman, and saw me sitting there counting my rosary beads, he was good enough to address a few words to me. What are you doing here, you old hangman? he asked with obvious hostility. He was kind enough to address these words to me. The colonel was referring to my cleansing. The young gentlemen should understand that as far as the colonel is concerned it is an act of considerable grace on his part to engage people like me in conversation at all. Having got so far it is almost a matter of indifference what he actually says. The joy of seeing him again was enough to pull the noble lady back from death's door. I had the opportunity of overhearing the exchange between them. After the first words of warm greeting the noble lady was quick to ask a question of the noble colonel. Where have you left your gold wristwatch? she asked him. The noble colonel gave a lengthy reply. I do not think it fit that I should apprise the young gentlemen, particularly young Master Tibor, of the full details of his answer. Young Master Lajos immediately came out to me with the request that I should seek out the young gentlemen and tell them the good news. He made me swear that I should mention the matter of the saddle to young Master Tibor."

Tibor started to laugh, waved his arms in the air, and took a few steps.

"My father is home," he cried. "Ábel! My father is home." He stopped and wiped his brow. "It's the end, Ábel. The end, you hear."

The cobbler looked around attentively.

"My son Ernő," he said in a flat voice. "He must be in there with the teachers, I suppose."

Béla pointed upstairs. Candlelight filtered through the window. Tibor turned to the cobbler.

"Your son, Ernő, is a traitor," he said quietly. "Look after him well. You know the fate of traitors?"

"Indeed I do," said the cobbler and nodded. "A bullet."

"THE SADDLE," CRIED BÉLA. "THE GLOBE! LET'S take what we can!"

Dawn was very faintly breaking in the valley. The cobbler raised his lantern and walked steadily into the house. He went up the stairs as though they were familiar to him. The stairs groaned and creaked beneath him. He went straight to the door, leaned his big shepherd's crook against the wall, carefully put down the lantern on the threshold, and opened the door. The cobbler's son sat at the table, his head on his arm. He was wearing a yellow frock coat as he lay over the table, the flame-red wig the actor had given him on his head. The cobbler stood calmly for a second, then, just as calmly, hobbled across the room, bent down, picked the revolver off the floor, examined it carefully, and threw it on the table. He lifted the body with surprising ease, laid it horizontally in his arms, and bent over the face with a smile of apology and whispered confidentially:

"Be so gracious as to look at him. You see? He is pretending."

He looked at the face and shook his head.

"He was just like this as a child. He always loved comedy."

He took him over to the bed, laid him down, and closed his eyes with his fingers, smiling playfully as though he didn't want to ruin a good joke. A scream issued from Ábel's mouth. The cobbler hobbled over to him, put his hand over his mouth, and pressed the hysterically shaking body down on a chair with irresistible strength, whispering:

"Let's not wake him up. Please be so good as to pick up the saddle. It would be best if we returned to town before dawn."

He picked up the saddle himself and threw it over Tibor's shoulders. He looked around and passed the globe to Béla. His stick and his lantern he handed to Ábel and whispered to him in gently cajoling tones: "If you would be so kind as to go ahead. The light is already beginning to break but the road is full of ruts."

He lifted the body in his arms and slowly descended the stairs. The landlord and the servants were standing yellow-faced in the glow of the gate. They drew back when the cobbler appeared with the body in his arms. He frowned at them disapprovingly.

"Psst!" he whispered and gave a wink. "Out of my way."

He crossed the yard undisturbed. Tibor followed him with the saddle across his shoulder. Béla's arms were full of the globe, and Ábel stumbled at the back with his lantern and the shepherd's crook that was twice as tall as he was. The cobbler pressed on with the body in his powerful hands, firmly hobbling, so fast that they struggled to keep up with him. Béla's shivering and crying gave way to loud sobs. At the end of the garden the road turned and from there they could see the lit windows of the bar of The Peculiar, and heard the laughter and singing drifting towards them in the cold silence. Ábel recognized Kikinday's voice. The road was steep and Ábel ran beside the cobbler, lighting the way. The light was growing brighter with every passing second. Down in the valley glimmered the town with its towers and roofs. They stopped for a second on a bend of the slope. The cobbler was quietly talking to himself. They heard him though their teeth were chattering. He was leaning over the face whose wire wig was hanging strangely independently of the skull, talking so quietly they couldn't make out what he was saying. Then he set off again and hastened down the valley, the town becoming clearer with each step, and so they dropped as through a trapdoor out of the panoramic land-scape, into a street, the cobbler's feet tapping unevenly on the paving stones. And that was how they proceeded down all the streets, the only noise the knocking of the cobbler's shoes and Béla's regular sobbing.

A NOTE ABOUT THE AUTHOR

Sándor Márai was born in Kassa, in the Austro-Hungarian Empire, in 1900, and died in San Diego, California, in 1989. He rose to fame as one of the leading literary novelists in Hungary in the 1930s. Profoundly antifascist, he survived the war, but persecution by the Communists drove him from the country in 1948, first to Italy, then to the United States. His novel *Embers* was published for the first time in English in 2001.

A NOTE ABOUT THE TRANSLATOR

George Szirtes is the prizewinning author of thirteen books of poetry and several translations from Hungarian, including Sándor Márai's *Casanova in Bolzano,* and also poetry, fiction, and drama. He lives in the United Kingdom.

A NOTE ON THE TYPE

This book was set in Adobe Garamond. Designed
for the Adobe Corporation by Robert Slimbach,
the fonts are based on types first cut by Claude
Garamond (c. 1480–1561). Garamond was a pupil
of Geoffroy Tory and is believed to have followed
the Venetian models, although he introduced a
number of important differences, and it is to him
that we owe the letter we now know as "old style."
He gave to his letters a certain elegance and feeling
of movement that won their creator an immediate
reputation and the patronage of Francis I of
France.

Composed by North Market Street Graphics,
Lancaster, Pennsylvania
Printed and bound by R. R. Donnelley,
Harrisonburg, Virginia
Designed by Virginia Tan